Evely

Evelyn James has always been fascinated by history and the work of writers such as Agatha Christie. She began writing the Clara Fitzgerald series one hot summer, when a friend challenged her to write her own historical murder mystery. Clara Fitzgerald has gone on to feature in over thirteen novels, with many more in the pipeline. Evelyn enjoys conjuring up new plots, dastardly villains and horrible crimes to keep her readers entertained and plans on doing so for as long as possible.

Other Books in
The Clara Fitzgerald Series

Memories of the Dead

Flight of Fancy

Murder in Mink

Carnival of Criminals

Mistletoe and Murder

The Poison Pen

Grave Suspicions of Murder

The Woman Died Thrice

Murder and Mascara

The Green Jade Dragon

The Monster at the Window

Murder Aboard Mary Jane

The Missing Wife

Murder
and
Mascara

by
Evelyn James

A Clara Fitzgerald Mystery
Book 9

Red Raven Publications
2018

Chapter One

Clara had not seen Abigail Sommers for at least two or three years. Not since her old school chum had gone to Liverpool to pursue a career. This was very much a novelty among the women of Clara's generation. Most of her school friends had fully believed that their education was merely a way of passing the time before they found a husband, produced children, and swiftly forgot every unimportant fact about algebra and capital cities they had ever learnt. A few, such as Clara and Abigail, had aspired for greater things. Clara had rather fallen into her own career choice by chance, but she had always intended to do something with her life.

Abigail's story was somewhat similar. Abigail was a dreamer with pragmatic leanings. She knew her academic talents would not lead to university. She was not stupid, but her head did not retain facts like other girls' heads did. And she was not much good at mathematics. That ruled out quite a few feminine career choices, including becoming a pharmacist or doctor. Not that she had wanted to tend the sick, anyway. Abigail wanted a practical career that would suit her and would make her independent. Rather like Clara, she had a horror of being utterly dependent on a man for her entire life.

Abigail's own parents had demonstrated the flaws in this arrangement. Her parents had separated when she was thirteen and she rarely saw her father. Rumour had it, at least among the teaching staff at her school, that he had found another woman. Abigail's mother was constantly agitating about money, and always writing letters to her absent husband or spending hours with a solicitor to ensure the bills were paid that month. Abigail had come to the conclusion from this unhappy experience, that being reliant on another person was a recipe for disaster.

But what career was there for a girl with brilliant common sense, but limited academic ability? Nursing or teaching neither appealed, nor did becoming some sort of secretary (Abigail was a hopeless typist anyway, on that she and Clara were united). In the end, it was during a visit to London in her final year of school that Abigail found her inspiration and saw an opportunity. The school had arranged a trip to a London showcase event, a careers fair for those girls who wanted to do something with those brains their school had so carefully nurtured. Most of the stands were what one would expect; secretarial schools, the Shopgirls' Association, midwifery courses. Clara recalled that occasion as being one of disappointment, for she had seen nothing that appealed to her abilities. Naturally there was no stand for female private detectives. There were not even female police constables until the end of the war.

While Clara had walked away feeling disheartened, Abigail had come away with a sense of purpose. For she had found a company that employed women in a fashion that was not heavily reliant on mathematics or grammar, but was very focused on practicality. The company was Albion Industries. They made cosmetics and beauty aids, hundreds and hundreds of lines of make-up, stockings and girdles. Not to mention tools for curling the hair or plucking disfiguring eyebrows. Their customer-base was primarily composed of women and they employed female representatives to distribute and sell their products across the country. Abigail recognised this as something she could do. Not only that, but it would give her the opportunity to travel about the country and become a free woman. She was sold that very morning and, when she turned seventeen the next month, she submitted an application to the company. Within six months she was a trained Albion Industries' representative, with a handsome wage and the exciting prospect of travel and adventure ahead.

Nearly ten years later, Abigail Sommers was one of the top representatives in the country, known for her skill in sales and unrelenting drive for improvement. Her region regularly topped Albion's yearly sales charts. She was the woman all others aimed to beat. Natural then, that when Albion Industries decided to host its first ever conference and trade fair in Brighton, Abigail was put in charge of running it. Three hundred ladies and industry professionals had been invited down. All the regional representatives were in attendance, along with members from their various suppliers and offices. And that was just for the conference. Albion expected thousands of visitors to their trade fair which was to be hosted over an entire week. Invitations had been sent out to every cosmetics company, corset maker, hair stylist and health pill supplier Albion Industries knew of, and the fair was to be open to the public on Tuesday and Thursday. It was set to be the biggest challenge Abigail had yet to face in terms of organising the arrangements and ensuring everything went off without a hitch. She was well aware that this event would be telling on her future career with Albion. She could not afford to fail in making this a success. Which was why a recent problem had her worried and had driven her to seek out Clara.

This she had all explained over a cup of tea in Clara's cosy office; a couple of rooms above a haberdasher's shop that Clara rented at a very reasonable rate. Abigail drank great quantities of tea and the teapot had already been refilled once.

"You see why I am worried about our little problem," Abigail said as she began on her fourth cup.

In appearance she was not much changed from the girl Clara had remembered. She had grown up, naturally, but her face was still a delicate heart shape that could make Abigail look quite pensive and her hair was still a natural golden brown, though she now kept it neatly arranged in a bun. Perhaps the main difference Clara noticed was her heavy make-up. Abigail wore kohl about her eyes and had carefully curled her eyelashes and blackened them with mascara. Her eyelids were dusted lightly with a dark brown eye shadow which gave them a slightly bruised look. Her cheeks were faintly reddened with blusher and her lips had been carefully adorned with waxy lipstick. She looked like one of the girls Clara had seen on various cosmetics advertisements, right down to the delicate and extremely fashionable short dress, black coat with fur collar and shiny black kitten heel shoes. She carried it all off perfectly, being as skinny as a rake and not suffering from the feminine curves that made Clara's figure so out-of-fashion.

"I can understand your reasons for being concerned," Clara said to her. "But you have yet to explain what the problem actually is."

Abigail Sommers sighed and stared at the garish lipstick mark she had left on her teacup.

"I think someone is trying to sabotage the trade fair," she said at last. "Such an attempt could ruin my career with Albion. I have rivals Clara, rivals who would like to see me fail at this."

"What has happened so far?" Clara asked patiently.

"There have been a handful of incidents. At first I wrote them off to natural accidents and the carelessness of workmen but now, with the fair so close to opening, I don't feel I can be so complacent," Abigail pulled a face. "The first thing could have been a misunderstanding. We have ordered large quantities of samples for this event.

Albion has supplied boxes and boxes of its own products. One of these boxes contained two thousand lipsticks in Albion's latest shade, Pearl Pink. As samples go, these are some of our most important as we are promoting the product heavily. All the boxes are supposed to be stored in one of the side rooms. We have hired out the entire Brighton Pavilion for this occasion, plenty of space for storage when we need it. The samples arrived last Tuesday night and I personally saw them put into the room we had set aside for storage. However, the following evening I found an entire box of Pearl Pinks sitting in one of the side rooms being used by the workmen for their breaks. It was being used as a table, which was annoying but not harmful. The unfortunate thing was the box had been set next to the portable oil stove the workmen have been using to make themselves cups of tea.

"The heat from the stove had radiated out across one side of the box. Clara, do you know what happens to lipstick when exposed to high heat over a period of time?"

Clara was not a great user of lipstick, but it did not take much of a stretch of the imagination to perceive how the sticks of oily colour would gladly melt when exposed to heat.

"I assume many of the samples melted?"

Abigail nodded sadly.

"When I realised what had occurred I pulled out some of the tubes. The lipstick inside had melted and then, when it cooled again, pooled into a misshapen oblong. Those samples were worthless to me. Thankfully the heat had only penetrated one side of the box and I was able to salvage nearly two thirds of the contents. But I still lost several hundred tubes of lipstick. I complained to the foreman in charge of the workmen. He claims none of his men moved the box and that it just appeared in their room one day."

"That is an unfortunate mishap," Clara sympathised. "And, as you say, it could have been done in error."

"Indeed. That was how I first took it," Abigail pressed together her lips. Clara couldn't help wondering if the colour she was wearing was this famous Pearl Pink. "The next incident was more serious in nature. The workmen have been renovating the parts of the pavilion we will be using for the fair and also putting together the trade stands and advertisement displays. Some of this involves being up on scaffolding as we have banners hanging from the ceilings. On Thursday afternoon one of the men was up a scaffold fixing a banner when the entire thing collapsed. He was badly hurt as metal poles and wooden planks crashed down on him. We had to dig him from the debris."

"Another accident?" Clara asked.

"The foreman was certain it could not be. He had supervised the building of the scaffolds himself. But, when a closer look was taken, it appeared some of the bolts were missing their nuts."

"Possible sabotage?"

"I put it down at first to sheer negligence. But the foreman was so insistent," Abigail paused. "And now we have this morning's incident. Today the Albion ladies have been arriving. They will be promoting our own products during the fair. I was taking the girls around the pavilion and showing them the different rooms we would be using when I heard an awful commotion. We all headed to the main hall and found the big Albion banner, the one our workman had so unfortunately been putting up when he fell, lying across the floor, ripped to shreds, and…" Abigail gave a small gulp as the memory came back to her, "…written across the floor in Pearl Pink lipstick was the word 'betrayal'. I can't ignore this now, can I? Someone is trying to sabotage our event, who or why I just don't know."

"Fortunately, that is something I am good at," Clara said in the hope it sounded reassuring. "I will need to come to the Pavilion and talk with everyone and be allowed the freedom of the building to investigate."

"Of course," Abigail nodded. "I was told you are very good at this sort of thing. You are on the committee for the Brighton Pavilion as well, so I hear? It was how your name was first told to me."

Clara nodded.

"I am indeed. In fact, I was at the meeting where it was decided to allow your trade fair to be held at the Pavilion. I think it sounds a good way to bring people to the town and I certainly don't want to see it end in disaster. You have my word I will put all my energy into tracking down who is behind this series of misfortunes."

"Thank you," Abigail released a sigh of relief. "I have been so worried. That is not like me, at all."

"Can you supply me with a list of everyone who has been working at the Pavilion during the preparations for the fair?" Clara asked.

"Naturally," Abigail said. "And, I insist you come to our pre-opening banquet to be held tomorrow night in the Pavilion."

Abigail rummaged in her tiny handbag and produced an invitation. She pushed it across the desk towards Clara.

"You must save the trade fair Clara. Please."

After Abigail had left to go back to her arrangements for the fair, Clara shut up her office and headed for home. It was close to the time Annie served dinner. Annie was Clara's friend and also her housekeeper. Annie did not like people being late for dinner, even when they had a very good reason, such as solving a crime.

Clara studied her invitation as she walked. If she was going to be around all those pretty and presentable ladies, she might have to consider donning a little make-up herself. Else she would stand out like a sore thumb. Oh dear, thought Clara, who had always banked on her natural prettiness to get her by without the need for cosmetics. Oh dear.

She opened her front door and strode into the parlour where she expected to find her brother Tommy. He lived with her in the home that had once belonged to their now deceased parents. Tommy was not present.

"Clara?"

She heard Annie calling her from the kitchen and headed down the corridor. She was surprised to enter the room and to see Inspector Park-Coombs sat at the kitchen table with Tommy and Annie. They were all looking pensive.

"Is something the matter?" Clara asked, feeling a pang of worry creeping over her.

"I wanted to let you know in person," Inspector Park-Coombs said very formally. A man in his late forties, he had plenty of grey hairs in his black crop to mark the worry he had felt over many a case. "I didn't want you to read about it in the papers."

"You are worrying me," Clara said, glancing at all their faces. "What should I not read about in the paper?"

"It's all very hush-hush at the moment," Park-Coombs explained. "But this morning I and some of the constables went to the hospital to oversee the discreet transfer of an important patient. We were there to ensure the man's privacy."

"What man?" Clara asked, her mouth dry as dust from the tension.

"Captain O'Harris," Park-Coombs said solemnly. "The man's alive, Clara."

Chapter Two

Clara didn't know how to feel as the news slowly sunk in. Captain O'Harris. The reckless, but oh so charming airman, who had attempted to fly from England to America in his biplane The White Buzzard. Clara had watched him go, her heart breaking all the time, and when she heard that the plane had vanished and no one knew what had become of it, she felt as though someone had punched her in the chest.

She had only known O'Harris for a brief spell. But in that short time she had come to both admire him and fear for him. He was everything you would expect from a man who had survived a war, both heroically brave and terribly tormented. He was also a fool. Clara had called him that not long before he had vanished. A fool because he could not be satisfied with a peaceful life on land and had to keep pushing to be in the skies. She had felt a dread in her stomach at the prospect of him making that challenging flight. None of his reassurances could numb the awful sensation of anxiety that flooded Clara, and when his plane crashed in the ocean, so Clara felt that her gut instincts had been horribly correct. She also felt guilt that she had not tried harder to deter him.

"Sit down, Clara," Annie insisted, propelling her friend

from the doorway of the kitchen to a chair.

Clara had gone very pale and silent. It was hardly surprising considering the news. It was why they had all been anxious about telling her.

"Perhaps..." Clara started to speak and her voice sounded hoarse, so she paused and licked her lips. "Perhaps someone might explain how this is all possible? It is nearly a year since..."

The sentence hung in the air unfinished. No one felt the need to add to it.

"I can explain as much as I know," Inspector Park-Coombs declared. "I was sent an official letter on the subject, but I dare say I only got the bare bones of the matter. As we know, after the crash of Captain O'Harris' aeroplane a search was conducted of the area of ocean he was most likely to have landed in and his co-pilot was found. This gave hope that O'Harris would be nearby, but the ocean is vast and currents can take a man or object caught in them miles from where they should be. O'Harris was not found during these searches and it was eventually agreed that he must be declared lost."

"I remember that well enough," Clara said almost breathlessly. "The newspapers were very vivid on the matter."

"Newspapermen like sensation," Park-Coombs grumbled. "One of the reasons I was asked to ensure there was a police presence at the hospital when Captain O'Harris arrived. This official letter arrived on my desk last week. It was from my superiors. The letter explained that Captain O'Harris had been found alive and initially transferred to an American hospital where his identity remained a mystery for some time as he would not speak. When it was discovered he was our lost airman it attracted a lot of unwelcome attention, and the Americans were very keen to have O'Harris shipped back to England as soon as possible. He arrived at Cardiff a few nights ago and was just transferred by private ambulance to Brighton General Hospital."

"And that is all you know about what happened to him?" Clara pressed.

"I'm afraid so, Clara," Park-Coombs shook his head apologetically. "I knew you would want to know all this as soon as possible. I have prepared a list of authorised visitors for the captain which I have supplied to the hospital staff. I ensured your name was on it, so if you wish to visit…"

"Wait, wait," Clara stopped him. "Visit? I… I just learned he was alive, I…"

Clara had spent the best part of a year putting O'Harris firmly out of her mind. Did she want to bring him back into her life? To potentially allow him to destroy her happiness again? O'Harris was the sort of reckless soul that has a tendency to cause disharmony in both their own and other peoples' lives. But Clara could also not deny that many nights she had lain in bed and wished to have one more chance to speak with him, to laugh with him, to share his vivacity for life. Clara was completely uncertain of what to think after all this.

"Well, when you are ready, you have the freedom to visit him," Park-Coombs finished. "I'm afraid I must be going now. The wife likes me home for dinner."

The inspector rose and nodded to them all as he collected his hat. He squeezed Clara's shoulder as he went past and let himself out of her house.

"You don't have to do anything," Annie told Clara firmly.

Annie had always been of the opinion that Captain O'Harris was a dangerous influence on her friend. He was far too flighty and impulsive for her liking. She just wished Clara could see things as clearly as she did. Someone like Oliver Bankes would make a much more sound and stable husband. Not this reckless lunatic and his flying machines.

"I have dinner ready. I think we should eat and let this information sink in," she commanded bluntly. She was looking at Tommy too, for he was almost as put out by the news as Clara. Tommy had been firm friends with O'Harris and had been grieved by his loss. "I made a beef and kidney pudding. Don't tell me it must go to waste? Surely a man resurrected from the dead is something to celebrate, not mope over?"

"He isn't Lazarus, Annie," Tommy said wearily. "He was never dead, clearly. He must have washed up somewhere and no one knew who he was."

"But am I wrong to say that is something to be glad about not sad?" Annie persisted.

"You are not wrong," Clara agreed. "I think we are both just in shock."

Clara looked up at her friend's petulant face. She knew Annie was concerned this news would cause all her hard work in the kitchen to go to waste, a crime of epic proportions in the woman's mind. Clara was also astute enough to know Annie was unhappy about the possibility of Clara becoming embroiled again with the captain. Well, for the moment that was not a worry as Clara could not say for certain whether she intended to become embroiled or not. She was just trying to get her head around everything.

"Serve dinner Annie. I am still hungry."

They sat at the dining table and ate beef and kidney pudding, served with boiled potatoes and peas. Clara could not deny that it was a very good pudding, crafted with Annie's knack for good suet pastry and perfectly tender meat. But her mind was elsewhere as she ate, as were the minds of her companions. Even little Bramble, their scruffy small black poodle, was oddly sombre. Clara decided after a while that this would not do.

"Have you heard of Albion Industries, Annie?" she asked to enliven things.

"I believe I have a pot of hand cream made by them," Annie nodded. "Oh, wait, aren't they something to do with that thing you are hosting at the Pavilion?"

"The trade fair, yes. Turns out one of my old school friends is organising the event and she is in a pickle because someone appears to be trying to sabotage things."

"Oh dear!" Annie declared with an appropriate degree of shocked horror in her tone.

"Wait," Tommy interrupted, "didn't you say Albion make cosmetics and beauty aids? Why would anyone want to sabotage that?"

"Precisely the question I have been asked to answer," Clara nodded. "After dinner, I propose a walk to the Pavilion to take a look around. I have full access and the workmen should still be there getting things ready for the grand opening on Sunday. With any luck we shall find someone who is happy to talk with us."

With that idea in mind Clara and Tommy set out after dinner to walk to the Pavilion. Bramble accompanied them on a lead, gambolling about like a lamb in his excitement. Annie opted to stay at home. She wanted to get the dishes washed.

Tommy had only recently learned to walk again after losing the use of his legs during the war. Many doctors had tried to get him on his feet after the incident, but most had focused on his physical capabilities. It was only when octogenarian Dr Cutt had started to look at the problem from a psychological angle, indicating that Tommy showed clear signs of shell-shock, that any progress was made. And even then it had been tentative, because Tommy did not like the idea that his problems were in his head and had taken some convincing to agree to Dr Cutt's plans. The result had been remarkable. After three years of disability, Tommy had stepped out of his wheelchair and, though still suffering the constraints of a slight limp, was walking about like his old self. He might be a way off from feeling up to re-joining the cricket team, (Tommy had been their star bowler) but just to be upright at all was a miracle.

Summer was slowly coming to Brighton. As they walked there was a warmth to the evening. Clara felt her soul start to lift, after all, there was hope in the air, was there not? The birds were singing, the sun was gradually setting and casting its long fingers over the houses. There was a promise of good things to come and surely she had already had a great gift today with the news about Captain O'Harris? Yes, now she came to think of it, there was a lot of promise ahead.

They arrived at the Pavilion, the building that divided the people of Brighton. Some loved its whimsical middle-eastern charms, others loathed it. Not so many years ago it had come within a hair's breadth of being demolished, which was when the committee was formed as part of a campaign to save it for the public. Since then it had been an ongoing ordeal to find events to encourage people into the building, and to keep the funds coming in for its maintenance. But it was iconic, no one could deny that, whether they thought it a hideous monstrosity or a work of architectural delight. It put Brighton on the map, for better or worse. The cosmetics trade fair was the biggest event to be held at the Pavilion in recent years. It was set to bring thousands of visitors to the town and the rental fee the committee had charged Albion Industries would go a long way to sorting out the leaky roof and a slight bit of subsidence in one of the corner walls. By all accounts it was going to be a productive affair.

For the moment, however, the Pavilion looked at sixes and sevens. The workmen were still installing the display stands and preparing all the large boards for posters and advertisement displays. The place looked nowhere near ready to be opened to the public. But, as Abigail had not mentioned this as one of her concerns, Clara had to assume everything was running to schedule. Once inside, having walked through the open gates and Pavilion front doors without being challenged by anyone, Clara glanced about for her friend. There was no sign of her.

On the other hand, there were plenty of other people about. Aside from the workmen who were all engaged in some piece of handicraft, there were a number of women dressed very smartly, who were chattering away and assessing the main rooms of the Pavilion with very business-like glances. Clara could only assume these were the Albion representatives, checking out their new venue. Over the next seven days these women would be selling Albion products as hard as they possibly could. They would be handing out samples, pigeon-holing traders, and courting potential customers. They were all ready for the challenge.

Clara and Tommy wandered among them. Clara was casting her eye over the workmen's various pieces of wooden construction. She was alarmed to see that one banner had been nailed into an ornamental piece of plasterwork that was over one hundred years old. Flustered at the sight, and feeling righteously indignant as a member of the committee tasked with protecting the Pavilion from such vandalism, she went in search of the foreman to give him a piece of her mind. She found him on the landing of the stairs, supervising the installation of a set of display shelves that would house expensive perfumes once the glass fronts were attached.

"Are you the foreman?" Clara demanded.

He turned and looked at her, annoyed by her sudden interruption.

"Who are you?" he demanded in return.

"Clara Fitzgerald, Brighton Pavilion Preservation Committee member," Clara said stoutly, putting plenty of weight behind the title. "We must talk at once!"

"I'm busy," the foreman grumbled.

"At once! Or I shall summon my fellow committee members and call a halt to this whole thing!"

Muttering and puttering about interfering women, the foreman halted his men and reluctantly followed Clara to the offending piece of woodwork. When she explained the cause for her anger he was nonchalant.

"We'll fill the hole back in," he shrugged.

"That is not the point! This building is over one hundred and thirty years old and is not to have nails knocked into it! Part of the agreement for this event was that no harm would be done to the structure of the

Pavilion! As it is, the committee will demand compensation for the damage and that bill will go first to Albion Industries, who will then turn to you and demand…"

Clara was interrupted in her rant by a loud, long scream. The foreman, who had been ready to respond to her complaint with some choice words of his own, also came to a halt. For a moment no one moved, then the scream was repeated and Clara started to move in the direction of the sound. It seemed to be coming from one of the side rooms. Several of the Albion girls were clustered about a doorway looking shocked. Another was standing just in the room and screaming repeatedly. Clara dragged her out of the room and then looked to see what had caused the commotion. It was not difficult to see why she was so distressed, for lying on the floor of the room, half covered by a pile of Pearl Pink lipstick tubes, was a woman. She was just lying staring at the ceiling, her hands splayed out either side of her.

"Good heavens!" the foreman had followed Clara and now he stood staring at the awful sight. "She's dead, isn't she?"

"Oh yes," said Clara, noting a pair of Albion shimmer brown stockings tied tightly about the woman's throat. "She is very dead."

Chapter Three

Dr Deàth, Brighton's appropriately named coroner, crouched by the body of the unfortunate woman and lifted her limp wrist.

"Can't have been dead long. She's still warm," he said, mostly to himself.

Inspector Park-Coombs stood a little way behind him, twitching his thick moustache. Clara was stood right next to him with her arms crossed over her chest.

"Who is she?" Park-Coombs asked her.

"One of the Albion girls. Someone has gone to find Abigail Sommers, the woman who is in charge of this event. She should know who she is."

"And you say there had been some trouble before?"

"Yes, but nothing to suggest anyone was contemplating murder, unless you want to count the scaffold incident. But, in truth, the scaffold was not high and it was unlikely anyone could be killed in the fall. This is much more deliberate, to put it bluntly," Clara stared sadly at the girl on the floor.

She was in her twenties, a natural blond with the severely streamline figure all the Albion girls sported. She was dressed smartly in a short, pale green dress and a rose pink cardigan.

"No one heard anything?" Park-Coombs was frowning as he flipped open his notebook.

"There is a lot of commotion going on in the building," Clara explained.

"Taken by surprise, I would imagine," Park-Coombs wrote down this assumption. "Wouldn't have been able to cry out much. Anything you can add, Dr Deàth?

Dr Deàth looked up thoughtfully from his work.

"I would say the stocking came from that box," he pointed to his right helpfully.

The room was full of cardboard boxes containing supplies and samples for the fair. One had been opened and plainly contained hundreds of pairs of stockings in paper bags that bore the Albion name. The remains of one packet was sitting on the floor behind the dead girl's head. It had been carelessly ripped open, a nasty tear running across the front of the paper and cutting through the company logo.

"Hmm," Park-Coombs mulled. "Doesn't strike me as something anyone planned, more an opportunistic killing. Wonder why this girl though? Was she known to the killer, or was it just extremely bad luck she came into this room by herself?"

There was a clatter of heels by the door and Abigail Sommers appeared. She gave a gasp at the sight of the body on the floor.

"Miss Sommers?" Park-Coombs asked her.

"Y…yes," Abigail regained her composure rapidly, though she could not take her eyes off the girl on the floor. "What has happened here?"

"I think that is rather plain to see," Inspector Park-Coombs said. "Can you tell me the name of the girl?"

"Um, yes, I think so," Abigail was trembling, but the initial shock had been softened because she had been forewarned by the girl who had located her and told her of the emergency. She had been ready to see something a lot worse than what was actually presented to her. In fact, the girl did not really look dead at all. "Esther Althorpe,

18

that's her name. She has been with the company a couple of years, I believe."

"Had there been any trouble with her?" Park-Coombs asked.

"What? No! Esther was reliable and very consistent with her sales figures," Abigail had become slightly defensive.

"Did she arrive today?" Clara interjected.

"Yes, all the girls did," Abigail pressed a hand to her lips, the shock of the whole thing starting to catch up with her. "This is awful. I never thought when I came to you Clara that something like this would happen."

"Clara has been explaining to me that there have been some odd incidents previously," Inspector Park-Coombs said. "But you have no idea who might be behind such a thing?"

"No, else I would not have spoken with Clara, would I?" Abigail was affronted. "Look, I have to get this situation under control. The girls are in shock, but I can't let everyone fall behind schedule."

"You are going to continue with the fair?" the inspector asked, though it was more of a statement than a question.

"I must. A lot of money and time has been invested into this. Besides, I refuse to be intimidated by this… this… person!" Abigail turned on her heel and marched away, looking about ready to conquer the world if needs be.

"She is determined," Park-Coombs said wryly.

"Women don't get far in this life if they are not," Clara replied. "They'll want to use this room, you know."

"I'll have photographs taken and the room searched from top to bottom for clues. Then we will let them remove the boxes, or rather I'll get my constables to remove them, and lock up the room just in case we have missed something," Inspector Park-Coombs scratched at his moustache. "What precisely is Albion Industries?"

"A cosmetics company, mainly," it was Dr Deàth who

answered him. "However, they act as a distributor for a number of smaller companies as well. If you pick up one of their catalogues you will find it contains everything a person might require in terms of personal hygiene and beauty products."

Park-Coombs gave him a curious look.

"And you know this, how?"

The coroner smiled, very little ruffled him.

"They produce a most excellent hand cream. It moisturises and protects the skin. In my line of work I spend a lot of time washing my hands and the skin between my fingers tends to crack something awful. My wife suggested Albion's hand cream and handed me their catalogue."

"Annie uses it too," Clara chipped in. "It is, apparently, very popular."

Park-Coombs scratched at his moustache again, thoughtfully.

"They sell moustache trimmers too, Inspector," Dr Deàth said jovially.

Park-Coombs scowled at him.

"I think I have seen enough here. Let's find the girl who discovered the body. I want a word with her."

"May I join you Inspector?" Clara asked.

Inspector Park-Coombs shrugged.

"I had already assumed you would. Just in case we are dealing with two separate incidents, the sabotage and now a murder, I imagine you will want to continue investigating."

"Absolutely!" Clara grinned.

"Yes, I thought as much."

The girl who had discovered the body had been upset badly by the experience, and her friends had settled her in the workmen's tea room. She was perched on an old wooden chair, sipping from a chipped mug containing very sweet tea. A friend was sitting with her, but when the inspector and Clara entered she rose and politely left. The three were left alone. Inspector Park-Coombs sat on a rickety chair that wobbled ominously, one of its legs being considerably shorter than the others. Clara perched on a stool near the oil stove that had caused such problems for the Pearl Pink lipsticks.

"I am Inspector Park-Coombs and this is Miss Fitzgerald," the inspector began. "You are the young lady who made the unfortunate discovery?"

"Yes," the girl said bleakly. She had been crying and looked fit to start again. "It was awful to see Esther like that."

"Ah. Your name, miss?"

"Ivy Longman," the girl answered.

"And you knew Esther?"

"We went on the same training course when we were first taken on by Albion," Ivy explained. "Then we both were placed in the South-East region as representatives. We travelled a lot, but I always kept in touch with Esther. We would arrange to meet up for tea once a month. This is a hard job, you know, not a lot of time for socialising, and it helps enormously having a friend who understands that."

Ivy sniffed miserably.

"I'm going to miss her so badly," her voice trembled, but she was not about to cry in front of strangers. She took out her handkerchief and dabbed her eyes discreetly.

"When did you last see Esther, before finding her in the room?" the inspector asked with his usual blunt approach.

Ivy winced as his words conjured up the image of Esther in the side room, but she answered clear enough.

"Perhaps half-an-hour before. We had been walking through the rooms set aside for the fair, taking note of the various trade stands. We wanted to be sure we would be in the perfect place to make our sales when the event opened. We had explored most of the building during the tour. Esther asked whether I had seen any of the samples, especially Albion's new lipstick. I said I had not. Esther said we ought to try out the product before we sold it. We always did that, it was part of our personal policies, to know precisely how the product worked and how it felt to wear," Ivy allowed a hint of pride to come into her tone. She was a professional salesperson and took her responsibilities very seriously. "Esther said she would fetch a sample from the storeroom. Some of the Pearl Pink lipsticks had been damaged and they had been put in a separate box. We were told we could take one of these damaged lipsticks to try. Esther went to fetch one while I was examining a corset display. She never came back."

Ivy had to take a deep breath before she could carry on.

"When she hadn't returned in such a long time, I started to worry. Well, perhaps worry is not the right word. I wondered what had become of her and I was bored with corsets. I thought I would go looking for her. It seemed logical to start in the storeroom where she had gone in search of a Pearl Pink sample and there..." Ivy gulped, "...there she was."

"I'm very sorry," Clara said gently. "You had no reason, I imagine, to think Esther was in any danger."

"None," Ivy agreed. "What danger would there be here? I never thought..."

"Did Miss Althorpe have any problems with anyone here? A work colleague perhaps?" Park-Coombs asked.

"Problems?" Ivy was bemused. "No more than anyone. We are all competitive here, naturally. We all want the top sales score. But no one is about to murder anyone over it! Or at least, so I had imagined..."

"Did Miss Althorpe have any male friends?" the inspector persisted.

"No. She never had the time. All of us are the same. We made a decision, Inspector, to have a career rather than a family. Some might think that a strange thing for a woman, we do not," Ivy's firm tone reminded Clara that she was a tough woman, someone determined to make a mark in a predominantly male world. Just like Abigail, she would not crumble easily.

"Miss Longman," Clara interrupted. "Can you think of anyone who might have cause to feel betrayed by the Albion company?"

Ivy looked puzzled by the question.

"Betrayed?"

"A message was scrawled on the floor of the main hall the other day in lipstick. It read 'betrayal'," Clara explained, making a note to herself to check the floor and ensure it had been cleaned sufficiently. After the plasterwork fiasco, she had lost all faith in the workmen.

"I can't think of anyone," Ivy shook her head. "No one has complained of such a thing to me."

They concluded the interview and Clara and the inspector wandered back into the entrance hall of the Pavilion.

"Rather puts a damper on events," Park-Coombs noted.

"Abigail will not let it deter her," Clara said loyally. "And the press need not get a whiff of this before the fair opens."

The inspector raised an eyebrow at Clara, indicating how naïve he felt that hope was. The press would latch onto anything, given half the chance. It would be difficult, considering the number of people who had witnessed the discovery of Esther Althorpe's body, to keep this under wraps.

"I'll know more after the post-mortem," Park-Coombs mused. "Do you know how unusual it is for someone to be killed without them knowing their attacker?"

"Very unusual, I would imagine," Clara guessed.

"Someone who attacks a stranger and thus commits a motiveless crime is very difficult to track. If you can't connect them to the victim, it is near enough impossible. Look at Jack the Ripper."

"But no crime is motiveless," Clara countered. "Jack was never caught, so he could not be questioned about his motive, but he most certainly had one. And that was a Victorian crime when the police force was very new and still learning its art."

"Meaning you still have faith in my abilities to solve this?" Park-Coombs smiled mischievously.

"More important, Inspector," Clara returned the smile, "I have faith in my abilities."

She winked at him. Park-Coombs laughed and said his farewells just as Tommy was appearing from one of the far rooms in the Pavilion. Bramble was trailing behind him, trying to sniff every item scattered on the floor as he went past and failing because Tommy had his lead firmly in his hand.

"While you were busy, I had the workmen carefully remove that nail from the plasterwork and I took a quick look about to see if there was any further damage," Tommy said as he approached.

"Thank you," Clara said gratefully. "That is one less thing to worry over."

"Abigail swept past me while I was sorting things. I remember her now, I am sure she visited us one summer."

"She did," Clara concurred. "She stayed for a week."

"Well she swept past with a scowl on her face that looked as though she was fit to bite someone's head off. Personally, I would not want to anger her. I think her reaction to a threat would be both swift and dangerous."

"You aren't suggesting she killed Esther Althorpe?" Clara asked him as they walked out of the Pavilion and towards the road.

"Was that the girl in the storeroom? No, I am not suggesting that. Just that this saboteur and murderer ought to be careful about who he offends."

They wandered out of the Pavilion gardens and through the gates. It was dark now and the stars glittered overhead. Clara stared skywards and paused.

"I'll go visit Captain O'Harris tomorrow," she said abruptly.

Tommy wasn't sure if she was talking to him, or just muttering to herself. He responded to be on the safe side.

"Good. Because I want to visit too, but I think it would

be best if you go first," Tommy hesitated. "Clara, the man has been through an awful lot. He has been missing a year and who knows the traumas he experienced in that time. Be aware of that when you go to see him. He might not be… like before."

Clara smiled sadly.

"I know. For a while it was that very thought that made me wonder if I should go at all. But I think I should. He needs to know there are still people around who care for him."

They turned up the road and walked home in thoughtful silence.

Chapter Four

The next morning Clara went back to the Pavilion first thing to see how events were progressing. She also wanted to keep an eye on the workmen and their slapdash attitude to old architecture. The trade stallholders had arrived on an early train and were setting up their various displays with alacrity. The rooms no longer looked bare, with just empty tables and plain hoardings. Now there was colour and excitement. Clara was beginning to understand how big an occasion this affair was likely to be. She mingled among the stallholders, largely ignored, until she came across Abigail.

"Have you time to talk? I know you are busy, but I thought we could try and get to the bottom of this little mystery?" Clara said as she spotted her.

Abigail looked anxiously at her watch.

"I think I have a moment or two. I've been going over this problem in my mind all night, I barely slept."

She directed Clara to one of the side rooms that had been set aside for the use of the Albion ladies. It was littered with handbags and coats, not to mention a vast array of cosmetics.

"The police want to take possession of Esther's personal belongings. I said I would arrange it," Abigail picked up a grey handbag with a pretty black sequin flower sewn around its catch. "This is hers, I am confident of it. Could I ask you to take it to the police station? I can't think when I will have the time to leave the Pavilion."

Clara said she could. Abigail handed over the handbag looking fraught.

"I keep thinking that it must be someone among us who did this dreadful thing," she said, finding a stool to lower herself onto.

"You have had the gates and doors open the entire time you have been here," Clara pointed out. "Anyone might have walked in."

"But this person has a grudge against Albion, and it is not correct that the doors have always been open. The last couple of days that has been the case, but previously in the week we have had the gates shut to prevent the press snooping about. You know I caught a newspaperman in here on Monday! He had slipped in posed as a workman! I sent him packing and since then have kept a better eye on the premises."

"Still, if he slipped in, perhaps someone else did too?" Clara gently hinted.

Abigail once more shook her head.

"I am certain Clara that I know everyone here. It was the reason I spotted the newspaperman at once. I didn't recognise his face. I am on top of all this, I really am," Abigail unconsciously brushed a strand of hair back from her face.

"What was the name of the newspaperman?" Clara asked, thinking she would find out from him just how impenetrable the Pavilion was.

"Oh, I don't know Clara," Abigail puttered. "I never asked his name. He babbled something about working for the Brighton Gazette."

"I'll check him out, just in case," Clara reassured her. "Now, if you are certain no one else could have entered the building, why don't we start putting together a list of potential suspects based on who was around?"

Abigail nodded wearily.

"The workmen, of course. Mr Taversham is the foreman. He will know all their names, I'm afraid I don't. Until yesterday there was no one else about, except for myself."

"How many workmen are there?"

"Ten, not including Mr Taversham. Could one of them really be responsible?" Abigail frowned. "What a ghastly thought. And to think they hurt one of their own in the process."

"You don't know the name of the workmen who was injured when the scaffold collapsed?"

"No. But Mr Taversham will."

"Abigail," Clara leaned forward. "Is there anyone specifically you can think of who might have a grudge against Albion Industries? The word 'betrayal' was a very precise thing to write on the floor, after all."

Abigail gnawed on her lip. She was thinking hard, trying to imagine someone who would be willing to go to such lengths over a grudge.

"It's no good," Abigail shrugged her shoulders. "No one springs to mind."

"What about you? Have you had cause to argue with anyone recently?"

Abigail laughed bitterly.

"Clara that is all I ever do some days! Don't get me wrong, mostly this job is about selling, but I have to be stern with some of my clients. They will take liberties if I am not, and I sometimes don't get everything I ask for from distributors. You see how it is with the workmen, every day is like that for me, it comes with the territory."

"But, have you had cause to speak to anyone more sharply than normal? About something outside work?"

"Clara if I even had the slightest hunch I would tell you, but I can't think of anyone. I speak to dozens of people most days. Perhaps some go away dissatisfied, but that is the nature of business. Nothing to take personally."

Clara was still convinced that either the person had a grudge against the company or a personal grudge against Abigail, which was why they were trying to sabotage the fair. But without a concrete lead, she was groping around in the dark for answers.

"You said you have rivals and one of those might be behind the sabotage?" Clara pressed.

"Every one of those ladies outside are my rivals," Abigail said plainly. "Each of them wants to beat me at my own game and become the top selling Albion representative for their region. I operate in the South-East, as do at least fifteen other ladies. All of whom would like to make more sales than me, but so far I am holding my own. Do you know the benefits Albion offers to their top sellers?"

Clara admitted she did not.

"Ten pounds, Clara. Ten pounds each month for the person who makes the most sales and I have been that person for the last twelve months. Ten pounds buys an awful lot of hot meals. I am putting it away and saving for a house, so I can move out of my little flat," Abigail smiled wanly. "I dream of having a little garden. Nothing fancy, but somewhere to sit on a summer's evening. And I thought I might get a cat to keep me company. If I have a dream and see that extra ten pounds as a means of achieving it, why shouldn't everyone else be the same?"

It was a fair point. Abigail's aspirations put her in a prime position to be despised by her fellow Albion ladies. Jealousy was a terrible emotion and there was nothing as good at creating jealousy as success.

"You said you operate in the South-East?" Clara asked.

"Yes, I do now. For the last year, in fact."

"Esther Althorpe also operated in the South-East, did you know her?"

Abigail was unfazed by the question.

"As I say, I have only been in the region for the last twelve months and I have yet to meet all my fellow representatives. We work alone, after all. It only tends to be at the annual Christmas conference that we come together. I had never met Esther, until this week."

"Is it possible that Esther had an enemy all of her own?" Clara continued. "Could it be the sabotage and the murder are unrelated?"

Abigail frowned again.

"I couldn't say. Esther was just another name on the list of sales representatives. She was good at her job, though. Top five most months. If she had an enemy, I was not aware of it."

Clara didn't feel she had gained much, other than a greater impression than before of the challenge now facing her.

"Are we done? I must get back to what I was doing."

"We are done," Clara nodded.

Abigail rose to her feet.

"I'll see you tonight at the pre-opening banquet. They are installing the table in a room upstairs as we speak. And I have to make sure the caterers have all they need," Abigail sighed. "I must admit, I'll be glad when this is over."

She departed from the room. Clara started to rise from her stool, then remembered Esther's handbag. She lifted up its flower catch and looked inside. The bag contained the usual assortment of belongings a woman would carry. There was quite a bit of make-up, all Albion. Clara counted at least three lipstick tubes. There was a crumpled tissue, a purse containing odd coins, and a photograph of another woman who looked much like Esther; Clara suspected it was her sister. There was a hairbrush and a small tin of mints. At the bottom were several crumpled pieces of paper which proved to be forgotten shopping lists and old receipts. Clara worked her way through them, but nothing seemed important. Clara was beginning to think Esther had just been in the wrong place at the wrong time. There seemed nothing, as far as she could see, that would make someone want to kill her. The handbag was a dead end for the time being.

She replaced its contents and would hand it over to the police as soon as she had the chance. In the meantime, she went in search of Mr Taversham the foreman.

Mr Taversham was a local man who had been employed by Albion Industries for the duration of the trade fair. Much like Abigail, Mr Taversham was feeling that the trade fair was causing him a lot of anxiety for very little return. He would be glad when it was over.

When he spotted Clara approaching him, he gave a slight groan. What had his men done now? Mr Taversham wanted to shake his head in despair. He had hired the men locally, as he always did, and had found them reliable to a point, but they clearly did not match up with the exacting standards of this damn Pavilion committee. He felt bad about the damaged plasterwork, that was a silly oversight, but he really could do without being further reprimanded by the prim young woman now heading towards him. He was contemplating disappearing among the various stands when he heard his name called.

"Mr Taversham, might I have a word?"

Taversham sighed.

"What is wrong now?" he asked with the weariness of a man who knows he shall be wrong whatever he does.

"Nothing, as such. I just wanted a word about this nasty business of sabotage and so forth. Could we talk?"

Mr Taversham found this a suspicious statement, but he nodded his head and followed Clara to the tea room.

"What precisely do you want to talk about?" he asked as soon as the door was shut behind them.

"The problems this event has been having," Clara said simply. "The misplaced lipsticks, the scaffold collapsing…"

"That makes me angry," Mr Taversham interrupted, wagging a thick finger in the air. "I have all these people looking at me with this expression in their eyes. They don't trust me, they think I am some shabby no-hoper who would neglect their duty and allow a scaffold to collapse. I did not, Miss Fitzgerald. I inspected every bolt on that scaffold and I can confirm that they were all secure and properly tightened. That scaffold was perfectly safe when I last looked at it."

"Then you are certain that someone came up to the scaffold later on and unscrewed the bolts?"

"It has to be that way. I know I checked them all, I know!" Mr Taversham pulled his lips back in a scowl. "I did not neglect my duty!"

"Do you think one of your workmen might have unscrewed the bolts?"

"I don't know. It's not the sort of thing you want to contemplate," Mr Taversham moped. "Someone could have been seriously hurt. This is a dangerous business and I can't imagine why anyone would put a colleague at deliberate risk. Accidents happen frequently enough without causing them deliberately."

"What about the box of lipsticks being moved?" Clara changed tack.

"I don't know who moved that and none of my men will admit to it. It could have all been the result of miscommunication."

Clara had to agree that was always a possibility.

"Have you noticed anyone suspicious about the Pavilion?" Clade hoped for something, anything. She needed a clue, a sign to let her know which direction to wander in to solve this crime. She was hopeful that Taversham could offer that clue.

"There was a newspaperman," Taversham shrugged. "Newspapermen are always suspicious."

"But he was picked out by Abigail swiftly enough and expelled.

"If you say so," Taversham shrugged.

Clara could see she was not going to get a lot from him.

The foreman was looking agitated and wanted to get on with his work. Clara insisted he give her a list of all the workmen at the site, just in case.

"None of my workmen did this," Mr Taversham grumbled.

"And you have proof of that?" Clara queried.

The way Taversham turned his head made her suspect that he was thinking she was a damn silly and interfering woman. And if she was not careful, he would refuse to speak to her at all in future. Clara let her last question go unanswered and agreed that they were done. Mr Taversham wrote out his list of names for her and departed from the room with an indignant grumble about being made to feel guilty just because he was a man. Clara would have liked to explain how everyone she interviewed came in for her own brand of suspicion, but she guessed now was not the time. She let Taversham go and set off for home. There was something very odd afoot in the Pavilion. Betrayal and murder, that was the gist of the matter. But who felt betrayed and were they the murdering sort, or had Esther been killed by someone else entirely? Clara concluded that knowing more about Esther might be helpful. If the woman proved to have enemies, that was something worth pursuing. In a way she hoped the crime against Esther was not as random as it seemed. It troubled Clara a lot to think of a person just killing someone else for no better reason than that it would delay Abigail and her tight deadline. It was an awful thing to think.

Clara walked home enjoying the warm sun on her shoulders. She would have to get her best dress out for the meal, but she had an ominous feeling that she was going to look very out-of-place among the Albion ladies. Never mind, she had work to do. A killer had to be found and the meal would provide the prime opportunity to get a good look at some of the suspects in this case. She just hoped nothing sinister would happen before that time came.

Chapter Five

The dinner did not begin until eight o'clock. Clara had a lot of time to burn that afternoon. Theoretically she could have been working on the case, not that she had much of a notion where to begin. Inspector Park-Coombs would be investigating the background of the victim and also making enquiries into disgruntled employees of Albion Industries. Clara had to make do with talking to people here, in Brighton, and she had a feeling everyone at the Pavilion would be too busy to speak to her.

Besides, there was something else she ought to be doing. Something that had weighed on her mind since she had learned that Captain O'Harris was alive and back in Brighton.

She had grieved for the Captain, nearly broken her heart over him. He had been so alive and so very enthralling. She could have a good argument with him, if she wanted. He had been a good counter to her sometimes overly determined investigating. For a man she had barely known, he had felt like an old friend. And then he had been gone, just gone. She had imagined all the ghastly things that could have occurred to him over the ocean, everything from his plane catching fire to him ditching into shark-infested waters. Those thoughts had been bad enough. To now know he had been alive but lost for nearly a year made her despair even more, for the authorities had stopped looking for him when they concluded he was dead, and all the time he had been waiting, hoping for rescue.

Clara could not be certain, after all this time, after being abandoned, that Captain O'Harris would want to see her, or that he would be the same man she remembered. The thought crushed her with dread and made her hesitate to go and see him. She considered this a type of cowardice, but she could not shake it from her heart.

Fortunately, Clara was pragmatic and sensible enough to know that this was not all about her. Whatever her feelings on the subject, Captain O'Harris deserved a visitor. There were few others close to him in Brighton to go to his hospital bed. Captain O'Harris' parents were dead. His uncle and aunt, who had offered him a home when he was orphaned, were also deceased. He had no other family and having only returned to Brighton shortly after the war to take up residence in the old manor house, he had yet to make any firm friendships outside of Clara and her brother. Captain O'Harris was a self-confessed loner. His personal demons, created by the war, prevented him from easily making attachments to others. O'Harris kept his distance from the world and, in return, it kept its distance from him. Clara doubted he had had any visitors to the hospital, except perhaps for Colonel Brandt; an old family friend of the O'Harrises. If Clara did not pay him a call, who would?

Clara resolved herself to the effort. Perhaps O'Harris would not want to see her. That would have to be endured.

Clara arrived at Brighton's General Hospital in time for the afternoon visiting hour. She noted, as she walked up the steps to the front doors, that there were several suspect individuals loitering around. They looked like pressmen, probably hoping for a scoop. It reminded Clara that she had to find the newspaperman who was nosing about the Pavilion. She avoided eye contact with the loiterers. Most of them knew her on sight from her various cases and also knew she had been a friend of O'Harris. She expected to be harangued by them when she exited the building, but it did not worry her unduly.

Clara introduced herself to the girl on the hospital's reception desk. She explained the purpose of her visit and that her name had been supplied by Inspector Park-Coombs as one of those allowed to see the Captain. The girl double-checked, nonetheless, then agreed that Clara could go upstairs to see the patient. She was given the number of a private room on the first floor where O'Harris was residing. Clara thanked the girl and went upstairs.

The hospital smelt of bleach and various types of antiseptic. Clara had worked in a hospital as a voluntary nurse during the war and the smells were so familiar that they rapidly disappeared into the background for her and she no longer noticed them. Clara stopped an orderly and asked if she was heading in the right direction for the private room where O'Harris was staying. She was given new directions and hurried on. Finally she came to a door marked 115.

Clara took a deep breath. Even now her nerve threatened to leave her, but Clara was not to be defeated. She had come this far and she had a friend on the other side of this door. She rapped on the white painted wood. A voice from within croaked that she might enter.

The moment between turning the handle for the door and pushing it open seemed to take an eternity. It was an eternity filled with dread and excitement. Hope and fear. Her stomach went over as she trembled at what she might see when she was presented with O'Harris. As the door crept open so the hospital bed came into view, then the red itchy wool blankets the hospital provided, and then, at last, Captain O'Harris himself. Clara stood in the doorway and just stared. He was the same as always.

Dashing, dark haired, a handsome face that was etched with the woes of a man who has been to war. The lines seemed no deeper, but Captain O'Harris' smile seemed to take a while to reach his eyes. He slowly took in the person standing on the threshold of his room.

"Clara," he really did smile now.

Clara was filled with relief. She entered the room and shut the door before hurrying to his bedside where there was a chair set out for visitors.

"Inspector Park-Coombs told me you were here," she said softly. "I…"

Clara had to stop herself because her voice had cracked with emotion and she was not about to burst into tears before the captain. She had to remind herself that this visit was not about her, it was about him.

"I suppose I am rather a shock," O'Harris said. He seemed to have only just woken from a doze and his voice was hoarse. He coughed. "I am rather a shock to myself."

"You silly fool, where have you been?" Clara asked tearfully, her emotions disobeying her determination to remain in control of herself.

Captain O'Harris grinned at her.

"I missed you Clara. Thoughts of you scolding me for disappearing sustained me through many a long night. I did promise I would come back."

"You never said it would take nearly a year!"

The grin faded a little.

"I never expected that myself," the captain admitted. "Actually, until recently, I had no concept of how long it had been. It felt a lot longer."

"What happened?" Clara asked, desperate for explanations. "Where were you?"

"I don't remember all of it," O'Harris explained tentatively. "There are large blanks in my memory. One of the doctors said it was a normal side effect from the trauma I have been through. Considering what I went through during the war, you would think I would be able to cope better with one rather mediocre plane crash."

"Don't be silly," Clara told him stoutly. "None of us know how dramatic events will affect us. Even the bravest and most daring of souls can suffer. It is not something to be ashamed of."

"I missed you telling me off," O'Harris laughed. "You are the only person, aside from my aunt, who has been confident enough to do that!"

"It is not confidence," Clara replied. "Just honesty."

O'Harris fell silent. Suddenly he reached out and took her hand. He squeezed it tight.

"I was afraid, foolishly enough, that you would not come and see me. I thought that perhaps you had moved on, found someone else…"

Clara, who had very nearly not come, squeezed his hand back.

"If it is any consolation, I was afraid you would not want to see me."

"Right pair of fools we are then!" O'Harris gave her that boyish grin of his, that hinted at mischief, but yet was oh so enticing.

Clara smiled in return.

"What happened John? On that day when you disappeared?"

O'Harris pulled himself upright in bed a little more and took a moment to compose himself. He never let go of Clara's hand.

"The White Buzzard's engine packed up. I've thought about it over and over. The hows and the whys. In the early days I had almost convinced myself she had been sabotaged. Now, with a more rational head on my shoulders, I perceive it as just pure bad luck. Aeroplanes malfunction, it is one of the awful risks we pilots must take. We can check them and maintain them as often as we like and then, one day, something just fails or breaks," O'Harris gave a sigh. "I suppose it could have been worse. I mean, crashing into an ocean is pretty bad, but it is better than ploughing into the ground.

"She started to stutter the second day we were over

the ocean. I mentioned the issue to my co-pilot, but what could we do? We had nowhere to land and make repairs. We just had to carry on and hope. We debated about turning around, heading back to England. But we had a tail wind driving us on, and turning back into it would likely have slowed us down considerably. We thought it was about as broad as it was long, so we carried on towards America. The White Buzzard stuttered all day and as night fell I was certain she was losing momentum. The steering felt less responsive, it might have been my overworked imagination, but I felt she was no longer pulling so strongly.

"During the night we lost height. That might have been a coincidence, judging height in the dark over an ocean is challenging with a perfect engine, let alone with one that has developed a cough. When dawn came we were so close to the waves we could feel spray hitting us. I tried to pull the Buzzard back up, but the effort was too much for her. She spluttered and gave out a death groan, then her valiant engine gave up. She stalled. I knew that was the end. All I could do was try and glide her down into the water. She fell like a stone and we were both thrown from our seats into the cold water."

O'Harris paused, his eyes wandering to the hills and valleys of the hospital blanket where it rested over him.

"I lost sight of my co-pilot pretty quickly. We had life vests on, fortunately. There was a good chance we would not drown, at least not swiftly, and the water was not as freezing as I had feared. But the currents swept us apart and the wreckage of the Buzzard sank within minutes. It suddenly dawned on me, as I found myself alone, that I was now floating in a vast expanse of water. A mere speck to any chance passer-by. What were the odds someone would see me?" O'Harris grimaced. "I felt more guilty about my co-pilot, feeling I had dragged him on this foolish mission. That was all I could think about as I floated. I cursed myself, cursed my luck. That was when thoughts of sabotage started to spring to mind. I became convinced I had been the victim of a vindictive rival, no matter how far-fetched that seemed."

"How long were you floating in the sea?" Clara asked gently.

"I couldn't say," O'Harris shrugged his shoulders. "Time meant nothing and towards the end I slipped in and out of consciousness. The life vest kept me afloat, else I would have drowned. I mean to write a letter to the company that supplied them, informing them of the quality of their product."

O'Harris paused to laugh at himself.

"What nonsense I think of!"

Clara squeezed his hand, assuring him it was not nonsense.

"Anyway, at some point the currents took me to this little island where I washed ashore. It was somewhere off the coast of America, one of those little sandy places where indigenous people still make their home. I was starving and close to dying of thirst. Someone, one of those natives, kindly dragged me ashore and I was taken into a village. There I remained, I can't say how long. My memory of the time is hazy. I was tended by a native woman who, in my delirium, I sometimes imagined was my late aunt. Everything is so very muddled in my mind about that," O'Harris waved his free hand at his head, indicating how fluffy his thoughts had been back then. "I can't even recall if the woman spoke English or not. I think perhaps I had a fever, or some tropical sickness that clouded my thoughts. I know I was well looked after. Placed in a bed, fed with soups and stews, the like of which I had never tasted before, and given plenty of water. I had to be helped to eat and drink. I was helpless, all my strength gone. I was so racked with guilt over my co-pilot that a part of me did not even care if I lived. But half the time I was so out of my mind I could not remember who I was, let alone what had happened to me.

"Once a month a mission from the mainland would come to the island to deliver supplies and offer medical aid to anyone who was sick. One time they came and they were shown to me. I don't remember it, I was told about it later. Through the mission arrangements were made to take me to an American hospital…"

Captain O'Harris was interrupted by a bell that rang to let everyone know visiting time was over. Clara pulled a piteous face, she did not want to leave. O'Harris glanced at her sadly.

"Will you come again?"

"Of course!" Clara declared.

"Tonight?"

Clara felt her heart sink as she explained.

"I cannot. I have to attend a dinner being hosted at the Pavilion. But, if you would like, Tommy wants to visit you and he could come tonight?"

O'Harris had looked disappointed, now he brightened again.

"I would like to see Tommy," he agreed.

Clara left him with promises that she would soon return and that he would have Tommy for company that evening. She made her way out of the hospital with some haste, avoiding the newspapermen who, predictably, sprang on her the instant she set foot outside. She ignored them, refusing to answer their questions, and was soon on the pavement and hurrying home. Her heart was beating fast, a sensation of happiness and joy filling her. O'Harris had been glad to see her. Nothing could have made her happier. There was a new spring to her step as she walked along smiling to herself.

Chapter Six

Abigail Sommers stopped outside the doors of the hastily prepared dining room and turned to Clara.

"I hope you enjoy this. I am finding it hard to keep my enthusiasm going after…" Abigail tailed off.

It was half past seven in the evening and the specially invited guests were slowly arriving for the dinner party. Abigail had promised it would be a feast to be remembered, but it was apparent that she had lost all interest in the event after recent developments.

"When I have a chance, I am going to compose a letter to Esther's parents. I feel I should," Abigail pulled a face, it was clearly a task she did not relish. How could she explain that it was while she was in charge of the trade fair that Esther Althorpe had met her unfortunate end? "I really don't know what to say."

"Just say you are sorry," Clara answered her. "What else can you offer but your condolences?"

"Clara, if I had thought this was the way things were going to go when I came to your office, I would have informed the police at once. It never occurred to me that someone would die," Abigail dropped her voice, aware that other guests were now walking up the stairs to join them outside the improvised dining room.

"There is no point blaming yourself," Clara said calmly. "No one, except the person responsible, expected this to happen."

Abigail gave one last frown, before she forced her face into a smiling countenance of jolly non-concern and greeted the other guests now joining them. She opened the dining room doors and invited people to take a seat where they pleased. The room had formerly been one of the less extravagant bedrooms, but it had now been cleared of furniture except for a long dining table and a number of chairs. The walls, however, were still hung with the artwork collected by the first monarch to use this place as his private retreat. The Pavilion was not a huge building, considering its royal origins, and many of the rooms were relatively small. It was therefore quite cosy in the dining room and there was a real risk, Clara noted anxiously, that some of the guests might accidentally crack their chairs back into the ornate walls and damage some of the decoration. Clara hoped she would not have to explain such a mishap to the committee.

In fact, quite a few of her fellow Pavilion patrons were present, specially invited because they had allowed Albion Industries to hire the place for their trade fair. Other guests were businessmen within the cosmetics industry; important clients and contacts who were being wined and dined at Albion's expense to make them friendly towards future trade deals. Clara realised with a glimmer of disappointment that, aside from Abigail, she was the only woman present.

Abigail stood at the head of the table and welcomed them all. She was dressed extremely well in a Moroccan blue dress and turquoise silk wrap about her shoulders. She glittered with pretty jewelled trinkets on her wrists and around her neck and her make-up was immaculate. She blinked expressive kohl eyes at the room. Clara felt quite dowdy in contrast. She had opted for a pale green dress and a cream cotton wrap that sat about her shoulders unnecessarily, for the room was already quite hot. She did not wear make-up and felt as though this was an error considering the company. She was relieved when the first course was served and she could concentrate on eating rather than reflecting on her inadequacies before the other diners.

Abigail had given her a brief outline of the guests in the room, emphasising over and over that none could possibly have anything to do with the crime against poor Esther. Clara thought it unlikely that any man in the room might have been directly involved in murder, but could someone here have enough of a grudge against Albion to try and sabotage their first trade fair in Brighton?

"Which company do you work for?" the man on Clara's left asked her.

"Fitzgerald and Co," Clara answered automatically, Abigail had advised she not tell anyone at dinner she was a private detective.

"Are you quite a new company?" the man persisted.

"Rather!" Clara smiled. "And we are currently only operating in Brighton, but we do hope to expand."

"This is an ideal opportunity for you then," the man nodded. "Getting to meet some of the top names in the business."

"I hope so," Clara smiled. "Might I ask who you are?"

"Henry Forthclyde," Henry introduced himself. "Of Cushing's Corsetry. We have sold our products through Albion for a number of years now. What do you specialise in?"

Clara was almost flummoxed for a response, but something reminded her that Albion Industries also dealt in health products that could aid failing beauty.

"We bottle and sell Brighton water," she said with a flash of inspiration. "It has a remarkable array of health properties and can restore one's youthful appearance."

"Quite a niche market," Forthclyde noted.

"For the moment, but we have other products coming

to market soon," Clara felt that her imaginary business was being called into question and decided to change the subject. "Can you tell me about the others at the table?"

"Some of them," Forthclyde said. "Let's see, over there are two representatives from Holt and Sons, a manufacturer of perfumes. And several of the men at the top of the table are from Albion Industries. To our right we have men from Carters' fine cosmetics, Diamond Pharmaceuticals, Locke and Co. Cosmetic Dentistry and Anderson's Chemical Company, who produce a range of base products used in the manufacture of various cosmetics."

Clara surveyed the room as the names were mentioned to her. The men mostly looked middle-aged and used to eating well. Some of them looked rather in need of their own services, especially the chap from Locke and Co. who had a severe overbite.

"They rather sound like they have been involved with Albion Industries a long time," Clara said thoughtfully.

"They have. I don't think any company here, barring yourself, has been involved with Albion less than five years. Cushing's Corsetry has been providing unique products to Albion these last fifty years, I am delighted to say," Forthclyde looked pleased with himself.

"Have you a stall here, Mr Forthclyde?" Clara asked.

"I do indeed," Forthclyde preened. "We are introducing our latest range of flatteners, for the ample girl trying to attain the fashionable fit of today's dresses."

Whalebone vests to ditch the curves, Clara concluded. Ironic, considering that for much of its history the corset was designed to create a curved hourglass figure rather than straighten it out.

"I imagine many companies will be aiming to launch a new product this week?" Clara continued, roving her eyes over the assorted men about her and committing their faces to memory. None of them looked much like a saboteur.

"Absolutely! I would think, at such a prestigious event

as this, it would be preposterous not to! I hear tell that Albion is launching a new lipstick shade itself, a rather controversial piece, or so I am told."

Clara glanced up at this little nugget of information. Forthclyde had clearly said it to arouse her curiosity. He was a gossip, pure and simple.

"What could be controversial about a lipstick shade?" Clara asked.

"In itself, nothing," Forthclyde nodded. "But it is how they came about the shade that has led to rumours. The story goes that Albion stole the colour and its unique pearly appearance – which is produced using a secret ingredient – off a rival company. If true, it would be quite the show stopper. It could lead to a court case, of all things. The scandal would be immense."

Clara was always interested when the word 'scandal' came up in one of her cases. Such talk had the tendency to produce murder suspects, as well as offering motive.

"Surely Albion Industries would not be so foolish as to take such a risk?" she said to Forthclyde.

"This is a backstabbing business, beauty products," Forthclyde told her with a rather sad look in his eye, as if he despaired of her naivety. "If a company thinks it can get away with it, they'll risk a lot. Albion wants to be the market leader, it doesn't want a rival company producing a new inventive product and taking sales from them."

Clara's thoughts had revolved back to that scrawled word on the floor – betrayal. Was the person behind the sabotage and murder a disgruntled member of this other company which Albion had stolen from?

"I still can't believe it. What company are you referring to?" Clara asked.

"They are called The House of Jasmine. The owner is of Oriental descent and quite innovative, along with being very cutthroat. He and Albion have been at loggerheads for years."

It still seemed implausible that a big company like Albion would risk their reputation by stealing from another company.

"You don't believe me," Forthclyde said in amusement. "I think you ought to, especially if you wish to survive in this industry. There is no honour among beauty product manufacturers!"

Clara was starting to feel rather glad her health product company was entirely fictitious. She worked her way through the four-course dinner without extracting anything more from Mr Forthclyde on the subject of Albion's suspected treachery. Nor were her neighbouring guests much interested in talking about anything but their own business arrangements. She was soon exasperated listening to discussions on stock prices, disgruntled shareholders and profit margins. As the meal wrapped up, Clara was glad to be free of the talk. She did, however, stop Abigail in the main hall of the Pavilion and take her to one side before she left for home. Abigail had survived the evening despite her earlier anxieties, she looked strained however, and her make-up was not completely masking the weary lines across her forehead and about her eyes.

"What is it Clara?" she asked with a hint of hope in her voice.

"Just something I wished to ask you about, it may be nothing, but it was curious."

Abigail's weariness suddenly lifted as she was given this news.

"Anything, Clara, that could solve this awful tragedy, ask anything."

"It was something I overheard during dinner. A piece of gossip, possibly no more than a malicious rumour."

Abigail's enthusiasm faded again.

"Oh? Is that all?"

"Someone said, and I can't possibly think it true, that Albion Industries stole the recipe for their new lipstick shade."

"Pearl Pink!" Abigail gasped and then her face hardened. "That will be The House of Jasmine spreading gossip once again. So, it has gotten back to some of our supplies? I should not be surprised. In fact, it's just the sort of thing The House of Jasmine would deliberately tell them."

"It is untrue?" Clara asked cautiously.

"Of course!" Abigail threw up her hands in astonishment that Clara had to ask. "Albion have been working for years on a way to create a sheen to their lipsticks like the shine you get on a real pearl. They have tried all manner of ingredients to perfect the process but only lately have they had success. As it happens, The House of Jasmine caught wind of Albion's project and began their own work, hoping to create their lipstick first. Mr Mokano who runs the firm is very competitive and can't bear to think he is being overtaken. We suspected he had placed a spy in Albion's headquarters."

"We?" Clara picked up on the word rather sharply. Abigail was talking more like one of the businessmen they had just dined with than as a sales representative.

Abigail blushed. Her anger had made her indiscreet.

"You will think I have taken advantage of my position to further my career," she said, her face still flushed. "But it is not like that. The people in charge of the representatives' sales figures have no idea."

"What are you saying Abigail?" Clara pressed.

Once more her friend blushed bright red.

"I have been seeing a young man who works in product development at the head office," she admitted in a low voice, quickly glancing over her shoulder to see that the other guests had departed. It was now just her and Clara in the Pavilion. "But it has only been for the last six months and it has nothing to do with me being put in charge of this trade fair. I earned this role by my own merit."

Clara was not concerned whether that was true or not, unless it was cause for someone to feel betrayed and even to commit murder.

"That is how you know about the Pearl Pinks?"

"Yes, look, Davy, my young man, he works in the laboratory where they devise new lipsticks. He knows all about the development of Pearl Pink and it was never stolen from anyone. Mr Mokano has been pipped to the post, that is all, and now he is angry. So he spreads rumours."

"Would he go further than that?" Clara asked.

It took a moment before Abigail realised what she was implying.

"No! I mean," Abigail pressed a hand to her mouth. "No, I can't think it. It would be so petty to try and sabotage us, and to kill Esther…"

Abigail stood very still, close to brimming over with tears. Clara reached out a hand and placed it on her shoulder.

"I'm sorry to have pushed the matter," she said. "But these questions have to be asked."

Abigail nodded, taking a deep breath to still her emotions.

"I think…"

A tremendous clatter came from the recently vacated dining room. Both women fell silent and exchanged a glance, then Abigail turned and started to run upstairs. Clara followed behind. They entered the dining room to see a huddle of serving staff standing to one side of the room in shock. Before them all, lying sprawled across the dining table where he had knocked glasses and plates flying, was the unfortunate figure of Mr Forthclyde. Clara felt her breath catch in her throat. Protruding from his chest was a large, thin white object. His head was thrown back as he eyeballed the ornate ceiling helplessly. Abigail gave a slightly hysterical cry.

"I thought he left with the rest?" she said to Clara.

Clara could only shake her head. So had she, but here he was lying dead before them. Clara licked her lips and pushed her anxieties to the back of her mind.

"You better summon the police again, Abigail," she said.

Chapter Seven

Dr Deàth poised himself over Forthclyde. He was not the tallest of men and had required a stool to raise him sufficiently above the corpse on the table and enable him to look directly down on the victim. The police coroner had been staring at the dead man for some time, apparently trying to take in every detail of the scene. He was not alone; Oliver Bankes, police photographer when he was not working in his shop, was going around the room taking pictures from every angle. There was a lot of debris about the body, the service staff had not had a chance to clear the table before Mr Forthclyde met his unfortunate end. Oliver was taking pictures so at a future date the position of every plate, spoon and glass would be known. There was no telling if something like that might be important.

"Stabbed," Dr Deàth said steadily.

Clara glanced at Inspector Park-Coombs, he responded with a roll of his eyes.

"I think we could all work that one out," he rumbled.

Dr Deàth looked up and smiled at them lightly. He was an easy-going soul who rarely took offence at the inspector's gruff demeanour.

"Cumbersome weapon for the task," he said, pointing a

finger at the flat white object that had been thrust down into poor Mr Forthclyde. "I do believe this is whalebone. The edges of which can become surprisingly sharp if honed. Not the usual choice for murder, though."

"Whalebone!" Clara tutted at herself for not guessing what the material was sooner, it had just looked so odd and out of place. "Mr Forthclyde worked for Cushing's Corsetry. It would not surprise me if that article has come out of one of the new flatteners he was intending to launch here at the trade fair."

"Yes, it could be a whalebone stave," Dr Deàth agreed. "As I said before, not a convenient murder weapon. Though I suppose you imagine your killer was going for irony over pragmatism?"

The inspector gave a humph.

"I don't like it when murderers start becoming creative."

"What is truly alarming is how fast this whole thing occurred," Clara said. "The guests had only just left, and we assumed Mr Forthclyde had gone with them. I was just having a quiet word with Abigail Sommers when we heard a commotion and ran upstairs to find this."

"So, Miss Sommers has an alibi," Inspector Park-Coombs noted. "But we still have a Pavilion full of suspects. I'll need a list of the names of the service staff here tonight and also all the guests. If Mr Forthclyde hung back, perhaps someone else did as well."

"I just can't explain why he remained here," Clara sighed. "Was he perhaps waiting for someone? Or hoping to catch Abigail for a quick word?"

"Perhaps he just fancied finishing off this wine," Oliver pointed out several half-finished bottles of red wine on the sideboard. The party had been over-stocked and, since all the men had work to attend to in the morning, there had been a practical reluctance to avoid over-indulgence. They had mostly been older men with sensible heads on their shoulders, business was their addiction and wine could only run a close second. There had been a great deal of alcohol leftover, but could Mr Forthclyde really have come back up here for a drink?

"We best start the interviews," Park-Coombs said solemnly, ignoring Oliver.

They wandered downstairs to the front hall of the Pavilion where Abigail and the service staff were gathered, watched over by a pair of police constables. A couple of the staff looked eager to disappear the instant they got the chance, hence why the constables were supervising them. Abigail pounced on Inspector Park-Coombs as he appeared down the stairs.

"I have had the workmen's break room opened for our use," she declared. "If that is all right. And may we proceed? I am worried that the service staff might revolt if they have to remain much longer. They are all rather shaken up by events."

Park-Coombs agreed to take their statements first and directed the staff one by one into the room set aside by Abigail. The process, which Clara was privy to, was unenlightening. There were eight men on the service staff, ranging from two chefs to several waiters. They had been hired locally to prepare and serve the meal that evening, and the waiters were then expected to clear everything away afterwards. Four waiters had walked into the dining room and discovered the body sprawled on the table. They had heard a crashing noise and gone to investigate it. They had only just arrived when Abigail and Clara had appeared. Each man denied anything to do with the crime and since they had all been walking together to the room from the old servants' quarters downstairs, they could alibi each other. The remaining staff had been in the kitchen cleaning the various pots, pans, moulds, spoons and other implements the chefs had used to create their feast. As each item was cleaned and dried, so it was packed away, the chefs taking especial consideration over the process as some of the items were quite delicate. No one had been out of sight of someone else for more than a moment. Park-Coombs took the names of the staff and said they could go home. They would have to return in the morning to finish clearing the dining room and retrieve the rest of their culinary equipment.

That just left Abigail. She came into the break room looking extremely pale. Clara wished she could offer her a cup of tea, but the stove was out and the workmen had taken their mugs and tea home with them. She offered her instead her cotton wrap, to throw about her shoulders and warm her a little. Abigail thanked her.

"I take it you were speaking with Miss Fitzgerald when you heard a noise from upstairs?" Inspector Park-Coombs began.

"Yes," Abigail answered.

"And you both went upstairs?"

"Yes."

"You saw no sign of anyone else about?"

"Other than the service staff, no," Abigail clutched her hands together, they were threatening to tremble. "I was not prepared for what I saw, not at all. Poor Mr Forthclyde. I thought perhaps something had collapsed, a table maybe. That's what it sounded like, a lot of plates and things crashing down. Instead…"

Abigail fell silent.

"Did you see Mr Forthclyde leave with the other guests?" Clara asked.

Abigail paused, before she shook her head.

"I was going to say I had, but really I only had an impression of who was leaving. They went as a group and I did not say goodbye to each individually. It was negligent of me, but I had so much else on my mind. The Pavilion is still not quite ready for the opening and I was thinking of all the things still to do," Abigail looked ashamed by her hospitality failings. "I really didn't want to have to deal with this banquet. It interrupted my other work. But what does it matter now? With poor Mr Forthclyde…"

"Where was Cushing's Corsetry's stock kept?" Clara

continued before Abigail could dwell too much on what had occurred.

"I'll show you," Abigail rose and led them out of the room and down a short corridor to one of the smaller rooms in the Pavilion. She opened the door and motioned to a series of towering piles of boxes. "We have had to put several rooms aside for stock."

Clara walked into the room and looked about her. Most of the boxes were carefully labelled, and she easily found those belonging to Cushing's Corsetry. As she moved among the stacks, she saw one box that was sitting on its own behind the others. The seal on its lid had been cut through and the two flaps that formed the top of the box gaped slightly open. Clara pulled the box forward and opened it.

"Here is where our murderer found their weapon," she said, standing back so Abigail and the inspector could see.

A corset was lying heaped on top of a layer of tissue paper. It had been ripped open roughly and one of the whalebone staves removed. The irony, as far as Clara could see, was that someone had used a knife to remove the stave. Why make a second, inferior weapon to stab a man with when you already had one to hand? The only reason would be to make a point.

"Who has access to these rooms, Miss Sommers?" Inspector Park-Coombs asked Abigail.

"Everyone," Abigail shrugged her shoulders. "The room is not locked. It would be a nightmare to have keys made up for everyone who needed to come in here. We intended to place a security guard at the entrance to the corridor during the trade fair to prevent anyone wandering in and stealing goods. But that hardly seemed necessary at the moment."

Abigail looked bleak, clearly thinking that a security guard on site might have prevented a lot of tragedy occurring.

"Someone is determined to ruin this event," she said tearfully. "Must I cancel the fair, Inspector?"

Park-Coombs shook his head.

"We can cordon off the rooms where the incidents occurred. In any case, it is this fair that is keeping our killer around. If we cancel it then he or she will have succeeded and will have no further reason to remain. I would rather they did not escape so easily."

Abigail nodded, but Clara suspected she was half-inclined to cancel the event herself. The strain of everything was simply too much to bear.

"Could there have been any reason why someone would wish Mr Forthclyde harm?" Clara asked her.

Abigail shook her head.

"I did not know him well. I can no more say why someone would hurt him as I can explain why he did not leave with the rest of the guests," Abigail rubbed at her tired eyes. "I suppose I must send a telegram to Cushing's and let them know their trade stall will no longer have a representative. Someone is out to ruin me, Clara, I am certain of it!"

Clara put a comforting arm around her shoulder.

"Go home, go to bed," she told her. "Rest and put this out of your mind. This is not your fault. Some lunatic has taken a grudge against Albion Industries, that is awful, but out of your control."

Abigail smiled wanly, but she didn't seem to entirely believe Clara. It was all too easy to imagine that her employers would gladly blame this misfortune upon her and use her as a scapegoat. She agreed to go home anyway, there was nothing more she could do until morning.

They had only just said goodbye to Abigail when a voice called out for the inspector and they hastened back upstairs. Dr Deàth's assistants had just lifted up the late Mr Forthclyde and removed his body to a waiting stretcher. Beneath the body, amid the debris of dinner, the coroner had spotted some smeared writing. As Park-Coombs arrived he pointed it out.

"I think someone was writing a message when Mr

Forthclyde stumbled upon them," he said. "I can make out B, E, T, R, A."

"Betrayal," Clara finished the word. "The same message was written on the floor downstairs."

She stepped a little closer to the table.

"Written in Pearl Pink lipstick again. The killer's favourite."

"Are we now suggesting that Mr Forthclyde had the misfortune to stumble upon something he should not have seen?" Park-Coombs peered at the smeared letters.

"Perhaps, but the whalebone stave had been prepared as a weapon for a reason," Clara said. "Maybe it was not meant for him or maybe it was. We still don't know why he came back upstairs."

"Mr Bankes take a picture of this," the inspector commanded. "I'll get my men to check the room for fingerprints if you are done, doctor?"

"Done," Dr Deàth smiled at them. "I shall take our friend here back to his new residence and settle him in."

Inspector Park-Coombs grumbled at the coroner's strange sense of humour. He sent his men to work scouring the place for any other potential clues and also dusting for fingerprints. Though he complained mournfully that there must be hundreds to be found, and most would be irrelevant to his enquiries. Clara wandered downstairs with Oliver Bankes. The inspector wanted his photographs developed as soon as possible and Oliver was anticipating a long night of work ahead. As he walked next to Clara he glanced at her.

"Have you heard the news?"

Clara looked at him out of the corner of her eye. She had been friends with Oliver over a year now. He had been a shoulder to cry on when Captain O'Harris had vanished, though Clara had never taken liberties. She knew Oliver had always hoped they might become something more than friends.

"Do you mean about O'Harris returning to Brighton?" she asked him.

Oliver nodded.

"It's very good news, isn't it?" Oliver smiled at her. "You must be relieved."

"Relieved, surprised," Clara shrugged her shoulders. "It sometimes seems implausible. Yet, I have seen him alive and well. Somehow he survived."

"I'm glad," Oliver reassured her. "You haven't been the same since he was lost."

"I barely knew him," Clara countered, flushing with embarrassment that she had been so obvious in her grief.

"Still, you liked him," Oliver said gently. "And now he is back. The newspapers are desperate for an interview with him, you know."

"I know! They attempted to nab me as I left the hospital earlier today," Clara complained. "You would think they could find other stories to interest them."

As she said this, she realised that the very story that would distract their attention was the one they were trying to keep hidden from them. At least until the trade fair had concluded.

"How long before they learn about this?" Oliver read her thoughts.

"Not long," Clara sighed. "It's becoming too blatant now. I just hope we can find the culprit before things get out of hand, well, at least anymore out of hand than they already are."

Clara paused.

"Might I get a copy of your photographs too? They might prove useful."

"I'll have to get permission from the inspector, but I don't see why not. You are clearly involved in this case," Oliver agreed. "Would you mind if I walked you home? It's on my way back to the shop and with this maniac on the loose I would feel happier if I saw you home safely."

Clara almost laughed. After all the adventures she had been through, it was about time people started to realise she could take care of herself. But she supposed that would never happen, not when she was a woman and her friends were men. It was too engrained for them to be protective.

"I tell you what," she smiled at Oliver. "I'll walk you home as far as my house, so I know no madman is coming after you."

Oliver laughed.

"Deal!"

They wandered out of the Pavilion and into the night.

Chapter Eight

Clara made her way to the Brighton Gazette's head office the following morning. She wanted to locate this rogue newspaperman and find out just what he knew about the events at the Pavilion. So far, she had a lot of questions and very few answers. No one had suggested a suspect or a likely motive for the crimes. Without those connections it was hard to know what to make of this whole affair.

The Brighton Gazette operated out of a strange building that had once been a chapel. It rose up between the usual Victorian terraces with a domed roof and a tower at the front that suggested it should have once housed a bell. The offices were spread over two rather cramped floors and the editor of the paper, who was also the owner, had a room at the front of the building where a circular stained glass window overlooked the street. Clara found herself sitting in this room, listening to the noise of traffic outside and admiring the precisely cut pieces of coloured glass. Whoever had designed the window had gone for an abstract pattern that was more about creating a rainbow of colour than illustrating a Bible story. Mr Pontefract sat right before the window in his big leather chair, and rays of different colours danced across his white shirt.

"Now, Miss Fitzgerald, what can I do for you?"

Mr Pontefract had started the newspaper at the turn of the century, having dabbled in the world of writing for several years beforehand. The money for the business venture had come from an inheritance left to him by a distant great aunt. Mr Pontefract had relished the idea of being a free man, able to run his paper as he wished, employ the people he wanted and write the things he wanted to write. Of course, none of that had actually happened, for he had to run the newspaper within the strictures of the business world, working with printers and advertisers and distributors who had their own ideas of what a newspaper should be like. And he had to employ people he did not always agree with because they were good at what they did and would make his paper a success, and some of the more radical souls he had thought to employ proved hopelessly inadequate when it came to producing regular articles. As for writing the things he wanted to write, well, there were times he could, but mostly he was constrained by what his readers wanted to read, and what his advertisers were happy sharing column space with. The wrong article could offend a lot of people.

Mr Pontefract, fortunately, was a pragmatic soul who rather liked his office and his role as editor, and could live with the limitations imposed on his work by an inconsiderate world. Now, settling nicely into his forties, with a pleasant paunch that spoke of comfortable living, he was quite content and looking forward to many similar years of easy living. After all, there were advantages to knowing exactly what people wanted, it saved a lot of time that would otherwise be wasted being creative, for a start.

"I assume you are still happy with your advertisement in the Gazette?" Mr Pontefract asked, a hint of concern on his face. "I would hate to think that one of our customers was dissatisfied."

"I am perfectly satisfied with my advertisement," Clara

assured him. "I actually came to ask you about one of your newspapermen. He was hanging around the Pavilion recently and was unceremoniously kicked out."

"Ah, that would be Gilbert," Mr Pontefract nodded with instant recognition. "He had a whiff of a potential story over there. Something about an industrial accident? Gilbert is very concerned about the conditions endured by the working man. You may have seen his recent series of articles on the lack of safety regulations put in place at factories and building sites? He interviewed a number of fellows who were severely injured just doing their job."

Clara, who had very little spare time to read anything, apologetically admitted she had not seen these articles.

"Might I speak with Gilbert?" she asked. "I am hopeful he may be able to offer me help in a case I am working on."

"He should be at his desk," Mr Pontefract explained. "He is supposed to be typing up the obituaries. That is one of Gilbert's more mundane tasks at the newspaper. He complains about it a lot."

Mr Pontefract led Clara out of his office and down to the ground floor of the Gazette's headquarters. This was an open space filled with desks and the clatter of typewriters. Cigarette smoke hung in a haze around head level and discarded or lost papers covered the floor. This was where the real work of the Gazette took place, where she was composed and created each week in a fug of mild pandemonium and nicotine.

"Here he is, Gilbert McMillan," Mr Pontefract pointed out a man sat behind a desk. He was glaring at a sheet of paper lodged in his typewriter, as if he imagined this would cause the machine to operate itself. "Gilbert, this is Clara Fitzgerald and she wants to talk to you about your work at the Pavilion."

Gilbert jumped up from his chair so fast at the sight of Clara before his desk, that his chair was thrown back and fell over. He looked a touch stunned to see a woman in his workspace.

"How are you coming on with this week's obituaries?" Pontefract asked, ignoring the man's clearly disconcerted demeanour. "Hope you have done a suitably nice piece about the old major who just popped his clogs. I expect lots of stuff about his military record. Anyway, take a few moments off to speak with Miss Fitzgerald."

With a wave of his hand, dismissing both Clara and Gilbert and their problems, Pontefract sauntered off back to his office. Not missing the chance, as he went along the row of desks, to harangued various members of his staff over the slow pace of their work.

Clara lost interest in him and turned instead to Gilbert McMillan. Gilbert was a man in his late twenties who suffered from a bad case of short-sightedness and had to wear thick glasses all the time. He was a good journalist, very adept at rooting out information from people, but he was also very used to working with men. In fact, he had built his reputation writing articles on the working man, not woman. Gilbert would be the first to admit that he suffered a case of extreme anxiety when confronted by a member of the opposite sex. He put this down to having a rather overpowering mother and several dominating aunts. As an only male child among this female swarm, he had been both doted on and controlled in equally alarming measures.

"Mr McMillan," Clara held her hand out to shake. "Do not be concerned, I am merely hoping you might be able to help me with a case I am working on. You might have information I have not been able to get hold of."

Gilbert blinked at her from behind his thick glasses, clearly perplexed.

"Information?"

"Precisely," Clara helped herself to a chair that was placed before Gilbert's desk. From the pile of papers on it, it was clearly not often used for visitors. "I heard that you went to the Brighton Pavilion the other day because of an accident that happened there."

Gilbert relaxed a little. Talking about his work always

relaxed him. He sat down too.

"I did indeed go to the Pavilion. I am assuming you know the details of the accident that occurred there?"

"I do," Clara agreed. "But how did you come to know about it in the first place?"

"Luck," Gilbert shrugged. "That magic ingredient that can make or break a journalist. Mr Pontefract had posted me at the hospital because he had heard talk that Captain O'Harris, the daredevil pilot, was shortly due to be arriving there. I was to interview him as soon as I could. But instead of O'Harris turning up, there was this man carried in by his friends. From his overalls he was clearly a workman, which caught my attention. Here, have you seen my latest piece?"

Gilbert rifled through some papers and produced a draft copy of one of his articles. He handed it over to Clara and she saw that it was entitled 'The Great Working Scandal: How Modern Industry Costs Lives'.

"I have been working on a series exposing the appalling conditions many men have to work in," Gilbert explained. "There are very few safety precautions taken in these places, not even the basic ones, and men often fall foul of the most horrendous accidents. Then what? Well, if they are lucky they recover and go back to work, hopefully without losing too much time and money. But if they are unlucky and their injury is something crippling, they are simply abandoned to the mercy of their nearest and dearest. Whole families can be ruined by one moment of misfortune.

"Not that their employers much care. There is always another man to fill their spot. They go about deliberately oblivious to the problem. It is about time someone opened their eyes and the eyes of the wider world to this problem. They need to be made accountable for the accidents that occur in their places of work, only then will they take an active interest in preventing them!"

"A very noble cause," Clara said, handing back the paper. "And this was why you went to the Pavilion?"

"A man had fallen from some scaffolding. He wasn't badly injured, considering the circumstances, but he was hurt nonetheless and, from the way he talked, he suspected someone had deliberately sabotaged the scaffolding," Gilbert tapped his finger on the table. "His friends agreed, said the nuts and bolts holding the scaffold together had been loosened. According to them, some of the nuts were completely missing. Now, either this was a case of extreme carelessness on the part of whoever put up the scaffold or someone had tampered with it. I thought I would go take a look for myself."

"And what did you find?"

"At the Pavilion, not a lot," Gilbert said apologetically. "The foreman would not talk to me, other than to deny he would allow such negligence. He insisted he had double-checked the scaffolding himself, which naturally led me to conclude that someone had sabotaged it."

Gilbert paused and looked sharply at Clara.

"Why are you so interested?"

"For the same reasons, Mr McMillan," Clara said carefully. "I have been employed to investigate the possibility of sabotage at the Pavilion and who might be behind it."

"Nothing to do with the murder that was supposed to have taken place there, then?"

Clara looked at him perfectly blankly.

"What murder?"

Gilbert, who was rapidly overcoming his shyness around Clara, merely grinned knowingly.

"I guess that is just a rumour then," he shrugged. "I didn't get much at the Pavilion, but I am certain someone is running amok there."

"What makes you so certain?"

"After I was kicked out from the Pavilion by this lady who did not like me snooping around," Gilbert pulled a face to imply what he thought of the woman, "I went back to the hospital and spoke to the workman who was injured. He was most forthcoming. Seems that since the workmen arrived at the Pavilion odd things have been occurring. Initially it was just things going missing, but then matters became nasty. Someone deliberately turned over the oil stove and nearly set the whole place alight, for one."

Clara's heart started to beat faster. The thought of the historic Pavilion going up in smoke was enough to frighten half the committee to death, it certainly troubled her, especially as Abigail had not mentioned anything about such a thing.

"The foreman tried to keep a lot of this hushed up," Gilbert continued. "He was worried no one would believe him and everything would be blamed on careless workers. Then the scaffold collapsed."

"That was harder to hush up," Clara confirmed.

"Exactly my thoughts, but what I cannot say is why anyone would want to sabotage the trade fair, assuming that is their intention and not that they want to wreck the Pavilion. You are on the Pavilion Committee, are you not? Has anyone made threats against the property?"

That was an angle Clara had not considered, but she dismissed the idea rapidly. Now, with the two murders, it was plainly apparent that someone was after those involved in the trade fair.

"No one has designs on the Pavilion," Clara said firmly. "The question is, who is angry enough with those involved in the trade fair to wish them so ill."

"I have been digging into that angle too," Gilbert nodded. "Of course, Albion Industries is behind the trade fair and they have a number of rivals in the business world. The House of Jasmine springs to mind."

"I have heard of them before," Clara admitted.

"They are not to be sniffed at," Gilbert commented. "Mr Mokano is a ruthless businessman and he is very angry that Albion Industries appear to have stolen his idea for a new style of lipstick. There is a court case pending. That is more Mr Mokano's style than sabotage."

"Other than Mr Mokano, has anyone any reason to

feel they have been betrayed by Albion Industries?" Clara asked.

"I haven't found anything specific just yet," Gilbert answered, a sly look in his eye. "Personally, I would be turning my attention to the lady in charge, Abigail Sommers. That lady has been ruthless on her way to the top of her industry, she has hurt people along the way. Perhaps someone wants revenge."

Clara had to admit that was a possibility she had been considering from the start. It was the very reason Abigail had come to her in the first place.

"I haven't had a chance to pursue one particular avenue that recently came to my attention," Gilbert continued. "Perhaps it will interest you? I am told the lady in question could have a real grudge against Miss Sommers."

Gilbert handed over a piece of paper upon which was written a name and address. Clara recognised the name at once. Yet another of her old school friends. She slipped it into her pocket.

"Thank you, Mr McMillan."

"How about an arrangement? If I learn something else I'll let you know, in return I get the scoop on this story?"

Clara had risen to leave, now she paused. It was true Mr McMillan had contacts she did not, and it would be handy to have someone else working on the case.

"All right," she said, holding her hand out to shake once more.

"Goodbye Miss Fitzgerald, and good luck."

Gilbert's words rang in her ears as Clara left the building. It was time to pay a call on an old friend.

Chapter Nine

Clara had attended an all girls school from the age of eleven until she was sixteen. It had been an experience she would never forget, though not always for the best of reasons. Abigail Sommers had been one of her class mates, another had been Rowena Yardley – it was Rowena whose name Gilbert McMillan had handed to her. Rowena and Abigail had been best friends in the classroom. They had been the pretty girls, the ones who knew the latest dances, how to curl their hair to perfection and always managed to give their plain uniforms a fashionable twist. Neither were devoted academics, but they were bright enough in their own way. Clara had always considered them inseparable. Wherever one was, the other was bound to soon appear.

Clara had no idea the pair had fallen out so irreconcilably. But then, until the other day she had not seen Abigail in years and, although Rowena lived just outside Brighton at Hove, Clara had not kept in touch. She wondered what had gone on between the two of them.

Rowena lived with her parents in a modest manor house set in several acres. Her father bred horses and was a very well-known name in equine circles. A number of his best animals had been sent to France during the war; only a couple returned and his stud farm had suffered from their loss as a result. In the last few years he had been working to restore his stables to their former glory and, in the meantime, finances had been tight. The old manor looked in need of some repair work as Clara walked up the long drive. It was a dark grey building, rather uninspiring, something the Bronte sisters would have lived in while dreaming up their despair-riddled tales of bleak unhappiness.

Attempts had been made to alleviate this depression. Someone had put pots of pretty flowers by the front step and under the windows, they created a rather desperate riot of colour against the backdrop of continual grey. Clara stood on the doorstep and rang the bell. After a moment it was answered by an older woman who Clara vaguely recalled was Rowena's mother.

"Is Rowena in? I am Clara Fitzgerald, we used to go to school together."

Rowena's mother was a small woman prone to dowdiness in her manner and appearance. She almost mimicked the house in her dull, grey skirt and cream blouse. She had clearly been in the process of baking, as an apron tied about her waist was covered in flour where she had hastily wiped her hands.

"Yes, Rowena is in. Do come inside," Rowena's mother led Clara through to a small parlour. It was north facing and cold despite the sunshine outside. Clara gave an unconscious shiver as she entered the room. Someone had attempted to enliven this space too with fresh cut flowers. A blue vase was sitting on the mantelpiece full of purple and pink sweet peas.

"I'll fetch her," Rowena's mother said, giving Clara a quick sweep with her alert eyes. "She has been out with the horses this morning and only just got back. Take a seat while I find her."

Clara plumped herself down on a pale sofa that coughed a cloud of dust up around her. Apparently, this room was used rather infrequently these days. Well, so were many peoples' parlours. They were the room kept aside for guests and holidays and tended to develop an air of unloved elegance. Clara could imagine this room being very underused, considering its aspect made it rather a cold and dark place. She endeavoured to remove some of the dust from the sofa with her hands, patting the arms and cushions to make herself feel better about sitting there. The only real result was that she made herself sneeze.

Rowena Yardley appeared in the doorway.

"I despair that mother put you in this room Clara," she said with a grimace.

Rowena was dressed in women's riding trousers and a blouse. She still had her tall riding boots on and a whip in her left hand. She surveyed the scene before her with mild embarrassment. Rowena had always been pretty with her fair hair and big hazel eyes. Just having come in from riding, her cheeks were still flushed from the exercise and this heightened her natural charms.

"Come into the sitting room. Mother thinks it shabby, but it is much nicer than this room."

Rowena escorted Clara to the sitting room, which was indeed a much nicer room, if rather worn about the edges. For a start the sun fell fully through the windows and gave the tired furniture a warm aura. Clara was offered a seat on a sofa that was starting to develop tears in the arms. Rowena flopped herself down opposite with a sigh.

"Shabby it may be, but it is far more comfortable," she smiled at Clara. "Gosh it has been years since I last saw you! What brings you to our house?"

"I met a mutual friend of ours and it reminded me of our school days," Clara explained, hedging about the truth. "It's been too long since I last saw everyone."

"School seems a long time ago," Rowena shrugged. "So much has happened since and I have been working so hard with daddy to keep this place afloat."

"The war was hard on the stud, or so I heard."

"Hard is the word for it!" Rowena laughed. "Daddy volunteered his horses, so he might do his duty. Not having any sons to send off to fight for king and country, he considered the horses a suitable substitute. We lost some of our best blood overseas. And, of course, daddy has never pressed for compensation from the government. Probably they would not give us any, but it might be worth asking. Well, that suggestion always falls on deaf ears. We are having to rebuild from scratch and it has taken time. Without fine stud horses to encourage people to bring their mares here, we have been existing on savings. Fortunately, we have had several promising foals since 1919 and soon will be able to offer stud services again. One stallion in particular has already attracted acclaim from those in the know."

Rowena looked very proud of this information and smiled. Clara was glad to hear things were improving for them.

"Which old school friend of ours have you met?" Rowena asked, suddenly remembering the start of their conversation.

"Abigail Sommers," Clara answered, feigning innocence of the knowledge that the pair were no longer friendly.

"Humph," Rowena puttered, pursing her lips firmly together.

"Oh," Clara put on a good pretence of looking surprised. "I though you and Abigail were firm friends?"

"At school, maybe," Rowena nearly spat out the words. "But that was a long time ago, and now we are adults and…"

Rowena hesitated.

"I thought Abigail was working away from Brighton?" she said sharply.

"She was," Clara admitted. "But she has come to Brighton to host a trade fair. That was how I bumped into her, the fair is being held at the Brighton Pavilion and I am on the committee for the place."

"A trade fair?" Rowena raised an eyebrow in sarcastic curiosity. "What is Abigail doing involved in something like that? Last I heard she sold make-up to people."

Rowena clearly perceived this as a very down-market occupation and unbefitting a girl who had gone to the same school as her and had once been deemed a friend.

"The trade fair is for Albion Industries, who Abigail works for," Clara explained. "And, yes, they do sell make-up among other goods."

"I wouldn't know," Rowena said firmly. "I never bothered with powder and paint. But then I have enough natural charms to not warrant it. Make-up is for plain girls trying to improve themselves. I was always astonished Abigail became involved with such a thing. She had no real need for it either, at least not the last time I saw her."

"I hadn't realised you two had fallen out," Clara lied. "Seeing Abigail made me think of the past and I wanted to catch up with those I could. Perhaps share memories of those old days. I don't know, sometimes you get this hankering for looking back to the days before the war, before the world changed. You happened to be the only other friend I knew to be nearby."

"Have you mentioned me to Abigail?" Rowena narrowed her eyes, looking warily at Clara.

"No," Clara reassured her. "Abigail and I have not had a chance to discuss the past. She is very busy with the fair's arrangements."

"That was always Abigail's problem, being too busy for her friends," Rowena turned her head, but not before Clara noted her hurt look.

"What, if you don't mind me asking, happened between you two? I thought you would be friends for all time. The last occasion I saw you both was when we left school for the final time and you and Abigail were walking down the gravel drive together."

Rowena's own memory was sparked by this image and she briefly smiled to herself, before her face became sombre again.

"Abigail was supposed to be my friend, but when I really needed her she turned her back on me," Rowena scowled. "It was a couple of years after we finished school, right when the war was hotting up and daddy was sending off all his horses. Things looked bleak, without the stud farm daddy had no income. I persuaded him to let me find a job so I could help the family. Mummy isn't a lot of use at such things, no good asking her to go off to a munitions factory!" Rowena found humour in the notion of her mother working, but she shook it from her head at once as she returned to her thoughts on Abigail. "I knew at the time, from letters she had written to me, that Abigail had found herself a nice little job and I hoped she might be able to find something for me to do. I had this idea that we could work together and it would be just like school again. But Abigail kept making excuses for not being able to find me work with her. Some of them were ludicrous and I knew what she really meant was that she couldn't be bothered to help me.

"Perhaps she thought I would be so much better than her at the job that she would be replaced by me! Abigail always was a little jealous of me. Out of the two of us, I usually was the better at school work and received higher marks."

Rowena gave Clara a satisfied smile, as if this ability to out-best her friend was at least some compensation for their falling out. Clara was having a hard time, however, imagining Rowena working as a sales representative for Albion Industries. Perhaps Abigail had guessed this herself and had deliberately made excuses.

"In the end, I was the one who had to go to the damn munitions factory for work," Rowena's scowl had returned. "It was horrible work, truly. One of the girls was blown to pieces when the shell she was working on exploded. And, on another night, one of the sheds we worked in caught fire. It was awful. I still have nightmares where I hear the girls trapped inside screaming."

Rowena's voice fell away, she stared blankly at her hands, her energy and her stoicism had suddenly abandoned her.

"I don't think anyone realises the hell we girls worked in," she said softly. "All to make more bloody shells to kill the Germans with, while the German girls were doing exactly the same. In a way, we were killing our own menfolk in the process. It's a thought that keeps me awake some nights."

Clara could see the pain this experience had etched into Rowena. Her face had lost some of its vivacity, now she looked quite pale and sad. Clara saw how all this horror had left Rowena angry and wanting to lash out at someone. That someone had been Abigail, the friend who had failed to get her a job and thus spare her from the nightmare of the munitions factory. Rowena had clearly felt betrayed, just as the saboteur at the Pavilion had felt.

"I'm sorry," Clara said. "I didn't mean to stir up bad memories."

"Trouble is, the bad memories are too tied up with the good ones." Rowena shrugged.

"But things are improving now, and you are happy?"

A little colour came back to Rowena's face.

"Oh yes, Clara, I am very happy. I am doing what I love each and every day. The horses make up for a lot. Let me show you around."

Rowena took Clara on a tour of the stud and introduced her to the various horses. Clara politely nodded and smiled as she was given names and details of each equine in question's lineage. She didn't recognise the names of the famous sires and dams which Rowena babbled out at a pace, proudly indicating the great parentage of the mares and the foals. As the tour concluded, Clara had to admit to herself that Rowena did not seem a person interested in revenge. She was too busy for a start. Taking regular trips into Brighton to derail Abigail's work would simply be too impractical. In any case, Rowena seemed happy and happy people rarely feel the need to revenge past slights. Clara found herself reaching the conclusion that Gilbert McMillan had been wrong and that, despite their falling out, there was no real bad blood between Rowena and Abigail. That left her back at square one.

They walked to the front of the house and Clara made her farewells. Rowena insisted she stop by again and Clara promised she would. It had, in fact, been refreshing to catch up with an old school friend. But as distracting as the conversation had been, it had not shed any new light on Clara's case. As she headed back in the direction of Brighton, hoping to catch a lift off a passing horse and cart along the way, Clara reflected that she was yet to learn of anyone who had a serious grudge against Abigail or Albion Industries. Perhaps it was time to spread her net further afield?

Chapter Ten

Clara returned to the Pavilion to see how events were unfolding. The official opening was to be later that afternoon and the last minute preparations were well underway. She briefly caught sight of Abigail rushing by with an armful of papers, but there was no time to stop and speak with her. She didn't even see Clara. Clara decided to do some poking around instead. She wandered about the Pavilion, observing workmen finishing off stalls and advertising boards, and noting a number of well-dressed men and women who were setting the stalls with their respective goods. Bottles of perfume, tubs of make-up, mirrors, beauty kits, health aids and an assortment of devices Clara could only wonder at but which, no doubt, had some purpose in making one look amazing, all were appearing on the stalls and giving the Pavilion a feel of an upscale market. The rooms were already rather crowded and that was before the public was invited in!

Clara observed everything at a discreet distance, trying not to get in anyone's way. No one seemed unduly concerned that two people had been murdered on the premises. Many were perhaps unaware of what had happened, but others would know and could easily have let slip the information. Clara had to assume that those who were aware simply did not much care about the occurrences.

She found herself standing near the Cushing's Corsetry stand. A woman with a strained looking face was trying to get a torso dummy to stay upright as she put a corset upon it. She was failing and the dummy kept unerringly falling over as she attempted to pull the strings tight on the corset.

"Might I help?" Clara offered, propping up the dummy without waiting for a reply.

The woman nodded at her thankfully and fixed the corset in place. Clara noted the dummy, which in traditional corset shops would have displayed an hourglass waist, was of a completely tubular form, not requiring assistance from the corset to give it a straight waist. This was clearly a dummy especially made for Cushing's new line of flatteners.

"Thank you," the woman said as she propped the dummy on her display table.

"I'm Clara Fitzgerald, one of the Pavilion Committee," Clara introduced herself promptly.

The woman looked at her stiffly. She seemed reluctant to respond.

"I wasn't sure what would be happening with the Cushing's stand, after last night," Clara lowered her voice to a conspiratorial level.

"Oh, you know about that?" the woman said, looking worried now.

"I was here for the banquet and, rather unfortunately, was among those who made the discovery. Poor Mr Forthclyde."

"Yes. He was my superior," the woman took a handkerchief from her sleeve and dabbed at her eyes. She had the look of someone who had cried a lot in the last few hours. "It was a shock to learn that he was dead."

"Who told you?"

"Miss Sommers," the woman said. "She came to my hotel to see me. I was distraught at first, couldn't understand that not only was Mr Forthclyde dead but murdered..." she hissed the word through her teeth. "Then Miss Sommers reminded me that I had a job to do and that I must take over where Mr Forthclyde had left off. So, I am here setting up the stall and trying not to think about things too hard."

"I do understand," Clara reassured her. "Could I help you with anything else while I am here? It is no bother, and you appear to have a lot of heavy items to put out compared to the other stall holders?"

The woman looked at her barely begun display table and the boxes of goods, including two more dummies and a large display board, waiting to be put out.

"If... if you wouldn't mind?"

For the next half an hour Clara and the woman chatted away in fits and starts, as boxes were emptied and the dummies erected. Clara observed that corsets had changed a lot since she was a girl and the woman treated her to a lengthy explanation of the benefits of a Cushing's corset. It seemed that not only could they give you a very modern figure, but they could cure you of all ills, everything from poor lung capacity to flat feet, as they helped the blood to circulate. Clara took this all with a pinch of salt, as she doubted Cushing's actually employed doctors to prove the genuineness of these claims. At least, amid the sales spiel, she also learned the woman's name. She was Penelope Muggins, often called Penny as Miss Muggins sounded awful and Penelope was rather long-winded. She had opened up quite a bit from when Clara had first met her.

"How long have you worked for Cushing's?"

"Two years last Christmas," Penny explained. "But I have only worked with Mr Forthclyde for six months, since his last assistant resigned. We travel all about... I mean, we did travel all about..."

Penny fiddled with the lace trim on a corset.

"I can't fathom it. Why would anyone kill Mr Forthclyde?"

"No one had a grudge against him?" Clara asked.

"Not as far as I know," Penny shrugged her shoulders. "He was nice, but always very professional. My father was very particular about that, seeing as how I would be travelling all about with a man. He was a bachelor, but I never told my father that or he would have had kittens."

"Had Mr Forthclyde mentioned that he might stay behind after the meal?"

Penny shook her head.

"We last spoke as he was leaving the hotel. I wished him to have a good time then retired to my room. We had separate rooms, naturally. In fact, they were not even on the same floor," Penny's face clouded and her lips twitched downwards. "Mr Forthclyde was the most experienced salesman on the Cushing's team. He sold more corsets than any of his colleagues. I was proud to work for him. I wanted to be the best like he is… was…"

"I'm sorry, this has been such a shock for you," Clara placed a hand lightly on her arm. "Would you like me to fetch you a cup of tea, or something?"

"No, thank you, you have been so kind already. I must not detain you any longer."

Clara would have been happily detained if it meant learning more about Mr Forthclyde, though she rather felt he was a dead end, a man in the wrong place at the wrong time. Penny had returned to fussing over her corsets and Clara felt she had overstayed her welcome, so she started to prowl the rooms again, glancing at the stalls as she went by. She came across some very morose Albion representatives putting together a complicated display of the new Pearl Pink lipsticks in a prominent place in the main hall. She stopped to admire the construction which involved a pyramid of carefully balanced lipsticks rising up before a shimmering pink curtain. One of the women stopped stacking lipsticks and glanced at her.

"Have you had a sample?" she asked, though it seemed a rather perfunctory question and not made for the sake of politeness, but rather out of a sense of duty.

"No," Clara admitted. "But please do not deplete your stock on my behalf. I am Clara Fitzgerald from the Brighton Pavilion Preservation Committee."

This statement did not generate any sort of recognition from the women. They merely nodded and carried on with their work.

"You have had no bother today?" Clara asked carefully.

The women glanced up at her.

"Should we have had?" one retorted sharply.

Clara wondered what she meant to imply, that Clara was behind the trouble?

"No, I was just checking. Things have been difficult the last few days and the committee is naturally concerned."

"Mr Forthclyde's blood might have stained the Georgian dining table upstairs," one of the women sneered to the girl next to her. "That is what the committee worries about, isn't it? Whether your precious Pavilion will be ruined by our arrival?"

"Actually, I am concerned that someone has been killed on the premises," Clara said smoothly, ignoring the snide tone the woman had addressed her with. Clearly rumour had circulated that Clara had made a fuss about the damaged plasterwork. So be it, she was not about to let the Pavilion be damaged for the sake of a trade fair.

"Are you not concerned that we might be next?" one of the women snapped.

Clara fixed her gaze on her, she was the one that had offered her a Pearl Pink lipstick.

"I didn't catch your name?"

"Niamh Owen," the woman answered. "Top Albion Representative for the South-East, excluding Abigail Sommers from the count."

"She beats you on sales?" Clara asked provocatively.

Niamh glowered. She was a tall woman with dark black hair and intense eyes. She looked like someone with a temper.

"Abigail is in Albion Industries' pocket when it comes to these things. She can do no wrong, but you can't compare us to her, not when she has the advantages of knowing all the higher level managers on a first name basis."

"And, one has to ask, how does she come to know their names so intimately?" one of the other women joined the fray. "Abigail is far too friendly with some important men for my liking."

"Don't be fooled into thinking she keeps her top spot in the sales figures by hard work alone," Niamh added, with a smug sniff of her nose. "At least, not the hard work she makes out she is doing. No one before Abigail has retained the lead in the sales leagues for more than a year. They produce the figures monthly and it is ridiculous to think she is outstripping all us other girls by so much every time. Well, if you do believe that, you must be a naïve fool."

"Niamh is the best of us," another woman admitted. "Even so, she only just beats us each month and is always miles behind Abigail. It doesn't make sense."

"You think the figures are doctored?" Clara said.

"Think? I know so!" Niamh snorted again with glee at being able to rat out her rival. "I have been doing some digging and I have found evidence that the figures are completely fraudulent and that dear old Abigail is nothing more than a big fat liar!"

Niamh looked very satisfied with herself and Clara was reminded of her school days yet again when the girls would get into silly cat-fights over the most innocuous of subjects. Not that this was innocuous, not when you considered the extra money Abigail was earning each month she was the top sales representative.

"That is such a shame," Clara said, thinking if it was true then here would be a motive for Abigail to be disgraced and could explain the sabotage, though double-murder was going to the extreme. "Would it be possible to see this evidence?"

"Why should it interest you?" Niamh was altogether too sharp on the uptake, Clara reflected.

"Did I not mention? Along with being on the Pavilion committee, I am also a private detective and I have been asked to keep an eye on the situation here. Anything that could suggest a motive for these crimes is interesting to me."

The women looked taken aback, but only for a moment.

"Why would evidence for Abigail's disgraceful behaviour suggest a motive for these horrid murders?" one said, utterly aghast.

"I can't say for sure," Clara didn't want to give them ideas about someone trying to ruin Abigail. "But anything could be important at this stage. The saboteur was intent on leaving messages about betrayal, that seems to suggest a very personal reason for these crimes."

Niamh flashed her dark, clever eyes at the other girls.

"Betrayal," she hummed. "Who betraying who?"

"Exactly," Clara responded.

"Poor little Esther never betrayed anyone," one of the women said. "She was a sweet thing and such a hard worker. She never deserved to be strangled."

"And with a pair of those stockings too," Niamh grimaced. "And after she had had such a triumph increasing the sales of them."

Clara pricked up her ears. Was this just another coincidence, or was the killer playing games with them?

"The stockings were significant to Esther?" Clara asked.

"Esther had secured a number of sales agreements with department stores and smaller retailers for those very stockings," Niamh explained. "It was something of a victory for her, seeing as they had been one of Albion's poorer sellers until then. We all had a little celebratory party over it and Albion Industries published her name in the quarterly newspaper that is sent to each sales representative."

"Along with the sales figures?" Clara guessed.

"Exactly," Niamh nodded. "Esther was certainly in the limelight that month. There were high hopes for her. Poor thing."

"I don't want to end up like that," one of the women, the youngest in the group, began to cry. The others flocked around her.

"There, there, Mary. No one is going to hurt you," Niamh comforted her. "We promised, remember, to always stick together and never go about alone?"

Mary sniffled and leaned her head wearily on Niamh's shoulder.

"It has been a long day," Niamh told Clara. "And we still have a long night ahead of us. May I suggest you go investigate this murder business elsewhere and leave us to our work? The sooner this fair is over and we can get away from Brighton the better."

Clara did not argue over the dismissal. She politely hoped that Mary would feel better soon and then moved away. But her mind was working fast. Esther had been killed using the stockings she had made top sellers, and Mr Forthclyde had been stabbed with a sharpened piece of whalebone from one of his own corsets. Clara had assumed the weapons had simply come to hand, though why anyone would want to sharpen a piece of whalebone for anything other than sinister reasons eluded her. But the stocking had appeared to be something that had sprung to the killer's hand, as if he or she had acted impulsively. Now here was the information that there seemed to have been nothing impulsive about it. Clara came to a halt and gazed about the Pavilion, at the stalls and the busy people, at the riot of colours in the displays. What was at work here? A madman out for revenge? Or something far more calculated? And was this about Abigail, as she had first feared, or was this a wider attack at Albion Industries? Whichever was the case, it seemed the person behind the attacks was very aware of the internal politics of the company, how else could they have known about Esther's stocking success? It was all very disturbing and, with barely an hour to go before the trade fair opened, Clara was no closer to naming a suspect.

Chapter Eleven

Clara decided she had spent enough time at the Pavilion of late. She had other things on her mind. As the afternoon drew on, she set out to see Captain O'Harris at the hospital. The trade fair would just have to look after itself for a while longer.

Captain O'Harris had his eyes closed when she gently opened the door to his room, but he opened them the second she lightly called his name. For a moment he didn't seem to register who she was, then he smiled.

"Clara, back again? Surely I am boring you by now?"

"Never," Clara assured him happily, taking a seat beside him. "How are you feeling?"

"All right, I suppose," O'Harris frowned. "Sometimes I don't feel…"

He hesitated, trying to find the words to explain the strange moods and sensations that came over him at times.

"Sometimes it doesn't seem real, none of it. This room, this bed, you…" O'Harris' words caught in his throat. "It feels like I am dreaming and… and it is the most frightening of sensations. To not be sure this is reality…"

"But it is," Clara took his hand in both of hers. "Don't you feel my touch? In what dream could you ever feel me squeezing your hand? This is a real place, John, you and I are both real."

O'Harris' eyes had looked anxious, now they seemed to lighten. He relaxed a fraction.

"I spend too long alone in this room. Too much time to think. I would rather be on the wards where I could see everyone else, but they won't move me there because it is too public and they think some newspaperman will try and sneak in during visiting hours," O'Harris sighed. "They can control who sees me when I am in this private room."

"How long must you be here?"

"The doctors are cagey on the subject," O'Harris shrugged his shoulders disdainfully. "Aside from being exposed to the elements in the ocean and half-drowned, I contracted a foreign disease on the island and it continues to flare up. They don't like the idea of me going home to live alone while there is a possibility I could become dangerously ill again."

"You're a local hero," Clara told him with amusement. "They couldn't face the publicity if you came to any harm because they released you too soon. You are the talk of the town."

"I wish I wasn't!" O'Harris frowned. "Anyway, the matter is moot because my house is not fit for me to reside in just yet. Colonel Brandt came to see me and explained he had kept an eye on the house during my absence and because of fear of vandals or thieves breaking in while it stood empty everything was put into secure storage. The house has rather a reputation, you see, because of the deaths that took place there."

"I suppose the local youths imagine there are ghosts haunting it!" Clara laughed.

"Or it is cursed, or some such nonsense!" O'Harris joined in the humour. "Anyway, Colonel Brandt says that someone did break in and smashed several windows. Could have been a tramp, because they started a fire in the dining room hearth and made such a mess of it they nearly set the whole place alight. Fortunately, a passer-by spotted smoke and the fire brigade were called. The dining room was gutted sadly before they could put it out, but the rest of the house was saved."

"What a shame!" Clara exclaimed with genuine regret. She had dined at O'Harris' house and had vivid memories of the old-fashioned dining room which reeked of Victorian luxury, from the red flock wallpaper to the parquet flooring.

"In some ways it is not so bad," O'Harris smiled wistfully. "That room held a lot of memories of my uncle's sad fate."

"Yes, I can imagine."

They fell silent for a while, each lost in their own thoughts and uncertain how to restart the conversation. Clara finally could not bear to be silent any longer.

"You never finished telling me how you made it back to England," she said.

O'Harris glanced up, his hazel eyes becoming shadowed for a moment, before he lightly smiled.

"You know, sometimes when I sit here in the evenings, I think about all I have been through and I realise that some would envy my time on that island," he laughed. "In a way it was a tropical paradise. The sun was always warm and seemed to shine every day. Apparently I had missed the monsoon season when it rains continuously. I had been lucky in a lot of ways. The water they pulled me from was full of sharks, the islanders considered it quite amazing that I had not been eaten.

"There were great palm trees and all manner of tropical fruits to eat. The natives had a largely vegetarian diet, occasionally enlivened by fish they had caught, but the sharks made fishing a precarious business. They fed me well enough and were very hospitable, though I couldn't understand them and I failed to grasp the language even after being there several weeks. My excuse for such impoliteness was that I regularly slipped in and out of a fever and was delirious for a great part of the time.

"And then I caught some sort of tropical illness. The natives had a name for it which I can't pronounce. I became severely ill and there were clearly concerns for me among the locals. I would occasionally drift up from my delirium and see their worried looks. I have to say, all the time I was in their care they were extremely good to me and I must have been a nuisance for them. Anyway, as I told you before, there is a Christian mission that regularly comes across from the mainland to the island. They bring over supplies and goods, such as toys for the children and clothes. They also bring over a doctor and, naturally, a pastor who is endeavouring during these haphazard visits to convert the populace.

"The mission doctor was brought to me and presumably told how I was found and the sickness I had contracted. He was American and spoke to me in English, asking questions which I was only half able to answer. He finally decided I needed to be shipped to the mainland and taken to a regular hospital. I was stretchered onto the launch the mission had used to get to the island and taken on the short journey to the coast of America. I don't remember much. The journey exhausted me and I was hardly fit to begin with."

O'Harris shook his head, remembering that strange time.

"That was when I began to struggle to know what was real and what was part of my feverish delusions," he said. "Some of the things that happened... I still can't say for sure if they were actual events or mere dreams. I know I ended up in a hospital and there were a lot of doctors and nurses about me for a while. I don't think they knew if I would live or not. I was in a ward with other men, and I drifted in and out of consciousness. I lost hours that way.

"None of this was helped by the great sense of guilt I felt over my co-pilot. I kept thinking that if I had not planned this trip, if I had not had this wild idea about flying across an ocean, then he would still be alive. I had no idea he had been rescued and that everyone was mourning over me. I beat myself up over my failings. I made them my cross to bear and when I was sane enough to do so, I flogged myself over the accident and my co-pilot's imagined death.

"Around this time things became very strange. I sunk into myself and no one could reach me. I felt as though I existed in a bubble and everyone else around me was meaningless. When I was not delirious I was simply silent. People spoke to me, asked me questions, but I couldn't seem to hear them. I understood later that I had shut down so much that no one knew who I was or where I came from. The mission doctor was convinced I was English and my flying jacket suggested to him that I was an airman. A report was printed in the US papers asking if anyone might know who I was. Apparently, they intended to ask The Times to print a similar report over in England, but before that was necessary the notice was spotted by my co-pilot, who had also been recovering in an American hospital after the accident. He had stayed behind in the country for a while, lapping up the publicity he was gaining as a survivor of an air crash at sea."

O'Harris laughed to himself.

"All the time I was worrying about him being dead and he was telling the world about how he survived and mourning my loss! Anyway, he saw the notice and I suppose he hoped, as much as guessed, that the man they were referring to was me. He came all the way down to the hospital to see me.

"I remember the moment he walked onto the ward. I thought he was a ghost come to haunt me. I started to…" O'Harris paused, a flush of colour flooded his face. "I started to weep. I have to admit to it Clara, even though I am ashamed."

"I don't see why you should be," Clara told him firmly, squeezing his hand again. "You had been through an awful ordeal and to see the man you thought dead must have come as a dreadful shock on top of everything else."

"It was," O'Harris concurred. "There he was, standing before me, and I thought I was gone truly mad. But then a nurse came over and spoke to him, she must have been asking him if I was actually Captain O'Harris, because then she came to me and patted my shoulder and told me everything was going to be all right, and she used my name."

O'Harris stopped, the memory of that moment slipping back all too vividly.

"I came round after that. The nurse promised me that the man before me was alive and very real. He came and sat beside me and we talked, well, he mostly talked and I just listened and nodded. He said how when the 'plane crashed down he was flung into the water and lost sight of me quite quickly. We had both been wearing life jackets and his kept him afloat as he was washed about in the waves. He had lost all sense of direction, but as the sun sank he realised which direction was west and struck out in the hope of reaching land or something. Night came on and he was freezing cold and nearly passed out, then the sun rose behind him and he made one last effort to swim westwards. By chance he stumbled across a fishing boat, and he waved down the captain. They took him aboard and carried him to America.

"I was stunned to think that all this time he had been alive and well! We talked for what seemed like hours, but was no doubt merely half-an-hour, then the nurse politely removed him. But afterwards, Clara, I felt so much happier, so much freer in my soul! My guilt was lifted and I could unburden myself and concentrate on healing.

"I started to talk then, to the nurses and the doctors. I told them my story. Arrangements were made to send me home. Passage in a ship was booked and the hospital in Brighton informed I would be arriving. The rest, well, is blatantly apparent."

Captain O'Harris held out his hands to indicate his presence before Clara.

"I am so glad you came home," Clara said softly. "I

have missed you and I thought..."

Clara stopped herself and merely smiled.

"But what I thought doesn't matter now. Here you are."

"And it is good to see you well, too. And Tommy, I hardly believed my eyes when I saw him walking!"

Clara's smile broadened.

"Tommy has been seeing a new doctor who has worked wonders on him."

"Good for him! Now he can drive a car, I suppose? Hah! I shall have him in one of uncle's old motors! They are all still in storage!"

Clara recalled the collection of cars Captain O'Harris had had at his home; treasured possessions of his late uncle who had been something of a motor fanatic. She was not entirely sure about the idea of letting Tommy drive one. Cars, in Clara's opinion, were very dangerous things and far too prone to having inexplicable accidents.

"And once the house has been tarted up and restored, you will all naturally come over for supper. I am going to be lonely in that big place, especially without the Buzzard to distract me," O'Harris became sombre again. "I will miss her. I know she was only a biplane, but she was also a sort of friend. She was familiar, comfortable. I knew her inside out and when I was having a bad day I could always just fired up her engine and listen to her purring. Why she ditched like that I'll never know, but one thing is for certain, she will be my last pair of wings. Some other fool can risk that crossing, I have had enough of laughing in the face of death."

This was a revelation from a man who used to almost court death with a vengeance, feeling guilt that he had not died in the war like so many comrades. O'Harris had almost made it seem, before the events of last year, that he would be quite inclined to die in a plane crash. But then sometimes actually confronting your own mortality puts a different perspective on the whole thing. Clara was just glad to have him sitting beside her.

They talked for a while longer, then the bell rang to declare visiting time over. Clara rose, she turned to leave, then an impulse came over her and, after recent happenings, it seemed foolish to deny it. She leant over and kissed O'Harris on the cheek. Then she hurried away before she could see his response.

Chapter Twelve

Clara had only just arrived home from her visit to Captain O'Harris when the doorbell rang and Annie went to investigate. She soon returned to report that there was a police constable at the door asking for Clara. Clara rose from the dinner table and went to see what was the matter.

Police Constable Jones was one of the regulars she knew from the station. He gave her a polite nod before quickly reassuring her it was nothing to worry about, as such.

"No one is hurt, just a small incident at the Pavilion which the Inspector thought you might like to know about, miss."

Clara was curious.

"What sort of incident?"

"Miss Sommers has been arrested for assaulting another of the women there. The woman says she was trying to kill her."

Clara was surprised to hear that, so surprised she gave a start.

"Is Miss Sommers at the police station?"

The constable nodded.

"I best come at once," Clara donned her hat and

followed the constable back to the station. The evening was pleasantly warm and still light as they hastened down the road. Constable Jones was unable to enlighten Clara further as to what was going on, so she had to wait until they were at the station.

There she was greeted by the scowl of her old nemesis the desk sergeant, who looked upon her as a nuisance of unimaginable proportions. Constable Jones fortunately ushered her down a corridor to one of the station's small rooms set aside for interviewing suspects. He opened the door to the room without warning and was greeted by the gruff voice of Inspector Park-Coombs.

"What in blazes are you doing?"

"Sorry sir," Constable Jones flustered. "But you said to bring Miss Fitzgerald as fast as I could."

Clara appeared just within the doorway, having avoided showing herself earlier in case she might receive some of the inspector's outrage too. She saw that the inspector was sitting facing the door while, across the table from him, sat Abigail looking miserable and with her kohl make-up smudged from where she had been crying.

"You best come in Clara," the inspector said grudgingly. "I think Miss Sommers could do with a friend right now."

Abigail glanced up as Clara entered, her eyes made big by the smeared make-up.

"I haven't tried to kill anyone," she insisted. "But the Inspector seems to think I am behind all these awful deaths."

"Not entirely true," Park-Coombs grumbled. "But Miss Sommers does have a lot of explaining to do. I have finished my questions for the time being, perhaps you would like to sit with her Clara while I go supervise the search of her hotel room."

"Is that necessary?" Clara asked, wondering what the inspector could possibly hope to find in the woman's room.

"I think so," the inspector raised an eyebrow at her. "But if you think you know a policeman's job better than he does…"

"Not at all," Clara quickly corrected herself, not wishing to offend the inspector. "I am clearly not up to speed with what is going on here."

The inspector gave another grumble, then let himself out of the room. Clara was alone with Abigail, Constable Jones having vanished as soon as he was able to.

Abigail turned to her friend and gave a stifled sob.

"I didn't kill anyone Clara."

"Tell me what happened," Clara said gently.

Abigail wiped at her eyes with her hand, she had lost her handkerchief at some point during all the commotion and her arrest.

"I am ruined," she sniffed. "Oh Clara, how can things have gone so badly wrong?"

"Try explaining it all to me," Clara pressed.

Abigail stared at her thumb which was now blackened with wet kohl.

"It was all because of that cow, Niamh," she said sharply. "I shouldn't call her names, but she is nothing but a trouble-maker!"

She dabbed at her eyes again, putting the running black make-up all over her hands.

"Niamh has hated me since we first met. She can't stand the fact that I am the top representative in the south-east region rather than her and she thinks my sales figures have been doctored. They have not. I am just very good at what I do."

Clara, having heard the other side of this tale, kept her mouth firmly shut and continued to listen.

"Niamh claimed she had evidence that I was being inventive with my sales figures," Abigail continued. "She wanted to show me, I don't know what she thought to prove. Maybe she thought she could frighten me into letting her take top spot as sales representative. I was not frightened. The papers she had come across were nothing to do with the sales figures, though she thought so. She began claiming that the sheets demonstrated that I had added numbers to my sales, when clearly they did not."

Abigail shook her head.

"I shouldn't have lost my temper, but this week has been hell," Abigail groaned to herself. "My nerves are ripped to shreds and the last thing I needed was for Niamh to be spouting her lies about the place. When she showed me the papers I went to grab them off her and we struggled, nothing more, but in the process she was knocked over and sprawled on the floor. She began to scream and when people arrived she claimed I had punched her and threatened to kill her.

"The police have had a constable posted outside the Pavilion since we opened and he rushed in and heard Niamh's nonsensical story. Of course I denied it, but he insisted I come down to the station. Technically I have been arrested, and yet I have done nothing wrong!"

"Rising to Niamh's bait was not the best reaction," Clara told her steadily. "Though I can understand why you snapped."

"Jealousy is an awful thing Clara, and I am convinced it is behind all these awful events. But I am no murderer, what cause would I have to kill Esther or Mr Forthclyde? For that matter, when he died I was stood talking to you!"

That, at least, was very true.

"How do you manage to have such high sales figures compared to everyone else?" Clara asked. "Surely the others could achieve what you do?"

"I work hard Clara," Abigail said steadily. "I work evenings and weekends, as well as during the day. I won't take no for an answer and I have built up a very good client base. There is nothing fraudulent or dishonest about it. The other girls could do the same if they wanted to put the hours in, but they finish at six of an evening and avoid working weekends. Those are the times when I am most active and when I catch people unawares. In the evening people are tired and more likely to be persuaded to take on a large amount of stock, certainly larger than they would agreed to at another time. And at the weekend people don't want to be bothered and will say anything to be rid of me. I pick my moments well and it pays off for me."

"But that doesn't stop people from being jealous," Clara noted.

"Should I stop being successful for their sakes?" Abigail asked angrily. "My figures are not remarkable when you compare them with other parts of the country. I am easily matched and beaten by the girls who work the London and surrounding counties region."

Abigail sighed and looked at her spoilt hands.

"Niamh will make the most of this. She has wanted to ruin my reputation for so long."

"It is only her word against yours," Clara said calmly. "This will hopefully all blow over."

"But with the other events that have taken place, it looks bad," Abigail clutched her head in her hands. "Clara, this was such an important occasion for me. I won't deny I thought it might open doors, perhaps lead to a management role. There are no women in the management level of Albion Industries currently, but times are changing. Women are taking on traditional male roles and proving themselves completely adept at them. I thought… I hoped…"

Abigail gave a sob.

"But it doesn't matter now."

She began to cry and Clara rested her hand lightly on her arm. It was hard to know what to say, how to console the poor woman. She felt very sorry for her because events really had gone out of her control.

"I'm so sorry Abigail."

"If I knew how to change things I would do so. If I knew who was behind this catastrophe… but I don't. Someone is out to harm me, I am certain of it."

"Who?" Clara asked.

But once more Abigail shook her head.

"I don't know. I can list people like Niamh who dislike me, but is that enough to try and ruin me? Niamh might think to accuse me of being dishonest, but she is not about to go out and kill someone and blame it on me."

"Could it be someone from your past?"

"Like who?" Abigail demanded.

"I'm not sure, but it is easy to offend certain people. I was talking to Rowena Yardley only this morning for instance."

"Rowena," Abigail sighed deeply. "We were once such good friends, but she thought I would risk my position to help her. I would have liked to, but she was so very wrong for the job. She thought I could offer her work with Albion and we would travel about together like old chums, but that is not how this job works. I didn't like to say it straight out, but she was just not the sort of person cut out for this industry. She had no interest in cosmetics, in fact she was rather dismissive of women who used them. How could I employ her? But she kept insisting and it was challenging to put her off. Eventually she got the message and stopped writing to me. Our friendship cooled after that. But I don't consider her a murderer either."

"No, I agree with you," Clara nodded. "My point was that people can take offence over things that they shouldn't, and then that offence turns into festering hatred. But if you can't think of anyone who fits that description, what about someone who feels deeply betrayed by Albion Industries?"

"You have asked me that before and I said I just didn't know."

"Please, think hard. Some small detail could be very important."

Abigail obeyed and sat very still contemplating every rumour and word of gossip she had heard over the last few months, but nothing sprang to mind as being particularly sinister.

"Albion is very good to its employees," she said at last.

They were once more at a dead end.

"Never mind," Clara patted her hand reassuringly, "Maybe something will spring to mind."

"Will they release me now?" Abigail asked pathetically. "I need to get back to work."

"I'm sure…"

Clara was cut-off by the sound of the door opening and Inspector Park-Coombs appearing before them. His expression did not fill Clara with confidence.

"I wonder, Miss Sommers, if you might be able to explain how it is I found a knife in your room and some small pieces of what appear to be whalebone?"

"I…" Abigail looked from the inspector to Clara. "They are nothing to do with me!"

"We also found several tubes of used Pearl Pink lipstick and a small banner with the word 'betrayal' painted upon it."

"Inspector, surely even to you such a large amount of 'clues' must seem suspicious!" Clara declared, though her stomach had lurched over at the thought that Abigail could be behind these crimes.

"They seem to me like the objects a person planning to undertake a campaign of terror against her employers would need," Park-Coombs responded in his solemn tone. "The knife was necessary for opening the sealed boxes and removing packaging and, of course, for sharpening the whalebone stave. That was done hastily as a suitable message, plunging a corset strut into a corset salesman is very ironic."

"But Abigail was talking to me when that happened!" Clara insisted.

"We can't rule out an accomplice then," Park-Coombs was not to be deterred.

"And the shavings on the floor? Surely any sensible person would clean them up?" Clara countered.

"They were in the crack between the floorboards, my boys almost missed them. They could have been missed when sweeping up in the evening."

Abigail was watching this banter between the two with fresh tears streaming down her face. The case looked bleak.

"I did not bring a knife here," she said, choking on her misery and fear. "I never stole a whalebone stave, nor carved it into a sharp point and I never made a banner."

"That was under the bed," Park-Coombs explained. "It was when my lads spotted that and bent down to pull it out that they also noted the shavings. The banner was very neatly folded. Where were you intending to hang it?"

"I was not intending anything! I never made a banner!" Abigail denied the allegations furiously.

"And what about the several purloined lipsticks? Worn down as if they had been used recently, perhaps to write a message on the floor of the Pavilion?"

"They are samples Inspector!" Abigail seemed about ready to scream at him, but was restraining her frustration. "They were used because I have been taking them about to my clients and letting them test the colour. The new shade is being launched this week, but that did not prevent me from securing early sales agreements for it. I am a sales representative, it is what I do!"

Abigail suddenly burst into tears, sobbing heartily.

"Someone wants to ruin me! Can't you see?"

It seemed for the moment Park-Coombs could not see, or rather he could see plenty, but it all led in the wrong direction. There was nothing more Clara could do. Abigail would be detained and questioned further, her hotel room and belongings would be pulled to pieces and her private life exposed. The papers Niamh had found were now the least of her problems.

"Please, let me go," Abigail begged.

The inspector shook his head.

"You'll be staying here until this mess is resolved."

The inspector took Abigail's arm and gently led her from the room. She was to be escorted to the cells. Clara, feeling she had been of little help, wandered back to the front of the building and waited until the inspector reappeared.

"You realise she has been set-up?" Clara said to him.

"Maybe," the inspector shrugged.

"It has to be Inspector! I shall continue my investigations and prove it!"

Park-Coombs merely shrugged at her.

"I have convicted people on a lot less," he told her ominously.

Chapter Thirteen

Clara walked back to the Pavilion. It was late now, but the fair remained open until seven and most of the stall holders would be still there preparing for the next day. Clara hoped to catch Niamh and find out exactly what had happened between her and Abigail. She did not, for one moment, think Abigail was a killer. For a start, she would ruin her own career by acting out these peculiar acts of vengeance. In any case, why should Abigail feel betrayed when she was doing so well? No, someone was trying to implicate her and doing a good job of it, as far as the police were concerned. At least, Clara mused, while Abigail was in prison and appearing to take the blame, the murderer might cease their activities. For if another crime was committed Abigail would be immediately exonerated.

The lights were still on at the Pavilion. Clara wandered in with a nod to the police constable on duty outside. He looked tired and ready for his bed. The stall holders were tidying up after a long day, their displays needed restocking and neatening up. There was an alarming amount of discarded rubbish strewn across the floor – lost brochures, cigarette butts, sweet papers, empty product packaging and other assorted scraps of paper – which the regular Pavilion cleaner was endeavouring to tidy away. He glanced up at Clara as he went past with his broom pressed to the tiles.

"Miss Fitzgerald, have you seen this little lot?" he gestured with his hand to the debris.

"I know Mr Morris, it is disgraceful," Clara sympathised. "I shall have words."

"I wouldn't be so shocked if it had been the day the general public was due in," Mr Morris shook his head and scuffed his broom on the floor. "I could understand that. You get all sorts to a fair when its open free to the public. But today it was just those professional folk, all dressed smart and looking as though money falls out of their mouths. I thought they would have some manners. I guess not."

Mr Morris tutted as he stared at the forlorn mess lying about the hall.

"And it is such random things! I found a set of dentures in the gentleman's convenience. How anyone managed to walk away not realising they had lost those defies me!" Mr Morris' eyes went wide as he voiced his amazement. "Then I found all these little things that looked like wood shavings in the Prince's old bedroom which isn't even supposed to be in use. I suppose some workman went in there for a crafty smoke! I could smell it."

"I thought the prince's bedroom had been locked for that very reason?" Clara said swiftly. The stately bedroom of old Prince George, who had built and stayed at the Pavilion, was one of the main features of the building and retained its original decoration and some ornate and very expensive pieces of furniture. It was only very rarely opened to the public, though it was available for pre-arranged private viewings. It had been agreed by the committee that the room would be locked during the trade fair to avoid anything in it being damaged.

"That's what surprised me when I tried the door," Mr Morris agreed. "You see, there was this pink smear on the handle and I went to clean it off and as I did so the handle

102

went down and the door opened. I could smell someone had been smoking in there at once."

"I think I ought to take a look at this," Clara said, other thoughts swept from her mind in the face of someone desecrating the prince's bedroom.

Mr Morris led the way upstairs to the bedroom, which was off the same corridor where the impromptu dining room had been arranged. Mr Morris opened the bedroom door. There was still a hint of cigarette smoke lingering in the air and Mr Morris grumbled as he went to the window and opened it to allow in some fresh air.

"Thought I had aired it enough already, sorry Miss Fitzgerald."

"Not a problem, Mr Morris," Clara cast her eye about the room looking for any signs that someone had attempted to steal anything or had caused any damage. "Where is the key for this room?"

"Hanging on a hook in my broom closet," Mr Morris answered. "I do apologise that my cupboard is not itself locked. I had not thought anyone would go prowling in there."

"And there is no other key?"

"No. If you recall, the committee decided I should have charge of the key so I could come up and dust the room once a week. I fear they will want to remove it now," Mr Morris looked glum, feeling he had failed in his duty.

"Mr Morris, I don't consider you negligent in your duty," Clara reassured him gently. "You were not to know someone would go into your cupboard and steal the key."

Clara finished assessing the room.

"Nothing looks damaged, though these wood shavings you found are worrying. I hope no one was attempting some 'improvements' to the furniture," Clara could not fathom why anyone would want to come into this room and start causing havoc, but people were peculiar and not always respectful of the property of others.

"The shavings were by the bed, strange things they were. Very white," Mr Morris bent down and poked at the bed curtains that hung to the ground. "Here, look, I missed one."

He stood up and showed Clara what he had just found. It was a white, roughly triangular shard and she instantly saw that it was not wood.

"That is whalebone Mr Morris," she took the piece from him. "This is very interesting. Clearly someone has been very busy in the prince's bedroom."

"Shall I relock the room? The key is back on its hook in my cupboard. Someone decided to replace it but could not be bothered to lock the room door," Mr Morris sighed at the inconsiderate nature of the intruder.

"Lock the door Mr Morris and take the key home with you. Then I shall know it is in safe hands."

Touched by this act of faith, Mr Morris almost blushed and his earlier concerns that he had let the committee down evaporated. He promised he would do exactly as Clara said.

Clara returned downstairs deep in thought. It now looked very likely that the murderer had used the prince's bedroom to hatch their plot. They had sat and smoked in the room, hiding in a place no one would consider looking, because the bedroom was off limits for everyone aside from committee members. And there they had carved the corset stave into a lethal weapon, before travelling a mere few steps down the corridor to the dining room and using it on the unfortunate Mr Forthclyde. This also went some way to vindicating Abigail. The whalebone weapon had been created at the Pavilion, not in her hotel room. There was one last clue, though perhaps not as helpful as it might first appear; Clara now knew her killer was a smoker, and a heavy one by the smell that had lingered in the bedroom. She just had to find a suspect that fitted that description.

Back in the main hall, the diversion put to the recesses of her mind, Clara went in search of Niamh. The raven-haired woman was in one of the furthest rooms, (once a princely drawing room) where she was giving a talk to the other Albion representatives. It seemed that with Abigail's absence Niamh had neatly stepped into her place and had taken charge. Clara thought that all too convenient. She waited while Niamh finished her talk.

"…today was a good start ladies, but tomorrow I want to see more, I want sales, sales, sales! Especially of Pearl Pink. I saw some promising figures from your pre-orders, but we need to improve on that. If someone says they will take a dozen, sell them two dozen, that is our motto for tomorrow. Find out how many they want and then double it! We shall make this the most successful trade fair for Albion Industries there has ever been! Now, go back to your hotels and get some rest, tomorrow is another busy day."

Niamh dismissed the other ladies and then turned around. She immediately saw Clara and the satisfied smile she had been wearing evaporated.

"Have you had a good day, Miss Owen?" Clara asked politely.

Niamh started to scowl, then restored her professional demeanour. She had learned since their last encounter that Clara was an old school friend of Abigail's, and that instantly made her the enemy by association.

"It has been a fair start," she said cautiously.

"I see you have taken charge of proceedings?"

Niamh lost some of her business-like façade at the statement. Clara reflected that she was a little too temperamental and did not control her emotions well enough. That probably went some way to explaining why Abigail was always ahead of her. Niamh would let her passions get the better of her in a negotiation, while Abigail was always professional.

"Someone had to step up after Miss Sommers unfortunate breakdown," Niamh replied rather haughtily.

"Abigail broke down?" Clara said, feigning surprise. "I had not heard that. I heard you attempted to threaten her with those papers you were bragging about earlier."

"Threaten!" Niamh put on a good appearance of being

affronted. "There was nothing but truth in those papers! And Abigail attacked me!"

Niamh thumped a finger into her chest to emphasise her words. Her mask of calm had completely faltered, in her fury she had resorted to using first names.

"Are you satisfied your rival is in a police cell facing serious charges?" Clara asked stoutly.

"She is there through her own fault!"

"The way I hear it, Abigail tried to take the papers off you and you stumbled. You then chose to scream blue murder."

Niamh's eyes flashed with fiery anger.

"So, that is how it is?" she declared. "I'll tell you this, Miss Fitzgerald, I did show those papers to Abigail and I told her I knew exactly how she had been cooking the books. She became scared that I was going to reveal her and flew at me, trying to snatch the papers. She pushed me and I fell to the floor and I saw the look in her eyes, the murderous look! She was intent on harming me! Had I not screamed… well, perhaps we would not be speaking now."

Niamh thrust out her chin in surly stubbornness.

"You really think Abigail capable of murder?" Clara said in disbelief.

"For the right motive I do," Niamh pointed a finger at Clara. "You have spent too much time listening to her bleeding heart stories."

"Suppose I have?" Clara countered. "Why not prove to me otherwise?"

Niamh smiled, rising to the challenge. She picked her handbag up off the floor and pulled out two sheets of paper.

"I got these from a friend," she waved the papers at Clara. "These show the number of sales a girl has made. The girls fill these in and send them to Albion's accounts department. These are Abigail's most recent sheets, you can see where she has filled in the figures."

Niamh thrust the papers at Clara.

"Take a note of the names of the retailers and distributors she claims to have sold this number of goods to. Now look at these," Niamh rummaged in her bag and produced another sheet of figures. "This is from Albion's shipping warehouse. This paper shows the actual number of boxes of products sent out to the shops and people Abigail made sales to."

Clara took the second sheet and compared the figures. She felt her heart sink a bit when she realised the figures differed. Not hugely, but always by a box or two, to make it appear that Abigail was selling just a fraction more than she really was.

"Why has Albion Industries not realised this?" Clara asked.

"The accounts department and the shipping department are two different things," Niamh shrugged. "Each month the accounts department will receive the takings from the sales of stock each shop and distributor sells, but there is no reason to assume they will sell everything, so if the figures are lower than those the representative stated they actually sold to the shop, well, that is to be expected. The shop or distributor holds on to the goods they are sent until they are all sold and there is always going to be a certain amount of products that either do not sell or can't be sold due to being damaged or even stolen from the shop. Albion accepts these losses. The only way the accounts department could know that Abigail was cheating was if they did exactly the same as I have done. But they have never done that. They rely on the good faith of the representatives, rightly or wrongly."

Clara stared at the papers and the blatant evidence they provided. The first sheets were signed by Abigail and there was no denying that they differed from the second set. If both sets of figures were genuine, then something very odd was occurring.

"So now maybe you see that Abigail is not the great innocent she makes out?" Niamh's tone put Clara's back up again. It did look likely that Abigail was cheating, but

Niamh's snide satisfaction still rankled. She had not sought out this evidence for the sake of Albion Industries, but because it would further her position and disgrace someone she had come to jealously hate.

"Could I keep a set of these figures?" Clara asked. "I would like to show them to the police and to Abigail, so I can hear her explanation."

Niamh hesitated, looking about ready to snatch the papers back.

"You have two months' worth of evidence," Clara pointed out. "You retain one set and I can borrow the other. I don't intend to destroy them. You have my word on that."

Niamh didn't seem to think Clara's word worth much, considering she was friends with Abigail Sommers, but she conceded anyway.

"So be it," she said grumpily.

"Whatever this does or does not prove," Clara said steadily, "I do not think Abigail a murderer or a saboteur. These papers in fact prove that Abigail is determined to keep her place at Albion by whatever means necessary. Sabotage and murder are completely counterproductive to that goal. They could destroy her career."

Niamh shrugged.

"I don't claim to understand her motives. I just say that she is dangerous," she took back her set of papers, leaving Clara with the other set, folded them into her bag and stalked off.

Clara was left alone to mull over what she had discovered. She was disheartened, but she had told the truth to Niamh, these papers did not make Abigail a murderer. Not yet, at least.

Chapter Fourteen

Clara didn't sleep easy that night, and when morning came there was a great deal on her mind, not least Abigail's apparent misdeeds with her sales figures. One of the problems she was struggling with was whether the two unfortunate murder victims were chance attacks or whether someone had always intended to kill them. There seemed hints that this was the case because of the choice of murder weapon, but how did that fit in with this betrayal business? Surely Clara was not looking for a saboteur and a murderer, two different people both out to cause havoc for Albion Industries or possibly Abigail herself? Clara decided that to try and answer that question she needed to know more about the victims.

She went first to the Pavilion to see how the morning was shaping up. Everyone seemed busy and uninclined to speak to her. She skirted the rooms, but everything seemed in order. She caught a glimpse of Miss Muggins near her trade stand, the woman looked pale and distracted. Having already spoken with her without achieving much success, Clara decided to leave her be. Clara turned around sharply and nearly bumped straight into a rotund gentleman in a grey suit. He laughed and apologised.

"My fault, I was in too much haste," Clara responded.

"Are you one of the stall holders?" the gentleman inquired.

"No, actually I am member of the Pavilion committee," Clara explained. "Miss Fitzgerald."

"Percival Grundisburgh," the gentleman introduced himself. "Of Albion Industries. I am one of their executives. I came directly down this morning from London."

Clara took another look at the man. Now she could see his suit was of a very good cut and the tailor had done what he could to mask his client's girth with the design. Mr Grundisburgh clearly enjoyed many working lunches, his paunch gave him away. But he looked robustly healthful despite his size and smiled broadly at the room about him. As far as executives went, Mr Grundisburgh was not terribly intimidating, rather he seemed the friendly sort with his round chubby face, bald pate and frizzy white hair about his ears. He was also considerably younger than a first glance might suggest.

"I was not expecting an executive from Albion Industries," Clara said. "Had I known I would have made suitable arrangements to welcome you."

Mr Grundisburgh brushed these remarks aside.

"It was a last minute trip, decided upon after we received some worrying news that there had been trouble at the trade fair. It was thought best if a senior figure came down to investigate and that job nearly always falls on me. My fellows seem to think I am rather good at sorting out this type of thing," Mr Grundisburgh was amused by this. "Now, do you happen to know where Miss Sommers is?"

News had clearly not reached Albion headquarters of all the trouble that had occurred at the fair.

"Mr Grundisburgh, might we converse somewhere private?"

The executive looked curious, but he had no reason to deny the request. He followed Clara to a side room where they could speak quietly admit assorted boxes of Albion Industries products. Clara perched herself on a box, Mr Grundisburgh eyed the room for a box that might be able to support his weight. Deciding there was not one available he contented himself with standing.

"What has happened that I do not know about?" he asked.

Clara took a deep breath before she began.

"Abigail Sommers has been arrested due to a complaint from one of the other Albion representatives. It is very circumstantial and I don't think any charges will stick. Sadly, the woman who has made the complaint has a very real hatred for her rival."

Mr Grundisburgh looked solemn.

"That is unhappy news. Albion does not like discord among its employees. Such a thing can be very bad for business."

From his tone, Clara guessed Mr Grundisburgh did not know the full extent of the recent problems the fair had suffered.

"What precisely was mentioned in the message you received?" she asked.

"The note was simplistic, but said there had been some attempts to sabotage the fair."

"No mention of murder?" Clara asked.

Mr Grundisburgh's eyes grew wide and round.

"Murder?" he hissed.

Clara gave a little sigh, then began to outline to Mr Grundisburgh the events of the last few days. Everything from the first attempts at sabotage to the recent death of Mr Forthclyde. She avoided saying too much about Abigail and the evidence found in her room. She didn't feel Mr Grundisburgh needed ideas put into his head. Clara was convinced that evidence had been planted by someone else and saw no reason to perpetuate the lies against Abigail. When she had finished outlining all that had gone on Mr Grundisburgh looked most morose.

"This is far more serious than I was expecting," he

said.

"Have Albion received any threats lately? Any disgruntled employees wanting to cause havoc?" Clara queried.

Mr Grundisburgh scratched at his head.

"Albion is not immune to hate mail," he admitted. "We are a big company, very popular, and some people are jealous of that success. Others just see us as a big target to attack."

"Has anybody made threats that stood out from the rest?" Clara rephrased herself.

Mr Grundisburgh considered this for a while, then slowly nodded.

"There was a very nasty letter the other week, full of expletives and threatening harm to anyone who worked for the company. The letter was typed and whoever wrote it had not been inclined to sign it. It was unpleasant, but no one took it to heart."

"What about someone who might feel betrayed by the company?"

Mr Grundisburgh paused. Then he glanced up.

"There was this one young fellow who caused us some bother. He was in the developmental section of the business, creating and refining products. Us executives laughingly refer to them as the kitchen boys because they are always cooking up new ideas," Mr Grundisburgh grinned. "This one fellow was a strange character. Came up with some good ideas, but struggled to work with others. Also, he was a little too prone to using the laboratories for his own experiments. He had to be reprimanded for it. He was dabbling in everything but cosmetics sometimes. Eventually the management grew tired of him despite his genius and fired him. He did not leave without a great deal of protest. But that was six months ago."

"What was his name?" Clara asked to be on the safe side.

"Jeremiah Cook, but I can't think he would harm

anyone," Mr Grundisburgh shrugged his shoulders. "I suppose he could have written that nasty letter."

"Is there anyone else you can think of?" Clara pressed. "Someone who would know the ins and outs of Albion's work, right down to how successful one girl was at selling an unpopular stocking."

Mr Grundisburgh opened his mouth, but nothing came out. He shook his head again.

"Who made the complaint against Miss Sommers?" he asked, changing the subject.

"Niamh Owen," Clara answered. "She claims Abigail pushed her, while Abigail states Niamh fell over her own heels when they were wrestling over some papers."

"Niamh Owen is temperamental," Grundisburgh said cautiously. "Only because she has been such an asset to Albion have we overlooked some of her more unpleasant aspects. She has despised Abigail Sommers for as long as I can remember."

"Has she ever caused problems?" Clara asked.

"A few," Mr Grundisburgh confessed sorrowfully. "She could be prone to upsetting customers when she first started, but she has moderated herself since we had stern words. She mainly upsets the other girls now. Abigail Sommers is one of her particular vendettas and we have been aware of it for a while. She would do anything to see that woman suffer, and we have informally agreed among ourselves that if matters become out of hand we will have to think about reassigning one or the other of them."

"Has she had problems with other girls too?" Clara was curious now, wondering just how far Niamh Owen might be prepared to go to discredit her rival. Might she go as far as murder in a fit of temper?

"We have had the odd complaint," Mr Grundisburgh admitted. "Nothing that required a great deal of our time."

"Might I ask if any of those girls are here at the trade fair?"

Mr Grundisburgh thought about the question.

"Now you mention it, yes indeed, Miss Esther Althorpe had cause to complain about her. Miss Owen was encroaching on her sales territory."

Clara's face fell. She had told Mr Grundisburgh about the murders but had omitted the identities of the individuals for the time being. Now her expression said everything.

"Has something happened to Miss Althorpe?" Grundisburgh asked cautiously.

"Miss Althorpe is sadly deceased," Clara answered.

Mr Grundisburgh became very quiet.

"That I had not expected. When you said two people had been killed I assumed they were workmen, like the gentleman on the scaffold who was injured."

"Would the complaint have given Miss Owen reason to hate Miss Althorpe?"

"My heavens!" Mr Grundisburgh tried to laugh, but the sound came out very brittle. "It was only a minor thing. Miss Owen was reminded that she was to stick to the area assigned to her. There was no nastiness, not really."

Mr Grundisburgh looked unconvinced with his own explanation, but Clara was inclined to think that it was a long way to go from encroaching on a person's sales territory to murder.

"Who... who was the other person killed?" Mr Grundisburgh asked anxiously.

"Mr Forthclyde of Cushing's Corsetry," Clara answered.

"Forthclyde!" Mr Grundisburgh gasped. "Why, the company has traded with Cushing's for years and he has always been their spokesman! I only conversed with him last week. We were finalising some stock figures for Cushing's new corset range. They want to sell them through Albion Industries' stores and we were most agreeable to it. Oh, this is just terrible!"

"I don't suppose Mr Forthclyde had any dealings with Miss Owen?" Clara asked, though she rather fancied that she was clutching at straws.

"Not that I am aware. Cushing's have their own representatives, so our girls only promote a few of their lines. No, I am sure there was nothing between them. I can't say if they even knew the other existed."

"Is there anyone you can think of who might have held a grudge against Mr Forthclyde or the Cushing's company?"

Mr Grundisburgh was clearly struggling to take all this information in. He became flushed and had to pull out a handkerchief and pat the sweat off his forehead.

"All this talk has made me feel queasy," he sighed.

"I shall fetch you some water," Clara offered.

"Please, no. I shall be fine. I must get this over with. Were there any problems with Mr Forthclyde? Let me see," Mr Grundisburgh thought for a long while, then he declared in a deep tone. "Mr Forthclyde was briefly at the heart of a scandal involving his former assistant."

"A scandal?" Clara was intrigued. "I have met his new assistant, Miss Muggins."

"Yes, she had to be taken on in some haste. The previous girl and Mr Forthclyde had had a fling which resulted in some unfortunate talk. The girl's parents were angry and wanted Mr Forthclyde to resign. He protested his innocence and, in truth, the girl's word was all we had for it. Nothing really happened except she left and we took on Miss Muggins instead."

It was scanty basis for murder, Clara reflected. So far neither of the victims seemed to have any real enemies.

"What of Miss Sommers relationship with either Esther Althorpe or Mr Forthclyde?"

"As far as I was aware it was purely professional," Mr Grundisburgh answered. "Esther Althorpe worked an area removed from the one Abigail Sommers was assigned. They would meet at certain functions, I dare say, but aside from that I don't suppose they saw a lot of each other. And Mr Forthclyde coordinated directly with Albion Industries, he had no reason to go through our sales representatives. Its highly likely neither had even been introduced until this very week."

So that was that, at least Clara could say there was no reason for Abigail to want the two dead.

"I come back to my original theory then," Clara said. "That someone has a grudge against Albion Industries. The word 'betrayal' has been used a number of times. It was written on the floor and underneath poor Mr Forthclyde. If it is not directed at the victims themselves, or Abigail Sommers, it seems likely it is aimed at the company. Who has Albion betrayed Mr Grundisburgh?"

The executive shook his head. He pulled anxiously at his tie, his colour had risen alarmingly.

"Miss Fitzgerald, we are a business. Businesses make tough decisions and sometimes people feel they have been treated badly."

That was close to an admission that the company had mishandled some past trouble.

"Can you think of anyone in particular?" she pushed.

Again Mr Grundisburgh wrenched his tie.

"Betrayal is such a peculiar word," he muttered. "We stopped trading with a face cream company whose products contained an unhealthy amount of Arsenic, but surely we could claim they betrayed us as they had mislabelled their products?"

"I think we are looking at an individual, rather than a company," Clara persisted. "Have you had to sack any employees lately?"

"Miss Fitzgerald, as at any large company, our turnover of staff is frequent and we do have to fire some from time to time," Mr Grundisburgh seemed to find it ludicrous to imagine a sacked employee could be the culprit. "Over the last three months I believe we have had to let go five individuals for various reasons."

"Might any of them have felt betrayed?"

"Angry, perhaps, but not betrayed," Mr Grundisburgh found the idea absurd. "No, Miss Fitzgerald, I just cannot help you."

Clara doubted that. She was convinced Mr Grundisburgh was holding back on her, but she didn't think he was going to reveal anything else for the time being. And he was looking very flustered and liable for a heart attack. She decided to leave her questions for the moment. Perhaps with time to think, Mr Grundisburgh would come up with new answers.

"I must send a telegram back to head office," Mr Grundisburgh muttered. "This is much more serious than I first imagined."

He moved to the door and Clara followed him. Back in the main hall it was cooler and Mr Grundisburgh's high colour started to diminish. He bustled off before Clara could say anything else to him. Clara watched the hall for a moment, looking at all the commotion as people bought and sold items and talked about the latest fashions. She decided it was time to go somewhere quieter. Time to seek out Abigail again and see if she was ready to tell the truth about all this.

Chapter Fifteen

Abigail clutched her head in her hands.

"Mr Grundisburgh," she groaned softly to herself. "I'm finished."

"Don't despair just yet," Clara reassured her. They were sitting in the quiet interview room at the police station, two strong cups of tea on the table. "This is far from over. Abigail, these attacks are not your fault, but we must talk earnestly and honestly. For your sake. Do you understand?"

Abigail put down her hands and looked up at Clara.

"Go ahead, what have I to lose now? I am facing the end of my career and I can't see how I can begin again. How many companies want to employ a woman in a significant position, let alone a woman who has been released from her previous employment in disgrace?"

Abigail looked abjectly miserable. Clara feared she would feel even worse by the time they finished their conversation.

"Let us begin with those papers Niamh referred to," Clara said. "She has shown them to me and I have borrowed one set."

Clara rummaged in her handbag and withdrew the papers, she placed them on the table before Abigail.

"Perhaps you might explain them to me?"

Abigail glanced at the papers and frowned.

"These appear to be my sales returns, the paperwork I send in to state how many products I have sold to a company," Abigail's frown deepened. "The second sheet is the record of what was actually dispatched to the shops and individuals in question. And it is plain to see they do not tally."

Abigail fixed her eyes on Clara.

"I did not write the first sheet like this. It bears my signature, I know, but I have never forged my papers. I swear on my soul to that!" Abigail became despairing. "Someone is trying to ruin me, that is plain to see. Here, look how this five has become a six in this column, turning 150 boxes of Glimmer Face Cream into 160. Please believe me Clara!"

Abigail desperately pushed the sheets back to Clara and indicated the changes. Clara had to admit that the numbers that differed from the dispatch sheet were indeed ones that could be easily changed. A zero became an eight with a stroke of the pen. The insertion of an extra one into a column turned a 2 into 12. The sheets certainly might have been doctored after they were sent in to Albion's accounts department.

"I can prove my innocence," Abigail persisted. "I keep copies of these papers at home for my own reference. Many of the girls do so. I could retrieve those copies and demonstrate that my figures tallied exactly with the stock dispatched."

"That is very good news," Clara assured her. "But who would doctor your papers?"

"Niamh Owen," Abigail said through gritted teeth. "She has a friend in the accounts department, I don't know who they are, unfortunately. Either this friend or Niamh herself changed my papers to make me look like a liar."

Niamh Owen certainly had plenty of motive to do just that and her personal dislike for Abigail biased any opinion she gave. If she, or her friend, had doctored the paperwork to discredit a rival it was very serious indeed. Before making such accusations, which could ruin someone else's reputation and cost them their job, Clara would need to be very sure of her facts.

"I suggest you send for those papers, Abigail," Clara said. "We can ask the inspector to request a police constable from another station to go to your home and retrieve them. I think that would be acceptable considering the circumstances."

Abigail seemed happy with that suggestion. She nodded her head in agreement.

"Tell me a bit more about Niamh," Clara took a sip of her tea. "I understand she is not all that popular among some of the girls?"

"Niamh is fiery, I think that is the best way to describe her. She acts like she has a lot to prove, perhaps she does, but it is mainly to herself," Abigail shrugged her shoulders. "She is underconfident and it shows in the way she jealously attacks others. I don't think she has any real friends among the Albion representatives, though there are those quite happy to trail in her shadow because they think it will do them some good. Niamh won't tolerate near her those she perceives as being a potential threat. I have always had to be guarded around her."

"What about her and Esther Althorpe?"

"The rumour was that Niamh had tried to take over some of Esther's better sales contracts. Esther was the representative for a lucrative area of the county. A number of larger stores came within her territory. Places where it was relatively easy to make high sales. Esther was perhaps not experienced enough to fully exploit that advantage, but she was learning."

"Niamh thought she could do a better job?" Clara guessed.

"Niamh wanted that territory very badly. She was not given it because she had had some confrontations with customers in the past. Albion was not prepared to let her erstwhile tongue spoil their relationship with these big stores. Esther was considered to be a potentially good saleswoman, if she could just be encouraged in the right direction," Abigail smiled sadly. "She had a good heart, did Esther. She was a little naïve to begin with, but she learned rapidly and rewarded the trust Albion had placed in her. Her improvement of their middle-range stocking sales is just one example of how she was developing and proving herself an asset."

"Which makes the irony of her being strangled to death by one of those stockings seem rather important," Clara pointed out.

"Do you think someone with a grudge against Esther killed her? But then that would not explain Mr Forthclyde. Why would anyone hate both of them? They were virtually unconnected."

"I hear Mr Forthclyde had his own scandal story?" Clara avoided trying to answer Abigail's question. She could not offer a solution even if she wanted to.

"Mr Forthclyde became a little too friendly with his former assistant. It was very common gossip among most of Albion's employees. Mr Forthclyde was a bachelor and some of the girls thought him rather dapper. His assistant was a stony-faced little thing, at least around us. I suppose she was somewhat different when they were alone. I hear she fell pregnant and her parents were furious, but that might just be talk. She certainly left in a hurry and her replacement was picked out swiftly. Poor Miss Muggins walked into quite a mess," Abigail tutted. "Though she does seem a good choice in comparison. Very upright and concerned about her reputation. So probably she won't falter as the previous girl did."

"Did the scandal cause anyone to bear a grudge against Mr Forthclyde?"

"Not among the Albion folk, as far as I know," Abigail answered. "Mr Forthclyde was not in Albion's employment. He seemed to weather the storm well enough and Cushing's was loathed to be rid of him, so decided to pretend nothing was going on. I suppose his old assistant might bear a grudge, but the story was that she received a sizeable sum of money from Mr Forthclyde and the company to keep her mouth shut. She probably is doing all right for herself."

Probably was not the same as a certainty, but even if this elusive assistant was responsible for killing Mr Forthclyde, there was still no connection between that death and Miss Althorpe's as far as Clara could see, and that was the sticking point of all her theories.

"I have not been very helpful, have I?" Abigail looked glum. "I have not offered you any ideas of who might be behind this all."

"I have ideas, but none add-up," Clara admitted. "Niamh troubles me. Her spite for you and some of the other girls could almost make me imagine she was behind the attack on Esther, but I can't think why she would try to sabotage the trade fair or why she would kill Forthclyde. The trade fair is as important to her as you."

"Maybe that is just it," Abigail suddenly had an idea. "What if all this was an attempt to discredit me so Niamh could take over running the fair?"

"Murder is a very drastic way of going about such a thing," Clara countered. "I could imagine the sabotage being an attempt to discredit you, but murder is another thing. It takes a callous person to kill someone just to cause trouble for someone else."

"Then I really don't know," Abigail sighed sadly. "I wish I did, so I could leave this place and get on with my job. If I still have a job."

"Please don't give up just yet," Clara interrupted. "There was one other name Mr Grundisburgh mentioned. A Jeremiah Cook who was sacked from the company about six months ago?"

Abigail mused on this name.

"He was one of the laboratory boys," she said at last. "I didn't know him well. Jeremiah was the talk among some of the girls because he was young and attractive. Well, to a degree. I always thought him a little creepy."

"He was not the best employee, or so I hear?"

"Jeremiah liked science but he was a terrible worker. I heard one tale that he had been tasked with testing a new face powder made by another company to ensure it had nothing hazardous in its composition and also so Albion could copy the recipe. He became side-tracked instead and started working on his own experiments. I hear he was very curious about the toxicity of certain heavy metals. He would waste the company's time by conducting his own work in their laboratory," Abigail rolled her eyes at the foolishness of the man. "I imagine if he had been a genius at his work and produced results for Albion, they would have overlooked his extra experiments. But he was not and he upset a few people. Well, more than a few. The crunch came when he failed to conduct the tests on the face powder after nearly four months of having the product. Albion showed him the door."

"Was he the sort of man who would feel betrayed by such a thing?"

"I don't know," Abigail had to admit. "I never really spoke to him. In any case, it was his own fault he was fired, he can hardly complain."

People did not always see things that way, Clara reflected.

"Tell me about Mr Grundisburgh? He seemed a nice enough sort."

"Mr Grundisburgh is lovely," Abigail briefly grew animated. "He is one of the most senior managers at Albion. I think he must have been with the company a good twenty, if not more, years. He used to conduct the training for new representatives, but I think he has probably risen to a position above such menial tasks now. I think nearly everyone likes him."

"Nearly everyone?" Clara asked.

"Well, no one is liked by the whole world, are they? Mr Grundisburgh has had to fire a few people too, that never goes down well."

"You are not surprised he was the one they sent down to investigate the problems here?"

"No, not really," Abigail agreed readily. "Mr Grundisburgh is the problem solver for Albion. If there was ever trouble with one of the sales regions he would be the one to go and sort it out. I believe it was Mr Grundisburgh they sent when Esther and Niamh had their difficulties."

"I am going to try and keep in close communication with him," Clara added. "I hope by doing so we can share information, and I will of course do my hardest to convince him you have been the victim of a campaign of hate."

"Oh Clara, I am so glad I came to you," Abigail dabbed at her eye with a handkerchief as tears threatened. "This has been the worst week of my life. I wish I had never been asked to conduct this trade fair."

"There is no reason to get upset," Clara reached out and patted her hand. "I am working hard to resolve all this."

"I thought nothing could stop me once I had set my course," Abigail continued morosely. "I believed I was unstoppable. I had come so far, clattered through so many obstacles that were against my succeeding. Why should I imagine things would go wrong for me now? I had not become involved in any scandals. I had avoided taking sides. Yes, there was the jealousy I sensed from others, but that was part of my success. I could do nothing about that. I thought I was safe, Clara, I thought I had made sure nothing bad could touch me."

Abigail coughed as tears caught in her throat.

"I was very wrong."

"Not wrong," Clara didn't like to see her cry. "Maybe a little too optimistic. But don't imagine for a moment that this is the end. I will find out who is really behind these crimes and you will be safe once again."

"I don't think I will ever feel secure in my position again," Abigail shook her head. "I will always be looking over my shoulder. I fear I have seen a very different side to the feminine character I had once considered so strong and irreproachable. Suddenly we seem far less noble creatures. When I see what my female colleagues have done to promote themselves, I feel quite ashamed to be a woman."

"We are all human," Clara replied. "Some of us are good, moral individuals, and some are less so. But no one is perfect and we should never imagine that to be the case."

"Perhaps my expectations for my fellows are too high," Abigail sighed. "I shall resign myself to disappointment in future."

Clara rather got the impression that Abigail was determined to be glum no matter what she said. She finished her tea, reassured Abigail once again that she was trying her hardest to resolve everything and then checked her watch.

"It is nearly visiting time at the hospital," she said. "I am going to pay a call on the workman who came so close to being another victim of this affair."

Abigail merely nodded. Clara was about to go, when a thought occurred to her and she paused at the door.

"I don't suppose you would know what this Jeremiah Cook fellow looked like?"

"I never met him," Abigail answered simply.

Clara thought that interesting. But whether Jeremiah was angry enough at Albion Industries to go in for murder was another thing altogether. She said goodbye to Abigail, promised she would do her best yet again, and then set her feet in the direction of the hospital. Time to talk to this workman who had come close to being the first victim of their saboteur.

Chapter Sixteen

Mr Timothy Briggs had worked in the building trade for the past fifteen years and, while there had been the odd mishap during that time, there had been nothing which had forced him to go to hospital. Oh yes, there was the nail that Dim Dave managed to hammer through Timothy's thumb one day, but it was a simple enough thing to remove. Painful, but simple. The foreman had taken it out with a pair of pliers. It had bled plenty, and hurt like hell, but once it was suitably bandaged and Tim had been given sufficient time to recover from the shock, he had got back to the day's work. And, of course, no one ever stood near Dave again when he was hammering something.

No, Timothy Briggs had been proud to say that he had never had to spend so much as an hour in hospital because of his work. Until, that is, he had climbed up that damn scaffolding. Looking back, Timothy reflected that the poles had not felt as firm as usual when he had clambered up. But he had been so fixated on fixing that nasty hole one of the other lads had carelessly smashed into the ceiling plaster before anyone from the Pavilion Committee saw it, that he had ignored his instincts. More fool him, he mused to himself. He could have saved himself a lot of bother and pain had he just listened to his own mind. But, then again, maybe he had not noticed the poles being loose, maybe that was just his way of berating himself later on. He should have noticed. That he might have failed to niggled him.

Timothy Briggs had broken a leg in the fall that followed. It was not so much that he fell from a great height, but rather that the wood and metal of the scaffold fell down on top of him. One plank in particular had come down across his leg with such force that he had heard a crack and searing pain had torn through him. His other injuries included a sprain to his lower back, a bump on the head which was annoying but not much else, and a smashed little finger on his right hand. Thankfully, Timothy had passed out pretty quickly.

Since being in the hospital Timothy had seen a regular crowd of visitors. Aside from his wife who popped over every evening while her mother tended the children, he had been visited by Mr Taversham, Miss Sommers, a representative of the Pavilion Committee and a newspaperman who seemed fascinated by his story. Timothy was rather revelling in his new-found popularity. But his nicest visitor by far had to be the young woman who came onto the ward that afternoon and introduced herself as Clara Fitzgerald.

Timothy was not much of a one for reading the newspapers, and he had no real notion of who Clara was. He just saw a nicely proportioned woman, with a pretty oval face and dark hair tied back in a loose plait. Clara was not yet smitten with this idea of very short hair for women. Timothy thought she was rather a fine thing to look at, though he doubted his wife would agree.

"Mr Briggs?"

"I am indeed," Timothy said.

"Could I bother you for a while to ask about what happened at the Pavilion the other day?"

"You can bother me as much as you please," Timothy grinned. "What precisely do you want to know?"

"Well, what really happened?"

Timothy laughed.

"The scaffolding fell down with me on it! Some bugger forgot to put the nuts on the bolts."

A nurse hastening by glowered at Timothy for his bad language. He grinned even broader.

"Has that ever happened before?" Clara asked, ignoring the nurse.

"Scaffolding being loose? Never!" Timothy's eyes became wide as if the mere idea amazed him. "Mr Taversham checks everything twice. I have worked for him on and off these last six years. I've never known him not to double-check everything. I dare say he double-checks his tea before he even contemplates drinking it! That's the sort of man he is."

"So, there is no doubt in your mind that the scaffold had been tampered with?"

"Should there be?" Timothy looked confused. "On another yard maybe you could say someone had been careless, but with Mr Taversham around there is no excuse. That man sees and knows everything that goes on among the workmen. So, I suppose, it had to have been tampered with.

"By whom?" Clara asked.

Timothy shrugged.

"How would I know? No one has confessed such a thing to me. Nasty thing to do though. I could have been killed."

"When did you know you were to be going up the scaffold?"

"That morning when Mr Taversham spotted me and told me what to do."

That ruled out Clara's tentative theory that someone might have had a grudge against Mr Briggs. No one could have known he would be the one to go up the scaffold.

"How long after he told you what job to do, did you climb up?"

"A few minutes, at the most," Timothy shrugged his sore shoulders. "I only went to pick up my toolbox before clambering up."

"No one would have had time to tamper with the bolts then?"

"No," Timothy said firmly.

"It is all very curious, don't you think? People taking nuts off bolts? The Pavilion wasn't open to everyone just then, either. It was closed off for you to work," Clara laid out an idea that was forming as she talked. "Someone already there had to have unscrewed the nuts. Strange in itself, as that person must surely have known what would occur."

"You would imagine so," Timothy agreed blithely enough.

"I take it you have no suspicions of anyone?"

The question brought another ripple of laughter from Timothy at first, but then he hesitated and his face fell. His grin turned upside down until the corners of his mouth seemed to droop dangerously.

"Have you thought of something?" Clara asked.

"I know most of the work crew," Timothy started to shake his head, then he paused. "Nearly all of them I have worked with before, but this one lad, well, man really. He was new. He was only recently come down from the north. He didn't look like much of a builder, no real muscle to him, but you can't go around accusing people of being scrawny once the bosses have taken them on. But he always seemed a little odd and when you said about someone seeming suspicious, well, he sprang straight to mind."

"What is his name?" Clara asked.

"Ian Dunwright," Timothy answered, the thought that one of his co-workers might have deliberately sabotaged the scaffold was only just sinking in. "He was one of those souls who never seems to have his mind quite on the job in hand. I had to teach him how to hold a hammer right. I really thought we had another Dave on our hands."

"Dave?" Clara picked up on the name.

Timothy shook his head.

"Doesn't matter. What does, is that I could imagine Ian being fool enough to borrow the nuts off the bolts to use for something else, without realising he was creating a real danger for everyone," Timothy gave a groan. "If it was him, I hope old Taversham gives him what for and kicks him out of the work crew! I'm going to be laid up for weeks, you know? And who is going to be bringing the money home to feed our Susan and our Daphne then?"

Clara had to admit she did not know. Timothy had become gloomy.

"I wouldn't have minded so much if I could get on with my work. I've never had a day off, never. Until now that is."

Clara didn't want to let him dwell in self-pity, that might defeat her purpose, so she asked another question to distract Timothy.

"What do you know about the sabotage incidents at the Pavilion?"

Timothy fell quiet. A sheepish look came over him.

"Are you going to tell anyone what I say?" he asked warily.

"No," Clara promised. "This is purely for my own reference."

Timothy still seemed uncertain and he looked up and down the ward, as if expecting all the other men in the beds to be eavesdropping on them.

"You really won't tell anyone?"

"Not unless it is forced out of me."

This seemed to satisfy Timothy, though he did enquire just what would constitute sufficient force to make Clara spill the beans. Clara was thinking that a cup of tea and a friendly enquiry from Inspector Park-Coombs would probably do it, but she didn't say as much.

"We kept quiet about a couple of things. Miss Sommers, she is the lady in charge of this affair, she only knew about the lipsticks and the scaffold."

"There were other problems?" Clara was deeply curious now.

"Yes, I mean, they might have just been accidents," Timothy was looking sheepish, as if he feared that Mr Taversham would walk in at any moment. "It was odd things that attracted attention. Tool boxes going missing and someone replacing the sugar jar with salt. The moved lipsticks Miss Sommers spotted. Then the scaffold. And all these signs going up everywhere makes you stop and think."

"Mr Briggs, missing tool boxes are not the sort of thing you feel the need to hide from someone like Miss Sommers," Clara said pointedly.

Timothy Briggs had the decency to blush.

"Ah, well…" he blew out his cheeks, then came to a decision. "All right, let me start again. It all happened shortly after the boxes of stock arrived. It seemed like someone was going in among them at night. Things were moved and boxes had been opened. Mr Taversham was scratching his head over it all. Who, he said, could be tampering with all the boxes? He locked up each night we left and assured himself we were all out of the building. Then we noticed that some of the stock had been stripped from its packaging, but not removed. As if someone were wanting to look at it, but not take it away. Mr Taversham was worried in case Miss Sommers heard about it and thought we had allowed someone to sneak in.

"Aside from that there was the dead cat business," Timothy hesitated again. "That might have been bad luck, of course."

"What sort of bad luck?" Clara pushed.

After huffing and puffing, and blowing out his cheeks once more, Timothy resolved himself to explaining.

"We used to leave the bigger tools out where we would need them the next day when we left at night. One of these was a saw. Don't ask me how, but it somehow got turned over and wedged on its back so the serrated blade was uppermost. None of us would have left it like that, but that was how it was. And it rather looked like the cat had fallen on it, perhaps jumping from some of the scaffolding."

Clara cringed. She didn't like to think of an animal hurt.

"Sorry, miss. That was another reason we thought not to tell Miss Sommers. But here is the thing, old Isiah, who has been working in this trade since before I was born. Well, he grew up on a farm where his father was a labourer. He said to me after we cleaned up the mess and he was making a good cup of tea, he said 'that cat was dead at least a week before it ended up here.'

"I asked him how he could know that and old Isiah said there had been places on the cat which looked like the open wounds maggots create, and also the creature had not bled much. Apparently already dead animals don't bleed a lot when you cut them. Old Isiah had watched a lot of animals butchered during his youth. I didn't like to tell Mr Taversham, but I certainly felt that someone was playing silly buggers with us.

"You know what worries me even more?" Timothy bit at his lip. "Mr Taversham came over and told me about the young lady and the man killed at the Pavilion. It struck me that those deaths were just like those first two strange incidents. The girl was killed in the stock room where all those boxes were moved and with a pair of stockings which was one of the things that had been tampered with before. And the man was stabbed and thrown back on a table, like the cat was."

"Try not to read too much into these things," Clara said gently. "It does however seem that someone is trying to make a point. What that point is remains unclear."

"If you ask me, that trade fair should be shut down!" Timothy suddenly said. "What do they want to be playing at risking peoples' lives?"

"The problem is, shutting the fair is precisely what the person behind all this wants," Clara knew that was rather a poor reason to risk all those people, but she had a hunch that none of the attacks was particularly random and the majority of the fair goers would be perfectly safe. "You said you knew nearly everyone on the work crew, was Ian Dunwright the only one who was new to you?"

"No, there was one other," Timothy was looking deeply worried now. "His name was Arthur Crudd, a young fellow just learning the business. Barely started to shave, he was that fresh faced. He's a good lad. Bit naïve, but then he is only young. Works hard and was always happy to run errands about the building."

Clara took note of these two names, though she had no reason to assume they were in anyway involved in the crimes, but new faces were always interesting in a murder case.

"Did you see anyone slip into the locked bedroom on the first floor while you were there?" Clara asked to conclude.

"There was a locked bedroom?" Timothy responded in surprise.

Clara concluded that she had learned all she probably would. As she was thanking Timothy, the visiting time bell rang and she saw everyone else rising from their chairs.

"I hope you are back on your feet soon, Mr Briggs," Clara said as she was going.

Timothy Briggs merely grimaced. Clara thought that it would be prudent of Albion Industries to compensate Mr Briggs for his mishap, considering that it was because of their presence he had been hurt. But what did she know? She hoped it did not take long for the poor workman to get well and provide for his family again. In the meantime she had a few more leads to work on, they might be further dead ends, but Clara always felt better when she had a plan of action, whether it was the correct one or not.

Chapter Seventeen

Clara returned to the Pavilion yet again. She was hoping to find Mr Taversham and ask him about his new workmen, what she found instead was everyone standing outside the building looking confused. A fraught police constable was trying to prevent them from going back inside. Clara pushed through the throng.

"Constable, what is happening here?" she demanded.

The police constable recognised Clara as one of the Pavilion Committee members.

"You best go inside, miss," he said. "There has been a fire."

Clara needed no further encouragement. She near enough raced into the building, envisioning scenes of charred 100-year-old wallpaper and ruined antique woodwork. The front hall, however, seemed quite peaceful. She stopped where she was.

"Clara!"

Glancing up she recognised Mrs Levington, one of her fellow committee members. The woman was waving at her and Clara hurried over.

"The police constable said there had been a fire!"

"Do not fret," Mrs Levington commanded. "It has caused no harm to the Pavilion due to the foresight of that gentleman."

Mrs Levington pointed out a man in a very smart (and therefore very expensive) suit.

"He has been most efficient about this whole affair," Mrs Levington continued. "Considering that he is an Oriental."

The gentleman in question was indeed of Asian descent. He was stood next to Mr Grundisburgh, about a head shorter than the robust Albion manager, and certainly a lot sleeker.

"I believe he is Chinese," Mrs Levington remarked.

Clara was already heading over to Mr Grundisburgh and the new gentleman. She had a hunch who the latter was.

"Mr Grundisburgh?"

"Miss Fitzgerald, please do not be concerned. The Pavilion is unharmed. There was a slight fire on one of the Pearl Pink displays."

Mr Grundisburgh motioned with his hand to a table upon which sat a charred mass of little tubes and an oozing, unpleasant pool of burned pink goo. Albion Industries had set up displays of their newest lipstick line all about the trade fair. You could not walk ten paces without seeing one. You certainly could not miss this ruined display. The stink of it was enough to attract your attention. To refer to it as a slight fire was rather understating things.

"What happened?" Clara asked.

"As yet we are not entirely certain," Mr Grundisburgh admitted. "We have only just put out the flames. Oh, might I introduce Mr Mokano to you? He has been most helpful in this matter."

Mr Grundisburgh held out a hand to the Asian gentleman, who responded by giving a bow to Clara.

"Pleased to meet you," he said in faultless English. There was the vaguest hint of an accent, but Mr Mokano had been in England a lot of years and it paid to not sound 'too foreign' when dealing with British businessmen.

Mr Mokano was actually Japanese, rather than Chinese. He had come to England in 1896 as a young man hoping to learn more about the Western world and their way of doing business. He had found a job, apprenticed to a London businessman who sensed he had potential. Mr Mokano had proved himself a good salesman with an eye for the market. He worked his way up in the Londoner's business until he found himself stagnating. That was when Mr Mokano decided it was time to take his future into his own hands. Persuading his employer to invest in him, he started his own business importing and selling on the newest cosmetics from Europe. It wasn't long before Mr Mokano was dabbling in creating his own lines of make-up and was setting himself up as a dangerous competitor to his English counterparts.

Now Mr Mokano owed a string of shops, a large factory, a research and development laboratory, not to mention his London head offices where his mail order business operated from. No wonder, therefore, Albion Industries felt rather uneasy when he was in their presence. Especially when there were rumours they had stolen the Pearl Pink formula from him.

Considering how he had been treated, Clara thought Mr Mokano was acting very decently over the whole affair. Unless he started the fire on the Pearl Pink display stand, of course…

"Mr Mokano," Clara held out a hand for him to shake and the businessman did not hesitate to take it, despite her being a woman. "I was very impressed with your conditioning shampoo for dark hair. I was recommended it by a friend and it worked wonders."

Mr Mokano smiled.

"Thank you, it is a very popular line. So many English ladies find their hair unruly. Black hair can be very thick compared to fair hair and requires a special formula."

Mr Grundisburgh looked sour-faced. Albion Industries did not yet produce a hair shampoo specifically formulated for dark hair.

"What happened to the display stand?" Clara returned to her former enquiry. "I would like to know if there is some hazard in the Pavilion liable to cause fires. We have electricity in some of the rooms, of course, I would hate to think we had faulty wiring."

As she spoke, she realised Mr Taversham had appeared and was carefully removing the mess of lipstick tubes from the table. When he heard her question he glanced up with his typically sombre expression.

"I would say this was the cause," he pointed to the table where he had cleared a space in the Pearl Pink mess.

It was not easy to see through the oily gloop of the lipstick, but there was a black patch in the cloth of the display and, just emerging from the pink mess, was the end of a cigar. Clara picked it up very carefully.

"Someone placed this right among the lipsticks with its lit end pressed into the tablecloth," she noted. "I suppose the cloth caught fire and the flames heated up the tubes before anyone noticed. If I recall correctly the lipsticks had their lids off to display the contents. They would have melted and the oil used in the lipstick would have helped fuel the fire."

Mr Grundisburgh grimaced as Clara postulated her theory. Mr Mokano merely stood back and observed silently.

"This was deliberate," Mr Taversham said what no one else wanted to. "Someone nestled that cigar right in the middle of the display."

"Our saboteur," Clara agreed.

Mr Grundisburgh was disheartened, but he was also an experienced businessman and there was a trade fair in progress.

"Clear the debris, Taversham," he commanded. "Throw the windows open and air the place, and let's get everyone back inside. Excuse me, Miss Fitzgerald."

Mr Grundisburgh left to organise the return of the visitors to the Pavilion. He was probably already working on a fine lie to explain away what had just occurred. A mishap, no doubt he would say, someone carelessly casting aside a match as they lit their cigarette, or something similar.

Clara found herself alone with Mr Mokano. The Japanese gentleman had the good grace to hide any pleasure he took in his rival's misfortune.

"I had not expected to see you at this trade fair," Clara said to him.

Mr Mokano looked up and smiled gently.

"Why would I not come and see what Albion Industries are introducing as their new lines? I have to know what they are doing, so I might stay ahead of them," there was a glimmer of satisfaction in his tone, as if Mr Mokano knew very well that he was leaps and bounds ahead of the competition.

"I have heard stories, that is all," Clara elaborated. "About the Pearl Pink lipstick."

"Ah, you know that Albion Industries stole the recipe from my own laboratories?" Mr Mokano said, seemingly delighted by Clara's knowledge. "Yes, that is a bad business. But my solicitor is taking good care of it."

"It is true then?" Clara said. "They really stole the Pearl Pink from you?"

"Mr Grundisburgh would say that it depends on your definition of 'stole'," Mr Mokano was highly amused by all this. "One of my laboratory researchers came up with the idea of the pearlesque sheen for a lipstick. It was a chance discovery, but it had the potential to revolutionise the way lipstick appears on a woman. We were all excited, but before the process had been fully devised, the researcher was lured away to Albion Industries, taking with them the secret. Albion claims it is perfectly fair that they now have the formula. My solicitor will remind them in court that all my employees sign an agreement that any ideas for new products they come up with during their time under my employ belong to my company.

"I expect to receive a sizeable sum in compensation

from Albion, enough to make them think twice about stealing from a rival again. Fortunately, my other researchers learned enough about the pearl formula before its creator betrayed us to recreate it themselves. We shall be launching our own series of pearl colours very soon and they will be even better than the Pearl Pink."

Mr Mokano sounded so confident in all this that Clara found it hard to imagine why Albion Industries ever thought they could get away with such a crime. Perhaps it was sheer arrogance on their part. But the thing that had really caught her attention was the one word that Mr Mokano had used so freely – betrayal.

"There have been a lot of troubles surrounding this trade fair," Clara said carefully. "It rather makes me think Albion Industries have upset more than just you, Mr Mokano."

Mr Mokano shrugged.

"These silly tricks," he motioned a hand to the ruined display of Pearl Pinks, "I don't see what purpose they serve. A businessman uses the law to his advantage if he is wise. Anything else is pointless games that could land a person in a lot more trouble."

Clara had to agree. She didn't think Mr Mokano was foolish enough to condone the sabotage of a rival's work, not when it could potentially be ruinous to his own business if he was discovered. He seemed too shrewd to dabble in such dangerous games.

"Well, my main concern is for the safety of the Pavilion," Clara said. "Naturally I want no harm to befall this building. The way things are going, I doubt the committee will ever dare allow other trade fairs to use the place."

"Let me assure you, Miss Fitzgerald, if my company was to hire your Pavilion, there would be none of these shenanigans. We would have many, many security men on duty."

Mr Mokano gave her a broad smile and Clara

suspected he was rather enjoying Albion's downfall. She also suspected that he was genuinely considering hosting his own fair in the venue to put his rivals in their place. Clara excused herself and went back to Mrs Levington.

"No harm done," she sighed to the woman.

"It has certainly been a queer business," Mrs Levington tutted. She was a middle-aged woman who dabbled in a number of philanthropic causes. She was one of those people who make a hobby out of belonging to committees. But she was also very good at what she did and had been one of the people who had pushed to allow Albion to use the Pavilion in the first place. "Clara, myself and the other committee members are very concerned about the terrible things that have occurred here."

Mrs Levington dropped her voice low. The trade fair visitors were returning and passing by them. She didn't want to be overheard.

"I am even more worried with tomorrow being the open day for the public," Mrs Levington continued.

"I understand," Clara nodded. "I intend to be here all day to keep an eye on things. It might not be a bad idea for other committee members to do the same."

Her statement was pointed. Several of the committee were well-known for making a fuss about things without being prepared to actually go and resolve matters for themselves. Clara might be trying to solve this crime, but she did not see that she had to guard the Pavilion alone.

"I shall have a word," Mrs Levington promised. "The press is invited tomorrow too. Heaven help us if something was to occur while they were here!"

Clara wished Mrs Levington hadn't said that. It suddenly made her feel deeply worried. It was all rather ominous.

The chatter of the returning visitors around her distracted Clara. The noise level had risen considerably, and to hear another person required their voice to be raised in a shout. Clara excused herself from Mrs Levington and went to get some fresh air. The stench of the melted Pearl Pinks was stuck in her nose and was making her feel slightly nauseous. She went to the front door and stood on the step in the sunlight, taking long deep breaths.

Mr Grundisburgh was smoking a cigarette on the grass outside, pacing about and looking unhappy. He glanced up when he saw Clara.

"It would happen when he was here," he snapped.

Clara smiled.

"You mean Mr Mokano?"

"I do, and don't think I have failed to notice the significance," Mr Grundisburgh went back to pacing. "Someone is attacking our new brand, I see that now. And they did it right in front of Mr Mokano. Oh, I might even think he was behind it all if I wasn't so certain he was not such a fool. To have him be the one to raise the alarm and throw a bucket of sand over the fire, well, it boils my blood. I imagine he is laughing at us all!"

"Mr Mokano seems convinced Albion stole the Pearl Pink idea from his company," Clara pointed out, thinking that perhaps the man had reason to be amused.

"No one stole anything," Mr Grundisburgh snorted. "An employee moved from his company to ours, bringing with him a very prototype idea. Pearl Pink would never have gotten off the ground without our researchers working on it in our labs. The fellow he is talking about, he would never have taken the notion any further without our help. As it was, it was about the only good thing about him. Probably a fluke he even had the idea."

"Who are we talking about?" Clara asked, curious now. Who was the person who had betrayed Mr Mokano?

"Didn't I mention that?" Mr Grundisburgh paced. "I suppose I forgot in the confusion. The fellow who had the idea for Pearl Pink was Jeremiah Cook."

Clara stared at him agog.

"The man you fired six months ago?"

"He was a hopeless case," Mr Grundisburgh shrugged. "Dead weight. You can't keep on a man like that."

"But he gave you his idea," Clara persisted. "You poached him from Mokano for it and then fired him!"

Mr Grundisburgh shrugged again.

"Business is business," he said. "Anyway, what does that matter?"

Clara thought it mattered a very great deal, but she wasn't going to say that out-loud to Mr Grundisburgh.

Chapter Eighteen

Mr Taversham was disposing of the rubbish from the minor Pearl Pink fire in a dustbin at the side of the Pavilion when Clara caught up with him again. He was looking to be in his usual morose mood, a cigarette nearly falling out of the corner of his mouth as he threw away the ruined lipsticks. Mr Taversham, Clara recalled, was a local builder that specialised in such temporary work as events like the trade fair afforded. He was the sort of man you employed if you wanted a stage rigged up for the midsummer gala, or needed a building spruced up before a wedding or party. He turned his hand to all sorts, usually for commercial venues, but occasionally for individuals too. Work was intermittent, and Mr Taversham could be quite depressive between contracts.

Clara had a vivid memory of the meeting the committee had had over who should do the work within the Pavilion. Albion Industries needed temporary display stands and other things built and had asked the committee to recommend someone. After a great deal of debate, the committee had concluded that Mr Taversham would be the name put forward. It was not a decision made without complications. Mr Taversham's last job had not been entirely to the satisfaction of everyone. He had been hired by the Town Council to construct a new procession float for them to be used in the Easter Parade. The Council had very specific requirements, and not all of these had been met. The final float was both fantastic and well turned out, but it lacked a certain sparkle and some of the council members had complained that Mr Taversham had failed them. These same council members happened to be on the Brighton Pavilion Preservation Committee and had tried to veto the motion that Mr Taversham take over the work for the trade fair.

Clara had decided to stay aloof from these proceedings. She had no reason to criticise Mr Taversham. She had thought the council float a fine piece of construction. What it lacked in imagination it certainly made up for in practicality. It rolled along beautifully. Clara rather felt that people expected an awful lot from a builder like Mr Taversham. Recent events, however, looked set to tarnish Mr Taversham's reputation further. Despite his protests of innocence, there would be those who saw the misfortunes at the pavilion as being in part his fault. He was not responsible for murder, of course, but the scaffold accident was likely to linger over him a long time.

"Mr Taversham, was there any damage caused by the fire?" Clara approached him, hoping she could catch the man in a reasonable moment, rather than when his temper was up.

"There is nothing damaged in the Pavilion," Mr Taversham grumbled. Clara suspected he was very tired of all the problems this job had caused him and the constant interferences of the committee members.

"That is good to hear. It would be awful if the Pavilion was damaged when we are trying to use this event to raise funds to preserve it," Clara kept her tone light-hearted, hoping Mr Taversham would not become defensive. "I wondered if I could ask you about some of your workmen?"

"What for?" Taversham scowled and it was obvious Clara's plan had not worked. Mr Taversham was too cynical for that.

"Necessary curiosity," Clara explained. "I am trying to discover who is behind these acts of sabotage at the Pavilion."

Clara did not mention the murders. She thought it best to leave Mr Taversham imagining those to be in the charge of the police, which of course they were. She hoped by avoiding talk of murder she would not put Mr Taversham's back up too quickly. He might become surly if he thought she was accusing one of his workmen of being a killer. He would see that as a reflection on himself.

"I do not blame you, Mr Taversham, for the mishaps that have occurred here. But the rest of the committee may prove less accommodating. As such, I hope to find the culprit swiftly and place blame where it rightly belongs and not upon your shoulders," Clara hoped she was making it plain enough that she was on Mr Taversham's side and that talking to her would be as much to his benefit as to hers. "I know you are not behind these curious happenings. Rather, I fear someone has misused you, so that they might gain access to the Pavilion and cause mischief. They have misused us all, naturally, but their deceit of you is the most cruel, for your reputation as a fine workman might suffer. I shall not let that occur Mr Taversham, if I can help it."

"It is a fine thing when a man just does his job and is left the worse off for it," Mr Taversham grumbled, feeling mollified by Clara's sympathy. "I have always endeavoured to do my best. I might not be the cheeriest of men, I might not smile and laugh like some, but I do a good job. I work hard and my work is done with care. Sometimes I think people would prefer if I smiled and joked and did a less good job. I don't seem to get any benefit from being conscientious."

"People are strange, but I, for one, appreciate your work ethic Mr Taversham. So, will you help me to help you? If we can resolve things, find the true culprit, then there should be no reason for this drama to stick to you."

Mr Taversham gave a long sigh. He clearly thought that whatever Clara tried to do to help him would not be enough. He was the sort of person who expects the worst and is rarely disappointed.

"I suppose I ought to," he complained. "I do need more work after this. A man can't live on his pride alone. What is it you want to know?"

"Tell me about your two new men," Clara said. "All the others in your team have worked for you for years, and are well-known in Brighton. But these two new men are of interest to me."

Mr Taversham scratched under his flat cap.

"You mean Ian Dunwright and Arthur Crudd? I took them on as last minute extras when I realised the scale of the job. Ian Dunwright said he had worked in the trade before, but he has proved a shoddy workman and I won't hire him again. Arthur Crudd is young and just learning. I only paid him half wages because he had to been shown what to do by someone else. I felt I was doing him a favour. He said he was orphaned during the war and was trying to make his way in the world," Mr Taversham frowned. "I like to give a fellow a start in life. I remember how it was when I was just a lad trying to find my way through this world."

"Do you suspect Ian Dunwright of lying to you about his previous experience?" Clara asked.

Mr Taversham surprised her by giving a hoarse laugh. His throat seemed unaccustomed to the sound.

"Suspect? I am certain of it! That man has never held a hammer in his life!" Mr Taversham snorted, amused despite himself. "Even Dim Dave is a better worker than him, and Dim Dave has to pull out half the nails he puts in and redo them. Ian Dunwright was a clown. I shouldn't have taken him on, but I was feeling desperate and he persuaded me. Said he was just out of the army and down on his luck. This job could mean the difference between having a meal in his belly or going hungry. I felt sorry for him."

Clara was amazed that beneath Mr Taversham's hard exterior was a sympathetic soul.

"Ian came to me one afternoon when I was working on some wooden planters for a customer. I do little jobs like that between the bigger ones to tide me over. Ian came to my cottage and he peered over my fence and asked for me by name. I asked what he wanted, because he did not look the sort to be hiring me," Mr Taversham shook his head, amused as much as annoyed with himself. "I should have known he was a right one. He sold me a good story. Just out of the army, desperate for work. 'I can hold a hammer and saw, Mr Taversham' he said in this little plaintive voice, 'I'm a reliable worker, I really am.' What tosh!"

Mr Taversham flicked off his cap and flapped it at a bumblebee that was getting perilously close to him.

"I never saw a man so useless. Spent most of his time daydreaming. I asked him to paint some planks of wood, I left him out here with the workbench all set up for him, and the paint and paintbrush at his side. When I came back an hour later that wood was as bare as when I left it. 'I was side-tracked,' Ian said, 'I saw this cloud that reminded me of a great bear and I started to ponder why clouds were clouds.' That was exactly the sort of nonsense he spouted to me! An hour sat wondering about clouds!"

Mr Taversham threw up his hands, demonstrating his exasperation for Ian Dunwright.

"Time and time again that was what happened. I started putting him to work with someone else. Old Isiah was good to pair him with because he took no nonsense, but even Isiah reached his limit and complained to me that the man was utterly hopeless. He was having to remind him to work every ten minutes. Reached a stage where Isiah refused to work with him anymore, he just didn't have the patience," Mr Taversham puffed out his lips, expelling the frustration that had built up in him over Ian Dunwright. "As awful as it sounds, I rather wish

Ian had been up that scaffold when it came crashing down. Him in the hospital would be no loss. Instead I am stuck with him, especially now I am a man short."

"Ian Dunwright is still working for you then?" Clara asked.

"When the mood suits him," Mr Taversham shrugged. "I'll be glad when this week comes to an end and I can be rid of him for good."

"What about Arthur Crudd?"

Mr Taversham brightened, or at least Clara thought he did. He was still frowning.

"Arthur is a good lad. Complete opposite of Ian. He asked me for a job when he saw my cart outside the Pavilion. That was about a week ago, when we first started to get to work here. Arthur strode up to my cart – barely tall enough to look in the back, he is – he asked me if there was any work going for an eager lad willing to work hard and learn," Mr Taversham clearly felt pleased about helping Arthur, he almost beamed with a certain pride over it. "I asked the lad who he was and that was when he told me about being orphaned. He had been living with an aunt in Hove, but had to find some work now he was out of school. I suppose he reminded me a bit of myself at that age. I took him on without hesitation, on half pay, that is."

"He has given you no cause for concern?"

"None at all!" Mr Taversham seemed offended Clara had asked. "He works like a little trooper. I can rely on Arthur to get a task done. He is so reliable that once or twice I have even left him in charge of locking up the place. Though, naturally, not after all the problems. I wouldn't want you to think I put him at any risk."

Clara was more concerned about the risks to the trade fair and the Pavilion; if Arthur Crudd was the saboteur he had been placed in a perfect position to strike.

"Could either of these men have been behind the vandalism in the Pavilion?" Clara asked carefully, expecting a quick response and getting it.

"Arthur? Never!" Mr Taversham would hear no wrong of his favourite apprentice, on the other hand Ian Dunwright was owed no favours. "I could imagine Ian causing problems by carelessness. Yes, in fact, I could imagine him being stupid enough to remove the nuts from the bolts of the scaffold. Probably because some idea came into his useless noggin about how he could use them to channel sunbeams or something. That's the sort of thing he comes up with! I caught him the other day with a glass of water and a slip of white paper, trying to create rainbows, or so he said. I wanted to despair!"

"I don't suppose you ever did discover what had happened to the scaffolding bolts?" Clara changed the subject slightly, she had wondered herself if the nuts were ever discovered.

Mr Taversham snorted.

"That's just it. I found the whole set in an old jam jar, perched on the mantelpiece in our break room," he replied. "I still can't fathom how they got there. I checked that scaffold myself the night it was put up. I made sure every bolt had a nut and that they were tight. I would swear to it. And yet the next day, after the accident, I found them all in that jam jar."

For a moment Mr Taversham looked worried.

"I was really concerned about Timothy. He could have been killed. I'll see him right while he is out of work."

"I would hope Albion Industries would do the same," Clara reassured him. "After all, it is someone out to get them who has caused this fiasco."

"That what you think?" Taversham mused. "The dead girl and man, were they part of it too? I think of them at night when I lay in my bed. Why them? I ask myself. What did they do?"

"They may have just been in the wrong place at the wrong time," Clara answered, though she was inclined to think there was a message somewhere among all this mess and that the deaths of Esther Althorpe and Mr Forthclyde had been planned. But she could be wrong.

"Now this fire," Mr Taversham looked at the debris in the dustbin. "Where will it all end?"

"It will end with someone being caught for these crimes," Clara said stoutly. "And your reputation will be untarnished."

Mr Taversham did not look inclined to believe her. He grimaced again, what little amusement he had found in their conversation had evaporated. Clara left him to his work. He had not given her any further reason to doubt either Ian Dunwright or Arthur Crudd, but she was curious nonetheless. Two strangers getting themselves involved in the Pavilion just before the trade fair rang alarm bells. Was either of them a killer? She would soon find out.

Chapter Nineteen

Clara took a break from investigating that evening and travelled over to the hospital to see Captain O'Harris. She had spent a considerable spell of time debating over what sort of gift to take him, until Annie had resolved the matter by handing her two freshly baked jam tarts. Annie considered food the finest gift and good, homecooked food the cure for all that ailed you. The jam tarts were in a neat little box, with a ribbon. Clara thanked her profusely.

It felt an age since Clara had last visited Captain O'Harris, though, in truth, it had only been a day. She headed up the stairs and came to the door of his hospital room. She was surprised to see it open, but even more surprised when she found the room empty. Clara stood gaping at the empty bed. Could O'Harris have been discharged? Clara turned around and went to find the matron.

The matron was a short woman who bristled with efficiency. She did not even have to pause to think when Clara approached her and asked if Captain O'Harris had been sent home.

"Certainly not!" she barked, as if Clara's question was an affront to her professionalism. "Mr O'Harris has been removed to a more secure room."

Clara was perplexed.

"Have the press been harassing him?" she asked, thinking that the only reason O'Harris would need somewhere more secure.

The matron gave her a pitying look, clearly thinking Clara was being incredibly dense. Then she relented and explained.

"Captain O'Harris took a bad turn this afternoon. For his own safety, and the safety of the staff, he has been moved to Ward D, where patients of questionable temperament are kept."

Clara was even more confused than before.

"Ward D? But, that was where the patients with psychiatric issues were placed during the war," Clara was flummoxed. "Are you saying Captain O'Harris has been deemed of so unstable a nature he has been placed there?"

The matron gave her that pitying look again.

"I am afraid so. It seems the captain's recent experiences have rather unhinged his mind."

Clara was so angry to hear such a blunt assessment of O'Harris that it took all her effort to bite her tongue. She had better things to do than argue with the matron. She turned on her heel and headed for Ward D.

During the war Clara had worked as a voluntary nurse in the hospital. It had been a job filled with horrors, especially when they started to take in wounded soldiers shipped over from the battlefields. She had seen things that could not be eradicated from the mind; men missing half their faces, or all their limbs. Men so poisoned by gas they could barely breathe. And then there were those whose minds had been so badly affected by the torment of battle that they had descended into madness.

Ward D was for these men. Prior to the war it had been a small emergency ward for ordinary patients deemed to be of unsound mind. But during those four bleak years the ward had been expanded and used to accommodate soldiers who screamed through fear in the night and hallucinated visions of the enemy during the day. There was limited effort made to help them, not because no one wanted to, but because no one knew how to. The nurses and doctors did their best, and occasionally a military doctor was sent in to assess the men and determine if any were malingerers. But when it came to mental conditions, most of the professionals were at a loss as to what to do.

Clara had only been into Ward D once. She had been running an errand for another nurse, and the ward had filled her with a sort of dread. The men about her were so tortured and out of their minds, it broke her heart as well as scaring her. When Tommy had been sent home suffering in a similar, if not so severe fashion, from shell-shock, the memories of that ward had flooded back and terrified her. She had been so scared Tommy might end up in such a place, and now here was Captain O'Harris, war hero and adventurer, shunted into that pit of insanity. Clara was almost in a panic when she finally found herself outside the ward doors.

Ward D was a secure ward for a number of reasons, not least that patients within could be a danger to themselves or others. Some were just prone to wandering away and could get themselves into mischief, others could suddenly be overcome by fits of violence. The double doors to the ward were, therefore, kept locked at all times. To gain entry Clara had to ring a bell and wait for someone to arrive.

A young man with spectacles appeared at the doors after a few moments. He peered through the small window in one of the doors out at Clara, then unlocked them. He opened the door just a fraction.

"Yes?"

"I have come to see Captain O'Harris," Clara, masking her anxiety and making her voice sound confident. She was all too aware that if she asked if she could see him she would be bluntly turned away. The only other option was to brazen out matters and act as if being allowed into the secure ward was perfectly normal.

"We don't let in visitors," the man said. He was dressed in uniform and Clara suspected he was one of the male nurses needed on occasion to restrain patients.

"I believe you will find my name on the official list of visitors for Captain O'Harris," Clara responded, keeping her cool. "As supplied by Inspector Park-Coombs. Now, might we move things along? I have already wasted twenty minutes of the visiting hour because no one cared to inform me that Captain O'Harris had been moved."

Clara glanced at her watch to emphasise her annoyance. She was endeavouring to channel the attitude of one of the ladies who was on the Pavilion Committee. A lady of good breeding who had never been turned away from anywhere. She did not ask to be allowed to enter a place, she commanded it. Clara had been amazed at how her stern, but non-aggressive, determination had enabled her to get her way at more than one meeting. Now Clara was hoping she could achieve the same.

"This is Ward D. We don't accept visitors without the express permission of Dr Patton," the man persisted.

"I am well aware it is Ward D," Clara said stoutly. "I worked in the hospital during the war. In fact, I have run errands on behalf of Dr Patton in my time and regularly set foot beyond these hallowed doors. Why not summon Dr Patton, if you must? Though I insist on you being speedy as visiting time is very nearly over."

The man was feeling badgered by Clara's persistence. Worse, he knew that Dr Patton had gone out to a dinner meeting with the hospital board and could not be found in a hurry. He knew his instructions, but he also knew how angry Dr Patton became when someone made a complaint against the hospital staff. The man was beginning to feel that Clara was the sort of person who would make a very forceful complaint and it might land him in even further trouble.

Clara leapt onto his indecision.

"I merely want to see if Captain O'Harris requires anything. I shall not disturb anyone and, as I say, I was a nurse here during the war. I have been on this ward in a professional capacity," that was stretching the point, her errand to Ward D all those years ago had taken less than five minutes. "If people had only been good enough to inform me sooner of what had occurred I could have arranged things through the proper channels. It is not my fault there has been a breakdown in communications."

The poor male attendant was now utterly disconcerted and uncertain of what to do or say. Dr Patton was not there to yell at him, but this woman with her stern attitude was. He decided it was easiest to concede to her.

"All right, come in. But be quick and don't disturb the other patients. It has been a bad enough morning already."

Clara hurried through the doors before he could change his mind. The ward was much as she remembered it; full of men who groaned and cried out random words. Some were tied to their beds and fought against their restraints. Others cried and shrieked, calling out for mercy or for their mothers. Some were old and their madness was a result of senility, others might have always suffered mental disturbances or seizures that robbed them of their normal senses. Among this confusion rested Captain O'Harris. Clara spotted him in a bed in the centre of the ward. She quickly went to him.

"John?"

Captain O'Harris was heavily sedated and looked at her with bleary, glazed eyes.

"Why is he sedated like this?" Clara asked the male attendant, who had hurried after her anxiously.

"Those were the instructions sent to us from his doctor. We follow those instructions until Dr Patton makes his assessment."

"And when will that be?" Clara took up O'Harris' hand, it felt cold and clammy.

"When he has a moment," the attendant shrugged. "Dr Patton is very busy."

Clara was furious. It seemed Ward D was where the

rest of the hospital deposited patients deemed too troublesome for normal wards and then gladly forgot about them. She was angry for O'Harris and for the other poor souls abandoned here, but she had to focus. She took up Captain O'Harris' medical chart and examined the details. She recognised the name of a ridiculously strong sedative that had been used on him, no wonder he seemed doped out of his mind. She read through the chart further until she found the name of the doctor who had sent him here in the first place.

"I shall see myself out," she told the attendant sharply.

Clara's foul mood had grown even worse when she had spied the name of Captain O'Harris' doctor, the man who had been tending him and had ultimately sent him to Ward D. The man was one she had clashed with before, during her time as a nurse. It looked very likely they were about to clash again. Heels clicking against the tiled floor furiously, Clara marched a familiar route along the hospital corridors, heading for the office of the man who had once been her daily nemesis. She had thought to forget about him. In a large hospital, what were the odds of her bumping into him by accident once she no longer worked there, but was merely a visitor? As it turned out, the odds were surprisingly high.

Clara found the door she had been searching for and hammered hard with her knuckles on its polished surface. The name 'Dr Holland' was displayed on a little brass plaque screwed to it. Clara waited impatiently until a voice asked her to enter.

Clara opened the door and strode in to face a man she had come to despise. Dr Holland was an arrogant, unfeeling creature who viewed patients as things and the nurses little better. Clara had argued with him so many times she had lost track of the number. He still made her stomach clench in righteous indignation the second she saw his face.

"You've grown a moustache," Clara said to the doctor, not bothering with introductions.

Dr Holland's face had fallen as he saw who entered his office.

"I thought you were Gladys with my tea," he gave a grim sigh. "Don't tell me you have applied to nurse here again, Miss Fitzgerald. Surely the patients deserve better than that?"

"I am here on a personal matter," Clara ignored the slight. "You are Captain O'Harris' doctor, yes?"

"I was, until two o'clock this afternoon," Dr Holland said languidly. "Then he became Dr Patton's problem."

"That I am aware of," Clara growled. "Might you mind telling me why you have sent O'Harris to Ward D and instructed him to be so sedated he doesn't even know where he is?"

"Are you making a complaint?" Dr Holland folded his hands before him.

"I am asking a question," Clara said bluntly. "Must I make a complaint to get an answer?"

"In the normal course of things I would want you to write out this question in a formal letter, then I might deal with it in a suitable fashion," Dr Holland had a slight smile on his face.

"You mean you would ignore it," Clara had her own smile appearing on her face. "I know the games you play Dr Holland, we have been here before. I can play games too. There are several newspapermen outside this hospital, all eager for a story. Shall I give them one about the war hero being mistreated by his doctor?"

"Do you think that will help O'Harris?" Holland grumbled, looking less amused.

"You tell me," Clara replied. "Why has Captain O'Harris been moved to Ward D? The last time I saw him he was recovering well, so I have to wonder what is going on."

They were interrupted by another knock on the door and Gladys appearing with the cup of tea. She eyed them both nervously, then vanished just as quickly as she had arrived. The pause had given Dr Holland time to think.

He was not really in the mood to lock horns with Clara, he had a stack of paperwork to deal with and he knew how obnoxiously persistent she could be.

"If you must know, Miss Fitzgerald, it was in my professional opinion that Captain O'Harris was suffering from a derangement of the mind. No doubt a result of his misfortune and the ill effects of a foreign clime," Holland shrugged, as if this was all perfectly logical. "This afternoon he became quite unsettled. He believed himself back in the ocean and started crying out for help. When a nurse tried to intervene he became violent, claiming she was a shark trying to eat him. It was necessary to sedate him and I considered it prudent to send him to Ward D for Dr Patton's attention."

"We both know Dr Patton is more interested in cosying up with the hospital board then assessing his patients," Clara folded her arms over her chest.

"That is his problem, not mine," Dr Holland waved away the issue. "I have submitted my own report with the recommendation that Captain O'Harris be discharged from this facility into the care of Mowbray Asylum."

A chill went down Clara's spine.

"O'Harris does not need to be placed in a lunatic asylum," she said, her voice tight.

"Really, Miss Fitzgerald? But, of course, you are an expert on these things. Now, I believe I have answered your question and can demand that you depart and leave me be."

Clara knew she was beaten for the moment. She took a pace towards the door, wanting to say something but not knowing what would be a suitable retort to the arrogant doctor. In the end she just let herself out of the room silently and stood in the corridor, trembling with outrage. She had to save Captain O'Harris. If they transferred him to the lunatic asylum, getting him out again would be difficult. She would not let that happen. Clara had to act fast, before Dr Patton could write one of his lackadaisical reports condemning a man to madness.

Chapter Twenty

On her way home Clara called round at Dr Cutt's house. She was greeted at his door by his housekeeper who was a dogmatic, though not unkind, sort of a woman. Dr Cutt's housekeeper was of the opinion that people took advantage of her employer just because he was always willing to help. With Dr Cutt now in his eighties, she felt it was high time he was a little more conscientious of his own health and so she guarded his front door against all possible late night visitors. Getting past her was a battle in itself.

"I must speak with Dr Cutt," Clara informed the woman. "It is most urgent and cannot wait until morning. I will take up as little of his time as possible."

"I have this same conversation with about three different people most nights," the housekeeper, appropriately named Mrs Wall, responded. "I shall tell you what I tell all the rest. If someone is dying call the ambulance. If someone has taken ill wrap them up warm and get them into bed and I'll have Dr Cutt pop over in the morning. If a baby is on its way there is the midwife. Anything else, make an appointment for the morning."

Clara was trying to keep her temper. She feared the morning might be too late if Dr Holland insisted on keeping Captain O'Harris drugged up to the eyeballs, and after her tense interview with him it was more than likely her nemesis would be pushing Dr Patton to sign O'Harris over to Mowbray Asylum just to spite her. By the time she was able to see Dr Cutt in the morning, matters could already be out of her hands.

"Mrs Wall," Clara said as calmly as she could. "The person I am concerned about is already in hospital, so I can neither call them an ambulance or get them into their own bed. And they are not having a baby, but I do fear that time is of the essence. By tomorrow it may all be too late."

Clara caught her breath. She was trembling all over, righteous fury having turned into cold dread. The sight of Captain O'Harris so incapacitated in his bed, so beyond her help, scared her to death. She had to put a hand on the doorframe, for her legs felt numb as her emotions heaved inside her.

"It is just so awful, Mrs Wall," Clara admitted, no energy for pretence left in her. "I have left a friend in hospital fearing for him. The doctor he is under has written him off as a lunatic, and nothing I can say will change that. I need Dr Cutt's help desperately, or else my friend will be declared a madman and sent to the asylum. He is not mad, Mrs Wall, he has just been through such an ordeal."

"Is he a soldier?" Mrs Wall's defensiveness had lessened. She relaxed a little. "A lot of soldiers have come back with problems."

"He was an airman in the war," Clara explained. "I won't say he came back from that unscathed, but he was coping. Sadly, a recent misfortune seems to have tipped the balance. Dr Holland thinks him dangerously unhinged..."

"Dr Holland!" Mrs Wall interrupted gruffly. "Don't tell me the poor sod is under that buffoon's care? The man is incapable of diagnosing a headache, let alone anything more complicated."

"You know Dr Holland?"

"My dear, I had the grave misfortune to be under his charge at one stage. I was suffering from a feminine complaint. I needed an operation, but Dr Holland was of the opinion my problem was all in my head. I spent weeks going in and out of the hospital, trying to persuade someone to listen, while all the time the pain grew worse and I became depressed," Mrs Wall's mouth hardened. "Dr Holland declared that I was becoming hysterical, that the pain was in my mind. I had three children, you see, and the complaint that was affecting me is not normally seen in women who have had children. Dr Holland wouldn't give me the time of day.

"I don't know what would have happened if a friend had not suggested I go to her doctor, Dr Cutt. My own doctor would not argue with Dr Holland, seeing him as superior to himself because he worked at the hospital. Fortunately, Dr Cutt is not so silly-headed. I told him my problems and explained the situation. He at once agreed I should be operated upon and rang the hospital to make the arrangements himself, bypassing Dr Holland. I had my operation and became a new woman. I was so grateful that when I learned Dr Cutt's old housekeeper was retiring I offered myself for the job and even said I would take only half the pay, as I wanted to return the favour Dr Cutt had done me. He would hear none of that, of course. Dr Cutt is a very good man."

Mrs Wall paused. She took a good look at Clara, assessing her with a keen eye.

"So now your friend has fallen foul of Dr Holland?"

"Yes, and I have done what I can but Dr Holland despises me. I was a voluntary nurse during the war and we failed to see eye-to-eye. He has never forgotten that. I went to see him this afternoon, for what little good it did," Clara sighed, she felt washed out by all the emotional drama she had just been through. She also felt she had failed Captain O'Harris.

"I admire anyone who is prepared to give that quack a

161

piece of their mind," Mrs Wall's eyes sparkled. "He has won this round, has he, dear? Never mind, we will soon take the fight back to him. You better come in and sit down. You look done in."

Mrs Wall took Clara's arm. Having decided that Clara was a fellow victim of Dr Holland, a man whose name Mrs Wall still took pleasure in cursing whenever she could, the housekeeper was now more inclined to help and had forgotten her earlier decree that Dr Cutt would not be seeing anyone after surgery hours. She deposited Clara in the front parlour and went to inform the doctor of his visitor.

Clara sat in silence on a sofa, listening to the clock in the hallway tick down time. Her stomach was in knots, she had not felt a fear such as this since she had heard Tommy had been shot. She pulled on her fingers unconsciously. She could not allow O'Harris to be sent to a lunatic asylum, she felt certain such a thing would destroy a man already become so fragile. Besides, if the doctors at Mowbray were anything like Dr Patton or Dr Holland, then he would stand no chance of recovery once committed. She couldn't bear to let that happen.

Clara was almost in despair when Dr Cutt opened the parlour door and gave her his gentle smile. Dr Cutt was a spry old man with pure white hair and the kindest face Clara had ever known. From the day they had met Clara had known the doctor could help her brother Tommy to walk again, and she had not been wrong. Dr Cutt had seen that Tommy's problems were far from physical, but had never made him feel ashamed about that. He had saved Tommy, now Clara desperately needed him to save Captain O'Harris.

"Good evening Clara, my housekeeper tells me you have a most urgent problem and since she rarely lets people through the door after six o'clock I can only assume it is something quite serious."

Dr Cutt settled himself in the chair opposite Clara.

"Why don't you tell me what is wrong?"

Clara started to explain, rushing a little and making herself breathless in the effort. She explained about Captain O'Harris' dramatic return, his adventures in the Pacific and his subsequent illness. When she came to the part about Dr Holland her voice hardened, she could not keep the dislike from her tone. She had just finished her explanation when Mrs Wall appeared with a tray of tea and sandwiches.

"You looked likely to need sustenance," Mrs Wall explained to Clara, handing over a cup of tea and a plate of sandwiches. Without asking she took a chair slightly to the side of the doctor. Clearly she wanted in on the action too.

"It seems you have a first-class pickle on your hands," Dr Cutt said lightly, taking up his own sandwich plate. "Dr Holland has his merits," Mrs Wall gave a huff in the background to this statement, "but he is not, and has never been, a very insightful man. He believes that pills cure people, and if a pill cannot cure them, well, then they have a terminal condition and he wants nothing more to do with them. Sad to say, he is not so unusual in the medical world.

"As for his views on mental health problems, the less said the better. He thinks that such difficulties as depression or phobias are caused by the sufferer's own self-indulgence. They should snap out of it, in short, and if they cannot then his only solution for them is Ward D, as you have seen. Dr Holland cannot abide patients with psychological difficulties, to the point that he prefers to hide them away rather than deal with them. I once remarked to him that he rather has a phobia about the mentally ill, which went down like a lead balloon."

Dr Cutt raised an eyebrow in wry amusement.

"Of course, that does not mean we must take this problem lightly. I just mean to reassure you that this is normal Dr Holland behaviour and not a direct attack against you."

As always Dr Cutt proved himself instinctively

insightful and had guessed one element of Clara's fears. Clara was at once relieved and a little abashed to learn her anxieties were so transparent.

"Now, as for Dr Patton," Dr Cutt mused. "He is a man dedicated to the desire for promotion. It is all he lives and works for. Ward D has suited him most admirably. For a start, it is a ward few doctors wish to become head of, thus cutting down his competition for promotion, while also gaining him the respect of other doctors who admire him for willingly taking on such challenging work. And then, of course, he has those patients who are so out of their minds much of the time, either through their illness or the sedatives delivered to them, that if they don't see their doctor from one week to the next they are unlikely to notice. And even less likely to complain or be taken seriously if they did. Dr Patton can thus ignore his patients without fear of a reprimand, which he would surely experience on any other ward. He is also quite happy to follow the recommendations of the other doctors in the hospital, rather than make his own diagnoses.

"This matter has concerned me for years and I have been lobbying the hospital board to do something about it. Unfortunately, Dr Patton has made himself very friendly with some of the members. But this should not distress you Clara, for I have other well placed friends who can help me get into the hospital to see Captain O'Harris."

Clara felt as though a weight had been lifted off her shoulders.

"You will see him and offer a diagnosis?" she said.

"I will, first thing tomorrow," Dr Cutt agreed. "From what you describe I believe the man is suffering from a delayed form of shock. I have seen a number of similar cases in returning soldiers. The hallucinations are particularly symptomatic. You say he imagined himself back in the ocean?"

"Yes, and thought the nurse a shark attacking him."

"Having met a few nurses in my time in the medical

profession I can see the analogy," Dr Cutt chuckled to himself. "But, in seriousness, this is something I have seen before and which can be worked through. There must be no more talk of asylums, however, and none of this sedative nonsense. That does no more than mask matters."

"Thank you Dr Cutt," Clara said, wanting to rush over and hug the old man, but restraining herself for the sake of decorum. "I was at my wit's end when I saw what had happened. Captain O'Harris is not mad, no more so than Tommy ever was. He has just been through such great turmoil."

"In more ways than one," Dr Cutt nodded. "The initial trauma of the crash and being lost in the ocean was bad enough, but then he ate himself alive with the guilt over his co-pilot which you mentioned. Now, the man was never dead, but the guilt was still very real. And, for over a year, Captain O'Harris was stranded among strangers. The fact that he fell into a deep depression and stopped talking to those around him tells me a great deal about his mental state during that time. I am not surprised he has suffered this episode, a wiser doctor than Holland might even have expected it."

Dr Cutt made everything sound so rational and Clara was reassured. She apologised for disturbing his evening and thanked Mrs Wall for the tea and sandwiches, which had indeed restored her. They rose together and walked back to the front door.

"Clara, one last thing," Dr Cutt paused her on the doorstep. "I must be honest with you. This problem Captain O'Harris has will not go away overnight. It could take months, years even. He must be prepared for relapses, and you must be also."

"I understand," Clara said. "But I am resolved to helping him."

"I never doubted that for a second," Dr Cutt smiled. "Now, go home and do not worry. I have this matter in hand."

Clara thanked them both again and waved goodbye from the pavement. It was growing very late and Annie would wonder where she had got to, but Clara did not regret making her impromptu stop. It had been necessary for O'Harris' sake. Now she set off for home, a new peace in her heart.

Chapter Twenty-one

Clara slept easier that night. When morning came she headed for the Pavilion to see what drama would unfold that day. It was the public opening and she had a suspicion that if the saboteur wanted to disrupt Albion Industries' event properly, they would pick today to do their worst. Clara had to admit her main concern was the old building this was all happening within. She didn't want any nasty damage befalling the fabric of the Pavilion. She was starting to regret agreeing to the fair being held there at all.

Mrs Levington was waiting at the gates of the Pavilion grounds, which had been locked overnight, to be let in. Clara joined her with a smile. It was a warm summer's day, the birds were singing in the trees and there was a happy atmosphere in the air, as if a promise had been made that all would be well. Mrs Levington nudged Clara.

"Look what I have," she opened her bag and produced a tube of Pearl Pink. "It really is a ghastly garish shade, but I couldn't resist. I am going to delight in wearing it to Committee meetings."

Clara was amused. Mrs Levington was an older woman who had never worn lipstick in her life. She had certainly decided to start with a bang.

"Grab yourself a sample," Mrs Levington persisted. "From the rumours I was hearing yesterday, it might be your last chance."

"What can you mean?" Clara asked.

"That Japanese fellow, the one in the very smart suit. He is suing Albion Industries, claiming they stole the Pearl Pink from his company. If he succeeds in his case, which from the gossip I was hearing yesterday seems very likely, then Albion will be forced to take the product off sale and pay him compensation. They will not be allowed to sell Pearl Pink lipstick."

That was a worrying predicament for Albion, Clara mused. They had put such energy into this product and its launch, to have it banned from sale could cause serious harm. Not to mention the bad press it would give the company.

She was distracted from this thought by the arrival of Gilbert McMillan.

"Good morning, Miss Fitzgerald. I finally get to see inside this legendary trade fair," he grinned. The press had been largely kept from the Pavilion (except for a chosen few) until the public opening. "I have been following the dramas concerning some of the Albion ladies with quite an interest."

"I hope you will allow this matter to be resolved before you print gossip," Clara said sternly, thinking of poor Abigail and the damage an erroneous newspaper article could do to her career.

"I am a newspaperman who believes in facts, Miss Fitzgerald, as strange as that might sound," Gilbert placed a hand on his chest in a 'hand on heart' gesture of honesty. "I was sorry to hear about Miss Sommers. It seems I may have been a little harsh in my judgement of her before. I have been doing a little digging and discovered she has made substantial donations to various charities over the years, and has assisted more than one girl in starting her career with Albion. I have heard several glowing reports."

"That is very good," Clara said, relieved that at last someone had a good word to say about Abigail.

"Now that Esther Althorpe who was murdered is quite another kettle of fish."

Clara pricked up her ears.

"How so?"

"Such secrets these ladies have," Gilbert tutted. "Why I heard from a reliable source that Miss Althorpe was embroiled in a scandal involving Mokano cosmetics. I hear Mr Mokano is here himself, so I fancy I shall pick his brains and see what is what."

"A scandal?" Clara said. "Precisely what did she do?"

"On that my source could not help. Perhaps it was something dubious enough to warrant her murder?" Gilbert raised his eyebrows in a speculative expression. "Well, all shall be revealed soon."

He stepped back as Mr Morris arrived to open the gates for everyone. There was now a crowd of people waiting to get in, including Mr Grundisburgh and the Albion ladies. The Pavilion had been locked up all night and everyone was eager to get inside and prepare for the day ahead. Mr Morris gave Clara a gentle smile as he removed the padlock. He would be glad when all this was over and the Pavilion returned to its usual quiet repose.

The group marched to the main Pavilion doors, where once again Mr Morris did the honours. Clara glanced about for Niamh Owen. She was usually the first here. She had her own copy of the key for gates and door. Mr Morris was a standby. But Niamh was nowhere in sight. Clara thought that odd.

Mr Morris took several moments to unlock the doors, he complained that the key seemed to be sticking. It finally turned and he swung back the doors with a grunt of satisfaction. This rapidly turned into a gasp of horror as the interior of the Pavilion came into view. His gasps were soon accompanied by the groans and cries from the other men and women gathered at the entrance. Someone had been very busy in the Pavilion overnight.

Clara stepped through the doors and looked about her. Mr Morris and Mrs Levington were quickly at her side. Banners had been draped from one side of the hall to the other and upon each was the same word – betrayal – written over and over again. The Albion trade stalls had been dismantled, or perhaps ransacked would be the more appropriate word. Someone had taken pleasure in smashing the displays of goods, turning over the tables and writing all over the advertising boards in Pearl Pink the same familiar message. Pearl Pink lipsticks were also scattered across the tiled floor. The culprit must have found every box of them and tipped them out into a heap. The Pearl Pinks had rolled to all corners of the room, but looked largely undamaged. Clara picked one up from beside her shoe and opened it. The bright pink lipstick seemed unharmed.

Mr Grundisburgh stomped into the hall, almost tripping over lipstick tubes.

"What is all this?" he declared, staring around him in anger.

Mr Morris was twitching, a deep desire to grab up his broom and start tidying the place almost overcoming him.

"I think we should check over the entire building," Clara said firmly. "So far nothing irreplaceable appears to have been damaged. Our saboteur at least has a conscience."

"Have you not seen the trade stand for the Baby Blonde Hair Dye?" Mr Grundisburgh spluttered. "Someone has drawn a moustache on the model in the advertisement!"

There was indeed a Pearl Pink moustache drawn on the pretty blonde girl advertising the 'easiest to use hair dye ever invented.'

"I said nothing irreplaceable," Clara reminded Mr Grundisburgh. "I was referring to the Pavilion."

"Naturally," Mr Grundisburgh grumbled. "That is all

you care about!"

"As it should be," Mrs Levington interrupted firmly. "The Pavilion is our concern, as the trade fair is yours. Just remember Mr Grundisburgh that if this building is damaged in any way because of the fair Albion Industries will be liable. Come on Clara, let's inspect the rest."

The scene of disorder continued through the building. While the independent trade stands had gone untouched by the hand of the saboteur, every one of the Albion stands had been demolished in some fashion. Products had been scattered and smashed, tables thrown about and the advertisements either ripped or defaced. The word betrayal was written everywhere and Clara was beginning to find the repetition tiresome. She rather hoped the saboteur could become a little more specific in his written admonishments. Perhaps he might write next time on what he felt betrayed over?

Thankfully the Pavilion was unscathed. Clearly the saboteur's attentions had been entirely focused on Albion and nothing else. Mr Morris was looking deeply unhappy as he prowled about with Mrs Levington and Clara.

"No damage," Mrs Levington sighed as they came to the end of their patrol. "Disturbing nonetheless that this could happen. Did you lock up last night Mr Morris?"

Mr Morris looked appalled by the suggestion.

"No Mrs Levington, it was that Albion woman who was given a key."

"Niamh Owen," Clara stated. "Who is strangely absent."

"Would she do such a thing?" Mrs Levington asked.

Clara had to admit she could not say for sure, though it was very true that Niamh had been present for all the crimes and had a motive for killing poor Esther Althorpe if nothing else.

"Personally, if I was behind this display, I would make sure I was about the next morning to unlock the doors and look shocked with everyone else," Mrs Levington mused. "To prove my innocence."

"Very true," Clara agreed. "And Niamh is smart enough to realise it looks more suspicious by her not being here than if she was."

Clara glanced at her watch. It was close to half past nine and the fair was supposed to be opening to the public at ten.

"I think we ought to find Niamh Owen and discover just what went on when she locked up last night."

Clara went in search of Mr Grundisburgh. He was still picking up Pearl Pink tubes and shouting at the Albion girls with him to do something about the ruined displays. Precisely what they were supposed to do was a question he left unanswered. Gilbert McMillan was hovering in the background, gleefully taking down notes on the scene of devastation.

"Mr Grundisburgh?"

The Albion manager glanced up at Clara and glowered.

"I am rather busy right now."

"I can see," Clara assured him. "I was wondering which hotel Miss Owen was residing in last night. She does not appear to be here."

For the first time Mr Grundisburgh noticed that Niamh was missing. He stood up from collecting lipstick tubes and glanced around him.

"That is very odd. Miss Owen is many things, but she would not neglect her duty, unless..." his eyes fell on the debris all about him and it was obvious he was coming to a similar conclusion to that which Clara had considered mere moments before.

"We ought to locate her," Clara hinted. "Just in case something has happened."

"Well, if she is still in Brighton she will be in room ten at the Crown Hotel," Mr Grundisburgh stated. "I shall show you there myself. Miss Owen has some explaining to do. For a start she can tell me why she has absented herself this morning."

Mr Grundisburgh handed his collected lipsticks to a

nearby Albion girl and headed out of the Pavilion with Clara in tow.

"Would there be any reason for Niamh to do something like this?" Clara asked as she matched Mr Grundisburgh's fast stride. He was operating on fury and his pace had quickened as a result.

"Miss Owen has had her ups and downs with the company. I recently had to reprimand her for being rude to some of her colleagues, but I can't see how she might feel betrayed," Mr Grundisburgh marched on. "But I see your thinking, Miss Fitzgerald. Miss Owen has had every opportunity to cause mischief here."

"And, in the process, two of her rivals have been effectively eliminated," Clara pointed out. "Esther Althorpe is dead and Abigail Sommers in a police cell, her reputation in tatters. Quite the success for Niamh, if that was her intention."

Mr Grundisburgh could not keep up his furious pace. His weight was catching up with him and he had become out-of-breath. He slowed as they came to a hill.

"When did you last see Niamh?" Clara asked.

It was several moments before Mr Grundisburgh had enough puff to respond.

"Last night as she locked up. We were the last two to leave the Pavilion. Miss Owen had had a difficult day and was feeling a little unwell. When she was locking up she became a little faint and I had to put an arm around her to stop her from falling. I accompanied her back to the hotel to see that she was all right," Mr Grundisburgh caught his breath. "Perhaps, after all, she has just been taken ill?"

"Possibly," Clara agreed. "Coincidences do happen."

They were finally at the Crown Hotel. Mr Grundisburgh explained their purpose at the front desk and asked if Miss Owen had checked out of her room. The woman on the reception went through the hotel registers.

"She has not checked out," she assured them. "Nor did she come down for breakfast this morning, though it has been paid for in advance."

"May we go up to her room?" Mr Grundisburgh asked. "We are very concerned that she has not turned up for work today."

The receptionist agreed that they could, but with the caveat that she join them. She took up the spare key for room ten and showed them both upstairs. Clara had that strange butterfly feeling in her stomach she sometimes got when she was sure something was wrong. If Niamh had not sabotaged the Pavilion, then why fail to show up the next morning? And if she had been behind the sabotage, why remain in the hotel where it was easy to find her?

They came to room ten and the receptionist knocked politely on the door and called out Niamh's name. There was no response.

"Should I open the door?" she asked Mr Grundisburgh.

"Indeed," he answered gruffly, despairing at her hesitation.

The receptionist unlocked the door and pushed it open. She was the first to look into the room and came to a dead stop on the threshold. Clara's stomach heaved over as she saw the colour draining from the receptionist's face. She quickly joined her in the doorway.

Niamh Owen was lying on her bed, still dressed in her Albion uniform. She was even still wearing her shoes. But the way her eyes were staring fixedly at the ceiling and the way she sprawled with her arms outwards gave away that all was not well. Clara stepped into the room and noticed the knocked over side lamp and the spilled contents of Niamh's handbag now lying on the floor. She reached over and felt for Niamh's pulse in her neck. There was none. Fallen by the side of the bed was a fluffy white pillow, there were slight marks on the fabric as if someone had dragged their nails across it. A picture began to form in Clara's mind. She sighed as she looked at the unfortunate woman lying on the bed.

"Mr Grundisburgh," she said sadly. "I think we ought

to summon the police."

Upon hearing that statement the reality of what had occurred reached the receptionist and she gave a sharp cry, before falling in a dead faint on the floor.

"Oh, for heaven's sake," Clara puttered.

Chapter Twenty-two

Inspector Park-Coombs stared at the dead Niamh Owen lying on the bed, very neatly dressed in her clothes from the day before.

"Well, at least your friend Abigail is excluded from this crime," he remarked solemnly.

Clara felt bad that for a moment this thought cheered her. She had to remember that Abigail's innocence came at the cost of another's life.

Dr Deàth wandered into the room with his leather medical bag in one hand.

"I haven't been inside the Crown in years," he remarked thoughtfully. "We used to have the mortuary staff's Christmas party here, until our budget was cut for such events. Now we hold it in the pub. There is a rather grand ballroom downstairs if I remember rightly."

"I don't think our young lady here will be doing much dancing," Park-Coombs said morbidly. "Looks likely by the same killer as before."

Dr Deàth tsked as he came about the bed and saw Niamh lying prone.

"Another Albion girl? Yes, that would seem rather a coincidence. Though I tend to keep an open mind," Dr Deàth had to rest one knee on the bed to lean over and examine Niamh. "Blood vessels have burst in the eyes, that suggests suffocation. The nails are rather damaged, looks as though she was clawing at something or someone. I rather think she would not allow such ragged edges to her nails normally."

Dr Deàth picked up Niamh's left hand and showed how the nails had been snagged and ripped.

"I do believe there is blood under this one," he peered closer, then plucked his penknife from his pocket and worked it under the nail. "Yes, looks like dried blood. Your killer will probably have scratches on them. She fought hard for her life."

Clara found this insight somehow more depressing. She could imagine the tough, fierce Niamh giving her all when faced by the possibility of death, but it had not been enough. The killer had overcome her.

"Is that a pillow I see on the floor?" Dr Deàth pointed to their feet. "She is quite blue about the mouth, I would suggest something such as that pillow was held over her face. She was not strangled, no marks about the neck. Hmm, what do you say Inspector, attacked while she slept?"

"She is still fully dressed," Park-Coombs countered.

"Perhaps she was taking a nap before dinner," Clara suggested. "It would seem odd otherwise that she was lying on the bed for her killer."

"The door was locked, but the key is missing," Park-Coombs nodded. "Suggesting the killer took it. Perhaps Miss Owen neglected to lock her door when she came in, fell asleep and was attacked?"

"All possible," Clara agreed.

"How long has she been dead, roughly?" Park-Coombs asked Dr Deàth.

The coroner was still propped on the bed examining the dead girl carefully.

"It will only be an estimate," Dr Deàth answered. "But she died several hours ago. Your surmise about her dying before dinner might not be so far off."

"What does all this mean?" Park-Coombs scratched his chin. "I have three corpses with no obvious connection between them, and someone sabotaging the trade fair. Mr Grundisburgh was keen to tell me about that as soon as I arrived."

"It would be interesting to see if Niamh's key for the Pavilion is missing," Clara added. "Perhaps our killer was after that and Niamh was unfortunate enough to wake up and see them?"

They searched the room as Clara had suggested. The key did not appear. It seemed there might be weight in Clara's theory that Niamh had been killed for it. Had the saboteur been so desperate to get into the Pavilion that they had been prepared to murder someone for a key? Well, the two other deaths might suggest just that. Perhaps Esther Althorpe and Mr Forthclyde had just happened to be in the wrong place at the wrong time too? Though it did not account for the very specific means by which they were murdered.

"I think I have seen enough here," Inspector Park-Coombs announced. "I suggest we go back to the station and inform Miss Sommers that she is off the hook for the murders, and with her accuser dead it is unlikely we will take the matter of her assault on Miss Owen any further."

Clara didn't think there had been an assault, but she remained silent. There was still the matter of the doctored accounts sheets to contemplate.

Mr Grundisburgh watched them leave, unable to resist extracting a promise that the inspector would come to the Pavilion as soon as it was possible. He seemed rather untouched by the death of Niamh Owen, he was more concerned by the destruction at the trade fair. Assuring himself that he was no longer needed, he headed to the Pavilion as fast as he could.

"There goes a man for whom business is all that matters," Park-Coombs huffed as they watched Mr Grundisburgh trundle off. "He doesn't seem much affected by these deaths."

"As you said Inspector, for Mr Grundisburgh life is about business and nothing else much troubles him. I rather think the same could have been said for Niamh Owen before this terrible turn of events."

They walked to the station slowly.

"So, this saboteur kills Miss Owen, steals her key and then spends all night wrecking the Albion displays because they feel betrayed?" the inspector clarified. "And no one can suggest who has been betrayed?"

"I rather imagine there are too many candidates," Clara joked without humour. "And the saboteur is being very vague with his or her messages. I suppose they do not wish to identify themselves, just disrupt the trade fair."

"It is all tied up with those damn lipsticks though," Park-Coombs scratched at his moustache. "What is all this fuss about a new shade anyway? Why does it matter?"

"In the wider scheme of things it does not," Clara agreed. "But in the narrow world of fashion it could mean everything. This new lipstick glistens in a way never seen before. The pearl effect, or so Albion Industries is advertising it as. It could be called revolutionary. It is certainly very new and very exciting for certain people. Revolutionary and exciting products can mean big sales and a high revenue return. Albion Industries is a business in a challenging market, they have a lot of rivals. To make money and to keep ahead they have to produce innovative cosmetics that no one has seen before."

"And do you believe the rumours that they stole the idea?" Park-Coombs asked.

"I don't need to believe them. I just need to know that Mr Mokano does. He wouldn't be here for any other reason and he wouldn't be suing Albion if he did not think he had a case. This business could be very costly for the company and this saboteur is not making things easier."

"Is Mr Mokano the sort to try a little sabotage to satisfy his ego?" the inspector proposed.

Clara shook her head.

"Mr Mokano strikes me as a sensible businessman, who is not about to indulge in such silly games. I think we can rule him out."

"So who does that leave?"

"I don't know," Clara admitted.

They had arrived at the police station and now headed down to the holding cells in the basement. It was a dreary place with more than a touch of damp lingering in the air. Abigail was all alone, sitting on the wooden bench along the wall that also served as a bed. She glanced up when they came down, but did not move. She looked scared.

"Abigail, I have good and bad news," Clara came to the bars of the cell and looked at her, as Inspector Park-Coombs took down a key and started to unlock the cell door. "The good is that we now believe you unlikely to be a murderer, not that I ever doubted your innocence. The bad news is that Niamh is dead."

"Niamh?" Abigail blinked rapidly. "When?"

"Probably last night. Look, if you are up to it, I will take you back to the trade fair and explain everything. You could speak to Mr Grundisburgh too, he will need some help to restore order there."

Abigail rose from the bench. Her fear had evaporated, she straightened her jacket and set her jaw in a determined line. She was back to being the confident businesswoman ready for anything.

"I shall head there at once. Why does order need to be restored?"

"I'll explain that too," Clara shrugged.

Abigail stepped out of the police station and smiled up at the warm sun on her face.

"Oh Clara! This does feel good! I thought I was condemned."

"You could have had a little more faith in me," Clara pointed out with amusement.

"Sorry, I know I should have, but I am not much used to relying on others," Abigail smiled and took a deep breath of air. "But now you must explain what has happened to Niamh?"

They started to walk down the hill.

"Niamh appears to have been murdered last night in her hotel room, though the motive is not entirely clear. It might be because the saboteur needed to get into the Pavilion and Niamh had a key."

"Killed for a key?" Abigail grimaced. "And just think, if she had not made that fuss and had me arrested, I would have been the one holding the key."

Abigail trembled as the thought came over her.

"The trouble is, we are no nearer knowing who is behind all this," Clara continued as they followed the pavement. "What can you tell me about Jeremiah Cook? He is someone who struck me as a possibility."

Abigail laughed.

"Oh dear, laughing sounds so callous under the circumstances," she gasped a little at her faux-pas. "Jeremiah Cook worked in the research laboratories of Albion Industries. He was the man behind Pearl Pink. We had a meeting at the head office about the new lipstick and Cook gave a talk about the science behind the pearl effect. In truth I only understood a little. The reason I laughed was that mentioning his name reminded me that Niamh had convinced herself that Cook was besotted with her and when she realised she was mistaken it was utterly hilarious. I'm sorry, but Niamh rubbed a lot of girls up the wrong way and it was amusing to see her ego get a little dented."

"What about Jeremiah Cook as a saboteur?" Clara suggested.

"I find that funny to imagine too. Let me paint a picture of him for you. He was tall and reasonably good looking, if a little prone to hunching up and not meeting your eye when he talked. He was rather quiet and forever drifting off when you were having a conversation with him. You would see his eyes glaze over as you spoke, he would suddenly be looking out of a window and studying the leaves on the trees rather than listening. He was really rather rude, though I suspected he couldn't help it," Abigail smiled to herself. "When he first arrived at Albion there was talk that he would become very important. He was some sort of genius, or so it was said, and could be worth a fortune to the company. I think that was why Niamh set her cap at him. She saw an opportunity she could not afford to miss.

"Niamh was as mercenary in her love life as she was with her friendships. You were only Niamh's friend if you could be useful to her, and not a rival. I suppose that was why we never saw eye-to-eye. Anyway, she thought Jeremiah Cook might be her ticket to promotion or at least to a lot of influence and money within Albion. But Cook would not give her the time of day, and it was just as well in the end because Albion only kept him on for as long as it took to develop the Pearl Pink and then they sacked him. Actually, it was pretty callous."

Abigail shrugged her shoulders as they walked along.

"But Jeremiah Cook could never be a saboteur," she laughed again. "That would mean becoming organised!"

Clara thought that anything was possible when revenge was fuelling your passions. Had Albion Industries made a dangerous and unpredictable enemy when they used and then abandoned Cook?

"I hear Cook and his idea for Pearl Pink were poached from Mr Mokano?" Clara said.

Abigail had the decency to pull a face that implied she had heard the same thing and thought it reproachable.

"Albion Industries is very worried about the success the Mokano Cosmetics firm is currently having. They heard a rumour that a researcher in the Mokano lab had come up with a revolutionary idea and they decided they would steal both the man and the lipstick. I don't know the full details, but the gossip among the girls was that Esther Althorpe was recruited by Mr Grundisburgh to be the bait," Abigail grimaced. "Esther was always very willing for Mr Grundisburgh, some people thought she behaved a little inappropriately around him."

"And she was to, what, lure Jeremiah Cook to Albion?"

"Pretty much," Abigail nodded. "She would flirt with him and snare him, then convince him to walk away from Mokano. It was all rather underhand and I think Esther felt guilty about it as Cook became rather besotted with her. It all ended rather badly and then months later Cook was sacked from Albion and Esther felt even worse."

Clara could imagine how that had upset Esther. She must have felt used too.

"Mr Grundisburgh was behind it all. Actually, if Esther was not already dead I could imagine her feeling very betrayed by him."

"I think a lot of people feel betrayed by Mr Grundisburgh," Clara asserted.

They were nearing the Pavilion. The trade fair was now open and people were wandering in and out.

"I have been desperate to get back to this place," Abigail said, abruptly pausing just outside the gates, "and yet now I am here I feel rather scared. There is a murderer among us, Clara."

"And I am working to find them," Clara reassured her. "The more help you can give me the more chance I shall have of succeeding in catching them before any further harm can be caused."

Abigail nodded.

"Well, I have a job to do and I need to prove to Mr Grundisburgh why I am the best representative in my region. Wish me luck Clara."

Clara squeezed her arm with her hand.

"Good luck, everything will be all right. I am on the case."

Abigail gave her a brave smile, then marched into the Pavilion. Clara just hoped she could keep her promise. She didn't want anything happening to her friend.

Chapter Twenty-three

Clara hoped the presence of the general public at the Pavilion would cow any would-be saboteur, (or worse, murderer) into forestalling any further dangerous activities. She was clinging to that notion as it made her feel better. She was on the hunt for Mr Taversham and his two new workmen. Recent events meant the work crew had had to return and begin repairs. Mr Grundisburgh refused to have a trade fair without Albion Industries' products being present. He had already sent out emergency telegrams and made several telephone calls demanding a new delivery of stock. Fortunately, much had been salvaged, the saboteur had simply not had enough time to destroy the vast number of goods Albion had brought with them. But they did need all new advertisements and certain product lines had been almost completely ruined.

Clara was coming around the corner of the Pavilion, following the sound of sawing and hammering that suggested Mr Taversham's work force were operating somewhere nearby, when she stumbled into Gilbert McMillan.

"Ah, Miss Fitzgerald, I have heard the ghastly news!"

Clara supposed it would not have taken long for

information such as the murder of Niamh Owen to be transmitted. The return of Abigail Sommers to the Pavilion would have caused curiosity alone.

"Poor woman," Gilbert said rather perfunctorily. It was quite obvious he had seen the potential for a good story and this was overriding any real sympathy he had for Niamh. "Any suspects?"

"I think it is safe to say that the one suspect most people would have favoured is safely out of the picture," Clara replied cautiously.

"Miss Sommers? Yes, difficult to murder someone from a police cell."

"Mr McMillan, I have found that Albion Industries has more potential enemies than Napoleon, but that is proving unhelpful. Narrowing the list is the key and I think that means looking more closely at those who have been targeted. After all, how did killing Niamh Owen really harm Albion Industries? In the scheme of things, the fact she was one of their employees is merely a side-note."

"You think this is more personal?" Gilbert extrapolated, a twinkle of excitement in his eye. "That would certainly make sense for the murders, except, what links the three victims? The only thing I can see is that they were all connected to Albion Industries."

"Or, perhaps, we could say they were all connected to someone who works for Albion?" Clara spelled out her suspicions for him. "I can make a case that the sabotage is a direct attack on Albion. But the murders puzzle me. How was killing Mr Forthclyde an attack on Albion? Even striking out at the Albion girls seems odd. If you wanted to hurt Albion Industries you would aim to go for someone important, such as Mr Grundisburgh…"

Clara stopped, because an awful idea had just occurred to her. Gilbert watched as she paused mid-sentence, her mouth dropped open as realisation dawned.

"Mr Grundisburgh," she repeated. "Oh, but what if this all was about getting someone important? What if the murderer saw this as an opportunity to strike at Mr Grundisburgh while diverting attention from themselves?"

Gilbert tilted his head to one side, attentive.

"Perhaps you can explain that Miss Fitzgerald?" he asked.

"Anyone can commit a murder, Mr McMillan, any fool can kill someone. It is the getting away with it that's the hard part. When someone is murdered the first thing the police look at is the person's known associates. The clever murderer goes to great lengths to disguise the fact that they despised the dead person, or that they could have been around at the time of the murder to commit the crime," Clara was into her stride now. "Supposing our murderer knew that in the usual scheme of things they would be suspected if anything was to happen to their victim? Supposing the only opportunity they might have to kill them would put them under instant suspicion? And supposing they concocted an idea of how they might kill that person in a manner and place that would lead to very little suspicion falling on them?"

"You mean, if they could lure their victim somewhere and make it look like he was killed for a very different reason to the one that was actually the motive?" Gilbert said. "Then, are you suggesting the deaths of Miss Althorpe, Mr Forthclyde and Miss Owen were mere coincidence?"

"As I have delved more into this case it has become plain to me that Mr Grundisburgh has the potential to be connected to every aspect. The betrayal messages, for instance, I can name several people who could have felt betrayed by Mr Grundisburgh, if we exclude Mr Mokano from our suspicions. He was betrayed by Albion Industries, but he is dealing with that in a very business-like fashion and I don't think he is foolish enough to play these silly games at the Pavilion and risk his position.

"So, our saboteur feels 'betrayed' and that betrayal could easily be felt to have occurred at Mr

Grundisburgh's hands. Then we have Miss Althorpe, who is intrinsically connected to Mr Grundisburgh. He used her in the whole Pearl Pink affair. Then there is Abigail Sommers, selected by Mr Grundisburgh to head this trade fair and hated by her fellow Albion girls because she was deemed to be his favourite. Our killer placed some very damning evidence in her hotel room and placed her in a very difficult position."

"Why not just kill her?" Gilbert pointed out.

"What, and lose such a useful scapegoat? Abigail was set up to take the fall for all these crimes, until Niamh was killed," Clara paused, here was the flaw in her carefully constructed theory. Had the killer not attacked Niamh then all these crimes would have landed at Abigail's feet. But the killer had attacked Niamh.

"What about Mr Forthclyde? What would his connection to Mr Grundisburgh be?"

"I don't know, but I feel as if I almost have the key to this all. The crimes occur with the full knowledge that eventually someone from Albion's head office will be sent down to find out what is going on. That someone will most likely be Mr Grundisburgh. There is a pattern here, I am sure of it!"

"Then, you think Mr Grundisburgh is in very real danger?" Gilbert suggested.

Clara hesitated. Was that what she was thinking? Perhaps, but so far no attempt had been made on his life, perhaps she was really grasping at straws.

"There is more to this than meets the eye," Clara persisted. "Maybe, Mr McMillan, you could investigate the matter and see if there is a connection between Mr Forthclyde and Mr Grundisburgh beyond that they worked together. And the same for Niamh Owen."

Gilbert nodded.

"Strange business, cosmetics," he mused, then he tipped his hat to Clara and headed off to begin investigating.

Clara carried on around the Pavilion and finally found

herself in Mr Taversham's temporary work yard. There was the building foreman, surrounded by his work crew, busily reconstructing or repairing the so recently damaged boards and stands for the fair. He looked particularly miserable today. He probably had Mr Grundisburgh breathing down his neck to get the work done as fast as possible, which of course was never fast enough. Mr Taversham scowled at Clara.

"None of the plasterwork was damaged by the banners, I checked meself," he snapped gruffly.

"I was actually hoping to speak to your two newest employees," Clara answered with forced politeness.

"You and me both!" Mr Taversham snarled. "Neither showed up today, though in the case of Dunwright that is hardly a loss, but the lad Crudd would have been a useful extra pair of hands."

"That is a shame," Clara agreed, thinking that the missing workmen suggested she was on the right track. "Where did they lodge, Mr Taversham?"

"Are you going to chase them up, now?" Mr Taversham mocked her.

"If it suits me to do so, what does it matter to you?" Clara replied. "May I remind you Mr Taversham that as one of the committee members I have an opinion about who gets future work contracts at the Pavilion and your recent behaviour and attitude towards me is hardly endearing."

Mr Taversham became abruptly silent. He had crossed a line and now realised it. He also realised the potential harm he was causing himself.

"Apologies, Miss Fitzgerald," he said at last. "It has been a trying week."

"And, until the culprit behind this mischief is located, I suspect it will continue to be trying," Clara assured him. "Which is why I am doing all in my power to find the scoundrel and stop them. Now, might you give me the lodging addresses of your two absent employees?"

Mr Taversham pulled a piece of paper out of his

pocket, it was folded and dirty. He spread it out and read off two addresses. Clara took note.

"When were they sent notice to come to work today?" Clara asked.

"This morning… wait!" Mr Taversham was staring over her shoulder in astonishment. "There is Dunwright right now! Well, I never, the silly fool turned up after all."

Clara turned around and saw a man in faded overalls wandering along the path beside the Pavilion. He seemed half lost in his thoughts as he came along, staring at the grass or the sky and not hurrying himself. He might have been out for an afternoon stroll.

"Oi! Dunwright!" Mr Taversham yelled furiously. "Get over here!"

Ian Dunwright looked up and gave an inane smile. He seemed undisturbed by Taversham's gruff tone and did not speed up his pace as he walked across the grass.

"Sorry to be so late," he apologised genially to his employer. "My landlady went out shopping and didn't give me the message I was wanted until she returned home a little while ago. I bet you thought I wasn't coming."

Taversham muttered something under his breath about wishing he hadn't come. Clara could just hear it.

"Look, now you are here, go make us all a cup of tea. And while you are at it, talk to Miss Fitzgerald will you? She's one of the Committee members."

Thus Taversham dismissed the two people who annoyed him the most that morning. Ian Dunwright did not bother to ask why he should talk to Clara, he just gave her a smile and amiably showed her the way through a back door into the workmen's break room. He turned on the stove and started to boil a kettle.

"Don't mind Mr Taversham," Dunwright said as he made tea. "He has a good heart really. After all, he gave me this job."

"You don't strike me as a workman, Mr Dunwright," Clara said, taking a seat on an old wooden crate that had once contained display materials for the trade fair.

"I like working with my hands," Dunwright answered.

Clara took a good look at him as he made the tea and hummed to himself. His overalls were faded, but extremely clean. No stains or tears that you would expect on work clothes. Aside from their paleness, they looked quite new. Clara started to wonder if they had been deliberately faded to give the appearance of use. Perhaps washed over and over to strip out the colour, without taking into account that work clothes did not just fade but suffered the marks of industry as well. Ian Dunwright did not strike Clara as someone who regularly worked in the building industry, but he did strike her as someone trying to pretend he was someone else.

"I think I will be glad when this fair is over," Clara said lightly. "It has been far too much complication, and all this sabotage has made me quite nervous. The Pavilion is my responsibility and preserving it for future generations is my primary concern. I would hate to see it damaged because of this event."

"I don't think the saboteur means any harm to the Pavilion," Dunwright said, offering her a cup of tea.

Clara took it. The mug she had been offered was badly cracked, but still held tea without leaking. She found Dunwright's statement curious.

"How can we know what this saboteur intends?" she said.

"I think he has been very careful not to harm the Pavilion so far. That is a good thing," Dunwright still had that placid smile on his face, rather like he knew some secret that gave him confidence. "I like old buildings. They feel like they have souls."

"This building certainly has one," Clara nodded. "That is why I worry about it so much. For instance, to my horror I learned that someone had secretly entered the most important room in the Pavilion, the prince's bedroom, and spent time there smoking and apparently carving a piece of woodwork."

Dunwright's face suddenly lost its smile and a frown crossed his brow. He looked upset too.

"That is awful. Smoke does so much damage to soft furnishings and wallpaper," an angry look flickered over his face. "Why would someone do that?"

"People do not think," Clara told him, surprised at his sudden appearance of outrage. "Do you not smoke, Mr Dunwright?"

"Never!" Dunwright looked offended. "I read a paper once about how a man's veins become clogged with soot if he smokes heavily. Why would I want that?"

"A paper?" Clara asked curiously. "As in an academic paper?"

Dunwright blinked, then seemed to fluster a fraction.

"I like reading," he said, trying to assuage her interest. "I read anything I can find. I ought to take Mr Taversham his tea out now."

He picked up a large wooden tray and set mugs on it, along with a sugar bowl, before heading purposefully outside. Clara followed him back out into the warm sunshine.

"I didn't mean to imply that it was odd for a workman to read," she said to Dunwright, trying to renew their conversation. "It is good to hear, that is all."

Ian Dunwright paused in the middle of the path. He stared at the assorted mugs filled with brown tea which he had haphazardly spilled as he walked.

"I know people think I am strange," he said softly. "I suppose I am a little peculiar. My mind tends to drift off and I have lost a lot of jobs because I become distracted thinking about this and that. But I know the difference between right and wrong, which a lot of folk can't say. For instance, one of the lads hammered the pin for a banner right into some ornamental plasterwork in the Pavilion. I told him that was wrong, though he didn't much care."

"I saw that," Clara said. "I complained to Mr Taversham."

"Not everyone understands right and wrong," Dunwright continued. "It's wrong to kill people, for instance."

Dunwright adjusted the tray in his hands.

"I don't do things that are wrong."

Ian Dunwright ambled off and Clara suspected that in his own unique fashion he had made it plain to her that he was not the killer in the Pavilion. That didn't let him off the hook for the other crimes, of course.

Chapter Twenty-four

Clara knew it was urgent she seek out Arthur Crudd and discover why he had not shown up for work that day. It could be that he had a perfectly innocent reason for not responding to Mr Taversham's message, on the other hand, he might just be the suspect she was looking for. The trouble was, Clara felt torn, because she also had a duty to Captain O'Harris and she wanted to go to the hospital and discover what had happened since her conversation with Dr Cutt. In many situations Clara put her duty as a detective first and her personal affairs second, but on this occasion she simply could not. O'Harris needed her and, unlike the murders at the Pavilion which had the Brighton police force also taking an interest, the brave captain only had her and now Dr Cutt. She knew where her real duty lay.

Clara arrived at the hospital on edge. She wasn't sure what to expect, but feared trouble. Dr Holland was not a generous or kindly person and he would know that Dr Cutt had arrived because she had summoned him. Dr Holland would be angry and would make life as difficult as possible for her. There were still a couple of newspapermen waiting outside the hospital, tasked by their editor to get an interview with Captain O'Harris.

Their comrades had fled the scene, getting whiff of a more exciting, or at least more accessible, story over at the Pavilion. Clara slipped past the remaining two without any difficulty. They seemed more inclined to smoke and enjoy the summer sunshine then to worry about who was going in and out of the hospital.

At the front desk Clara asked if Dr Cutt had been in. The receptionist admitted she did not know, having only just come on duty. It was close to visiting time, so Clara thanked the woman and headed in the direction of the wards, veering off at the last moment to head towards Ward D. If the receptionist noticed, she did not say anything.

Clara felt her stomach knot as she approached Ward D's locked doors. There was something so imposing and depressing about those doors, even though they looked no different to any others in the hospital. Perhaps it was just the thought of who was behind them that made her anxious? Clara rang the bell for assistance. A male attendant, not the one she had encountered before, opened the door a fraction to observe her. Clara guessed, with the nature of the patients in the ward, it was best to have male staff always on hand. There would be patients prone to fits who would need restraining, and those of a violent or simply difficult demeanour. Patients might need to be lifted or carried. Certainly, if they kept them drugged like Captain O'Harris all the time, they would be incapable of moving themselves. She supposed the main criteria for working on Ward D was to be of a strong physique.

"I have come to see Captain O'Harris," Clara said, trying to master some of the force she had had in her voice the night before. However, her anxiety was stripping it from her, making her sound noticeably more hesitant.

"We don't accept visitors," the attendant told her bluntly.

"I am not a visitor," Clara said, regaining some of her firmness. "I am a member of the committee and I am here to inspect the conditions in which Captain O'Harris is residing."

Clara did not illuminate the attendant as to precisely which committee she was on, she doubted the Pavilion Preservation Committee had much clout in the hospital.

"I have been informed of a complaint concerning Captain O'Harris' treatment and have come to inspect the situation for myself. With all the furore about the captain's miraculous return, the hospital does not need anyone spreading lies about the quality of care, do we?" Clara was beginning to sound more and more like her old mathematics teacher, she wasn't sure she liked it, but she had to admit the woman had been excellent at controlling even the most unruly of students, so perhaps there was something in it.

The male attendant hovering at the door was looking unsure. He clearly didn't like the sound of 'complaints' and 'lies'. Perhaps he was thinking of his own position. Ward D was a place where the forgotten were usually sent and no one paid much attention to what was going on there. Supposing the attendant felt his own behaviour had not been as exemplary as it could have been towards his charges? Clara decided to pursue that idea.

"I am sure nothing untoward has occurred here, but people come up with all sorts of strange notions, especially about locked wards," Clara explained. "People think the patients are treated badly, left sedated rather than actually helped. I have even heard Ward D referred to as the first step towards Mowbray Asylum. Such talk is always a worry. Rumours can quickly become established as 'facts' among the uneducated. Need I elaborate on the trouble that could cause us all? Why, it would be ghastly! People could lose their jobs for no real reason. Better to nip this all in the bud, don't you think?"

The attendant was looking pale now. Perhaps he had a guilty conscience, or perhaps he didn't like the idea of losing his job. Unemployment was not a pleasant prospect with England's economy in a slump. Who could afford to lose their job? Especially a well-paid one such as working on Ward D?

"People don't understand how hard it is in here," the attendant said as he opened the door wider for Clara. "The people here aren't like normal patients. Look at this, for a start."

The attendant rolled up the sleeve of his shirt and revealed a bite mark.

"The old fellow in the far bed did that this morning. All I was trying to do was check his temperature. The people in here are more animal than human," the attendant tutted to himself. "You'll soon get to understand it. Any of those folk complaining should try working in here for a day or two!"

Clara was no longer listening to him because she had spotted Dr Cutt sitting beside Captain O'Harris' bed. She was flooded with relief to see the two were talking and Captain O'Harris no longer looked drugged up to his eyeballs. Clara hurried over, abandoning the attendant.

"Clara," O'Harris smiled as she approached.

Dr Cutt looked up and gave Clara an amused smile.

"How did you wrangle your way in here?" he laughed.

"I pretended to be on official business," Clara hissed. "Don't break my cover!"

She winked at them both. O'Harris started to chuckle too.

"Now, I think we have talked enough," Dr Cutt nodded to his newest patient. "And you should rest. Clara, as much as you would like to be here, I think your presence may cause more harm than good."

Dr Cutt stood and took her arm.

"I have been assured that Captain O'Harris will be returning to a normal ward later today, where I shall be attending him daily to supervise his recuperation."

"Thank you doctor," O'Harris' eyes still looked foggy from the sedative. "It was good to talk to someone who understands."

"I shall see you soon," Dr Cutt told him, then he led

Clara out of the ward.

Once in the hallway outside he wagged his finger at her.

"Do you wish to raise Dr Patton's goitre?"

"I only wanted to see what was going on," Clara shrugged. "I don't trust them in there."

"But you trust me," Dr Cutt reminded her. "Now, will you please behave yourself. I would like to explain all this to you, so shall we go see if they serve edible sandwiches and tea in the hospital canteen?"

Clara followed the elderly but spry man along the corridor and through several turns until they reached the canteen. It smelt as Clara so vividly remembered it; of boiled cabbage and cleaning fluid. Dr Cutt paused before a glass case within which sat some rather bleak looking sandwiches.

"Might this one be cucumber?" he asked the girl behind the counter, who was waiting for him to order so she could retrieve the said sandwich for him.

"Yes sir," she said.

"And might that one be cheese?"

"Yes sir. And that one is corned beef, and that one is meat paste. We don't do any others."

Dr Cutt agreed to the cucumber sandwich, which looked the most likely to agree with his digestion, while Clara contented herself with cheese. The sandwiches were retrieved and a pot of tea fetched. Clara and Dr Cutt found themselves a spare pair of seats at a table and picked at their respective meagre lunches.

"Hospital food has not changed since my days as a medical student," Dr Cutt reflected with a half-smile. "It is still cheap and made by someone who has not the first notion of the way to present a sandwich to make it look appetising. Here, you see, I have the evidence of a ham-fisted chef; finger impressions in my sandwich where they have pressed down far too hard when cutting the bread in half. Sadly, someone with more finesse cut the cucumber, it appears with a fine razor as the slices are barely discernible against the butter."

Dr Cutt opened his sandwich to show wafer-thin cuts of cucumber, sliced so thin they had a translucent appearance. Clara preferred not to inspect her cheese sandwich too hard.

"What was your opinion of Captain O'Harris?" she asked instead.

"A sensible man of remarkable resilience," Dr Cutt responded at once. "I found him a pleasure to talk to. Just as importantly, he was acutely aware that he had a problem. So many of my patients are trapped in a spiral of denial that restricts my ability to help them. Captain O'Harris, on the other hand, accepts that his mental condition has not been of the best lately and has gladly agreed to my help."

Clara relaxed. She physically felt her shoulders drop down as the tension in them was relieved and her stomach eased.

"You were concerned he would not be so forthcoming?" Dr Cutt guessed.

"Captain O'Harris is a war hero and a proud man. I thought he might struggle," Clara admitted.

"I can't deny that a lot of men do, but I think Captain O'Harris has been so trapped in turmoil that he was only too relieved to find someone who might understand him. He spoke very honestly with me about his experiences over the last year. I am not surprised in the slightest that he is having some trouble adjusting back to ordinary life," Dr Cutt sipped his tea. "I find it baffling that so many within the medical profession are oblivious to the impact dramatic events can have on both the body and mind. It is not as though we do not have enough evidence for this after the last few years. There has to be a change, Clara. I must find others willing to help me make that change."

Dr Cutt's smile became sad.

"I am an old man thinking of starting a new crusade. Is it all too late?"

"Never," Clara insisted to him. "Whether you enact a

change yourself or inspire someone else to, this will be all worthwhile."

She had given up on her sandwich, her nerves were back as she asked;

"Can O'Harris be helped?"

Dr Cutt lost his moroseness as he reached out for her hand.

"Of course, my dear, everyone can be helped. Captain O'Harris is suffering from a condition I have seen several times among men and women who have experienced traumatic events. I have treated a number of former soldiers who have the exact same symptoms and they are now leading normal lives. I can't say I am an expert on the subject, as I doubt there are any experts as yet, but I know enough to be able to help," Dr Cutt squeezed her hand. "The brain is a surprisingly fragile object. I mean, most of us understand that we have a thick skull to protect our soft brains, and that beneath the bone is a very unique and easily damaged object. But, aside from the physical, so few appreciate how truly vulnerable our brain matter is.

"Look at those people in Ward D Clara. Each and every one of them has a damaged mind. For some that damage is caused by physical harm. Seizures that rattle the brain in the skull. Cancer that grows tumours on the brain. Even old age which, in some people, seems to cause irreversible damage to the grey matter. Thankfully, I do not have that condition!"

Dr Cutt chuckled to himself.

"Then there is other damage, which we barely acknowledge, let alone understand. This damage is internal and not caused by a blow to the head or a disease. Rather it is caused by emotional events that occur to us without leaving any physical scar," Dr Cutt threw up his hands. "How little we know! Science fails to explain how an organic mass of pink tissue that looks rather disgusting, I might add, can enable us to speak, imagine, dream. How this blob inside our skulls can enable some people to paint masterpieces, while others struggle to draw the simplest of things. If we don't understand how it even works, then how can we hope to understand why it breaks down at times? All we can do is devise ways to ease the symptoms.

"Captain O'Harris' brain has suffered a series of shocks that has left it traumatised. I think that is the best way I can describe it without there being more serious study of these things. Like a frightened animal his mind tried to hide away, so we have this period of time when Captain O'Harris refused to speak. His brain had shut itself completely down. But the world around him forced Captain O'Harris' mind to cease hiding. He has been forced to cope with the situation at hand, but because his mind is not in a fit state to do so, so sometimes it has these moments when it becomes overworked. We are only just beginning to understand the psychology of the mind, but it is safe to say that dramatic events can leave the brain so shaken that it needs time to heal. And if not given that time, then it develops these little blips. I like to think of it as a badly fixed broken bone, which causes the sufferer occasional periods of pain."

Clara had listened to this with a slight frisson of horror.

"What if Captain O'Harris cannot be healed?" she asked.

Dr Cutt shook his head.

"You haven't been listening. Brains can heal just like bones. Scars may be left behind, but they will be minor compared to the original damage. Captain O'Harris will recover."

Clara gave a sigh.

"I should not doubt you," she said.

Dr Cutt shrugged.

"Why should you be different to everyone else?" he said, amused. "People doubt, they can't help it."

"Well, from now on I shall put my trust in you," Clara said, utterly resolved. "And I shall not interfere."

"Oh Clara," Dr Cutt chortled. "Both you and I know that is a promise you will find impossible to keep!"

Chapter Twenty-five

Clara headed for Arthur Crudd's lodging address. It was in one of the less congenial areas of town. The families that resided in these streets were just clinging on to their veneer of respectability, but it wouldn't take much to tip the balance. People eyed her suspiciously as she wandered down the road. She looked far too well dressed for this part of Brighton.

Crudd's lodging house was in the middle of a row of terraces. It belonged to a widow who rented out two bedrooms to provide her with a little income. She lived on the ground floor and from the look of the worn paint on the window frames and door, the income her lodgers were providing was not entirely sufficient. Clara knocked on the door, noting the empty space where a door knocker had once hung. Perhaps in better times the lady of the house had been proud to display an iron or even brass knocker on the door, but it had long been sold for scrap to pay the bills.

The woman who answered the summons was wearing a long apron, and had a duster in one hand while the other held a chipped porcelain ornament that displayed the legend 'A Souvenir of Blackpool'. She was a tall woman, with little meat on her bones. Her hair was fiercely swept up and hidden beneath a large handkerchief, presumably with the intention of keeping it clean and out of her way while she worked. A cigarette lolled at the side of her mouth and she squinted at Clara with unpleasant narrow eyes.

"What do you want?" she demanded. It was immediately apparent to this woman that Clara was no prospective lodger, at least not in a dive like this. "If you are collecting for some charity you can sling your hook!"

"Actually, I am looking for Arthur Crudd," Clara said politely.

"You and me both," the woman scowled. "He went out late last night and never came back. I don't hold with that sort of thing. Only reason people go out and don't come back of an evening is because they have got themselves into trouble and I don't like trouble in my house."

Clara imagined that the landlady caused trouble enough for her lodgers without them trying to add to it.

"Hasn't paid me for today's lodging, either. If he intends to stay another night I expect to be paid by eight sharp in the morning. It's my rule. Else how am I supposed to support this place and buy food? If my lodgers pay me extra I even cook them a supper, now they can't say better than that. But I haven't had a penny from Crudd," the woman paused and glowered out her door at the world around her. "Gone and done a runner, that's what it is. I should have known when I first clapped eyes on him that he was trouble. Too many 'pleases' and 'thank yous' for my liking. Always fawning and being polite, didn't seem right for a lad like him."

"When did you last see Crudd?" Clara asked.

The landlady's forehead actually managed to furrow into a deeper frown.

"Would have been just after supper. I always make it for seven o'clock. That's another of my rules. I keep to a strict routine. Mr Brown, my long-term lodger, understands and appreciates this," the woman's tone softened as she spoke about her clearly most cherished lodger. "Crudd had paid for supper and ate it, though I didn't care for the look he gave my food. I made fried kidneys on toast. That is Mr Brown's favourite, but young Crudd gave it such a sneer when he thought I weren't looking! I asked myself, what does he expect? The lad acted as if he were used to much finer eating. Made me suspicious."

"Did Crudd say where he was going?" Clara asked, thinking that she might have difficulty consuming fried kidneys on toast too.

"No, he didn't. Why are you asking?" now the landlady looked at Clara curiously, clearly wondering what this smartly attired woman's interest could be in a working class lad.

"I should explain," Clara gave her an apologetic smile. "I am a member of the Brighton Pavilion Preservation Committee and Mr Crudd has been doing some work for us. He was asked to come to the Pavilion today as urgent work was required, but he failed to show. This has caused us some inconvenience and I was asked to seek out Mr Crudd and discover why he did not appear."

"Well he never got your message," the landlady said, looking almost satisfied by this statement. She was probably enjoying Crudd getting into trouble after he had looked down on her cooking. "I still have the note he was sent sitting on the mantelpiece."

"I am concerned about what might have befallen him," Clara said, genuinely worried. "He is a young lad alone in this world. He was taken on by the Pavilion workforce as it was felt he would benefit from the guidance and practical education. We feel responsible for him. I hope he has not found himself in serious trouble."

"Well, I don't know about that," the landlady shrugged. "I take no responsibility for anyone but myself. If you are that worried, you can go up to his room and look through his things. I glanced in this morning and saw that everything is still there, so if he has legged it he has left all his stuff behind. Better for me that way, I'll pawn the lot."

Clara hesitated, searching through someone's private things felt a little bit intrusive.

"Go ahead," the landlady noted her trepidation. "I'm only going to clear the stuff out of there myself shortly. I'll be letting out the room again as soon as I can and it will need a good clean. I was just getting my other chores done before I set to work up there. Don't go getting all precious about it, now."

The woman seemed amused by Clara's reluctance, she clearly saw nothing wrong about invading another person's privacy. Clara decided that with Arthur Crudd apparently vanished, there was a fitting reason to examine his belongings. Perhaps it would provide a clue to where he had gone and, if he was in trouble, it would be best for him if it was discovered where he might be. Clara overcame her reservations, especially when she saw the landlady smirking at her with deep amusement.

"I will take a look, seeing as he is missing."

The landlady almost laughed, clearly enjoying Clara's discomfort.

"Go on up, first door to the right of the landing," she instructed. "Mr Brown has the room straight ahead. Don't go wandering in there."

Clara thanked her, though she was not entirely sure what she was thanking her for, and headed up the stairs. There were two doors at the top, as the landlady had described. She ignored the one immediately ahead of her and turned right to the door just along the landing. She found it was unlocked and opening it she came into a small room with a bed, a dresser, a wooden chair and a small wash stand as its sole furnishings.

The room had been kept very neat by Arthur Crudd. The wash stand included a jug full of clean water, apparently unused. Presumably it had been placed there after he had left. The dresser was empty and the drawers smelt rather musty. Crudd had made no effort to settle himself in this room, almost as if he had always known he would be leaving again swiftly. Well, with the limited work he had available to him with Mr Taversham, that was a logical assumption, but Clara rather felt there was something more to this seeming desire to leave the place untouched.

The bed had not been slept in. It was of a flimsy brass construction with a very lumpy mattress. Clara bent down to look underneath and spotted a suitcase. She pulled the case out and the first thing that struck her was how nice a thing it was. The case was of tooled leather and relatively new. How strange, Clara mused, not the sort of thing you would expect a poverty struck lad like Crudd to be carrying. She flipped its clasps upwards and lifted the lid. Inside there was a shirt and a pair of trousers. Clara lifted them out and then she paused in surprise, for beneath the male attire was a pair of frilly and very feminine knickers, and just beneath them was a pair of stockings. When Clara looked at the stockings closer she realised they were an Albion pair just like the ones used to strangle Esther Althorpe.

Clara sat back on her heels. What was this? She emptied the case and found another pair of knickers and a fancy hairbrush, not the sort of thing a man would use. It was rather expensive as it was made from tortoiseshell. Clara rose and took another look around the room. Now she thought about it, there was a distinct lack of male accoutrements about the place. Where, for instance, was the razor that any man who did not want to grow a beard would require? Crudd was young, but not so young that he would not need to shave at least occasionally. Was it feasible he had taken his shaving kit while leaving his suitcase behind?

Clara started to put everything back into the case. Knickers and stockings were too outlandish in a man's suitcase to be ignored. Could it be, Clara wondered, that Arthur Crudd liked to wear women's clothes? Or, and this idea intrigued her even more, could it be that Arthur Crudd was actually a woman? It was not unheard of.

Women sometimes dressed as men to pursue careers only open to male candidates, though in general these were better professions than that of a jobbing builder. But if Arthur Crudd was an alias, then who was he or she really? And why were they in Brighton? Could it be all this charade was to enable them to commit murder?

Clara was almost trembling with excitement as she replaced the contents of the suitcase. She sensed that here was the key to all this drama, here was the clue she had so desperately needed. She was just picking up a cloth bag to place in the case, when it slipped through her excited fingers and expelled its contents. Clara was amazed to see what looked like long brown fingers protruding from the bag. They were, in fact, cigars. Expensive ones. Not the sort of thing young Crudd could afford. Clara picked them up and sniffed them. She was thinking of the cigar butt that had set the Pearl Pink stall alight and the heavy fog of smoke left behind by the probable killer in the prince's bedroom. Cigars were not everyone's cup of tea, find the person who smoked these and you would be inches away from solving this complicated affair.

Clara packed the suitcase, clicked down the clasps and walked back downstairs. The landlady was loitering in the hallway, clearly intending to waylay Clara on her way out.

"What are you doing with that?" she demanded as she saw Clara had the suitcase.

"These are Crudd's belongings," Clara answered simply. "I am taking them so I might restore them to him when he is found."

"Oh no you don't!" the landlady barked. "I need those to pawn! Crudd has left me in the lurch, those are mine fair and square."

Clara really did not have the energy to explain the realities of the law to this woman. She gave a sigh. The suitcase was coming with her.

"You have no claim over Crudd's belongings, but if it makes you feel better I shall pay his room rent for today, therefore you are not out of pocket."

The landlady started to open her mouth to protest, but Clara had produced her purse and the promise of money had silenced the irate words the woman had intended to yell. She fell quiet instead, clearly torn between demanding the suitcase and the thought of instant money. She was doing speedy calculations in her head as to the potential value of Crudd's belongings and whether their pawn value was greater than her usual room rental rates.

"How much do you charge for a day's rent?" Clara asked, her purse open in her hand.

The landlady seemed to gag a little, clearly indecisive as to what to demand. Her eyes jumped from the suitcase to Clara's purse and back again. Tired of the debate Clara took some coins from her purse.

"Here are five shillings," she said, handing the money to the landlady. "I should think that amply covers your rent rates, especially considering the low wages poor Crudd was earning. If you do happen to hear from him, you might inform him that his suitcase is in safe hands and he should go to the police station and enquire about it."

The landlady's eyes flashed greedily, she looked about ready to demand more money, but her fear that demanding too much would lose her what she already had stilled her tongue. Clara moved past her.

"There's enough here for supper too," the landlady seemed to have had an unusual pang of conscience. "I should make you something before you go. A cup of tea at least?"

"That won't be necessary," Clara assured her. "Thank you for your assistance."

She hurried out the door before Crudd's landlady started to think twice about letting his suitcase out of her sight. There was no knowing how quickly her fickle mind would start to turn over the potential contents of the case and just how much they might be worth. Clara wanted to be out of the way before that happened. She headed along the road as fast as she dared without actually running. People watched her go by, but Clara did not acknowledge them. She was heading in one direction alone, straight to Brighton's police station to show her find to Inspector Park-Coombs. Arthur Crudd, whichever way you looked at it, had some serious explaining to do about his luggage. Whether that made him a murderer was another matter. Clara clutched the suitcase a little tighter. She was on the right track, she was sure of it.

Chapter Twenty-six

"Can I see Inspector Park-Coombs?" Clara asked the desk sergeant at the police station.

They were not on the best terms and he was often deliberately awkward when she made a request. Today was no different.

"Not in, is he," the desk sergeant told her with great satisfaction.

"And where might he be, then?" Clara asked with the first hint of a sigh of annoyance.

"Not sure I should tell you that," the desk sergeant gave an exaggerated impression of lawful integrity.

They might have reached an impasse had not Police Constable Wood just then come rushing into the station.

"Am I too late? Has the Inspector already gone to the Pavilion?" the constable asked in a panic.

The desk sergeant glowered at him. Clara gave him a cheerful smile.

"Constable," she said, turning around, "I am now heading to the Pavilion, might you accompany me?"

Police Constable Wood, abashed by the desk sergeant's glare, was only too glad to help Clara and escape the station. They both emerged back into the summer sunshine and turned towards the Pavilion.

"What has occurred Constable?" Clara asked as they walked briskly. "There has been no great harm to the building I hope?"

"No miss," Constable Wood promised. "I was out on an errand when everything happened. I only knew something was going on because Constable Tuppin spotted me and said the Inspector had called out several names of constables who were to go with him to the Pavilion to make an arrest, and I was one of the names. I've been doing duty up there on the door. I was worried I would be in trouble when I learned I had been asked for when I was not there."

"You cannot be in two places at once," Clara reminded him. "I should know, I have tried. But you say the Inspector is about to make an arrest?"

"Yes miss."

"An arrest of who?"

"I don't know, miss."

Clara was wondering if the inspector had come to the same conclusions as her about Arthur Crudd, perhaps he had even been sighted at the Pavilion and the alarm raised?

They reached the Pavilion, it was now late afternoon but the trade fair was to be open for a couple of hours as yet. People were still milling in and out of the door. Clara excused herself as she pushed past a man and woman blocking the entrance with Constable Wood trailing her. Inside the main hall, she glanced around for someone who might know what was going on and sighted Abigail. She waved to her. Abigail came over looking excited.

"The Inspector knows who is behind all this awfulness," she declared in a whisper to Clara. "He is arresting the fellow as we speak."

"Who is he arresting?" Clara asked urgently.

"Why, Jeremiah Cook, of course!" Abigail announced. "He was caught red-handed trying to destroy one of the large trade stands. It is the one displaying hand cream. You must have seen it because it is so tall. Mr Cook had snuck behind it and was removing some of the nails holding the stand together. Had not a lady's small dog disappeared under the same stand then no one would have known. As it was, when one of the Albion girls moved the skirt of the stand to retrieve the dog, she spotted Cook's feet! She gave a cry and Mr Grundisburgh came over. He recognised Cook at once and it was obvious what he was up to because he had a hammer in one hand and a pocket full of nails that he had just removed. The stand would have collapsed when someone bumped into it and caused such a commotion!"

Abigail was elated by the discovery. She clearly now assumed the trade fair could carry on without any problems. Clara, forever cynical, was still in two minds about whether that was the case or not.

"Where is the Inspector?" she asked.

"Mr Grundisburgh escorted Cook into the workmen's break room and then sent the constable on the door to fetch the Inspector. He only arrived a moment ago."

Clara headed for the break room, wondering what she would encounter beyond its door. She knocked, deciding that now was not the time to barge in, and the inspector's familiar voice summoned her inside. Clara and Constable Wood entered the small room. It was already quite packed with Inspector Park-Coombs, Mr Grundisburgh and Mr Taversham surrounding Jeremiah Cook. Clara looked into the face of Ian Dunwright and nodded to herself.

"You never did strike me as a workman," she said.

Jeremiah Cook, alias Ian Dunwright, looked up and smiled wanly at Clara.

"I didn't damage the Pavilion," he assured her.

"Now, Mr Cook, I can continue what I was saying," Inspector Park-Coombs said gruffly, slightly annoyed at the interruption. "I am arresting you for criminal vandalism and for the murders of Miss Althorpe, Mr Forthclyde and Miss Owen."

"I haven't killed anyone!" Jeremiah Cook squeaked,

looking appalled by the suggestion. "I just hung banners and defaced Albion property. I don't know anything about these deaths, I swear."

"Really Mr Cook!" Mr Grundisburgh spluttered in amazement. "How can you deny it? You and only you have been in this building on a nightly basis causing so much harm. Quite clearly you turned your hand to murder when it suited you."

Mr Grundisburgh was so outraged that he had taken on a disturbing red colour and looked half ready to boil over or have a heart attack, whichever came first. Clara decided it was a good time to interrupt again.

"Supposing Mr Cook did not kill those people?" she said.

"Clara," Park-Coombs puffed out his cheeks in exasperation, "the man has been about this building causing havoc. I daresay he didn't plan the murders, they were probably spur of the moment things. Don't forget, Mr Forthclyde was lying on top of one of Cook's betrayal messages on the dining table!"

"I never killed him!" Cook said miserably. "And I never wrote a message on any of the furniture. That might damage it and that would be wrong."

"And Mr Cook has a very strong sense of right and wrong," Clara spoke, her voice softer. "Do you not, Mr Cook?"

"I haven't ever damaged the Pavilion," Cook bleated, helplessly looking to Clara for assistance. "I know someone else has been sneaking about the place. I have sensed them, but never seen them."

"So now we have an invisible killer on our hands?" Inspector Park-Coombs scoffed. "Come on Cook, no more lies!"

"I don't think he is lying Inspector," Clara said firmly. "Mr Cook is a very principled man, despite what we have seen him do here these last few days. And I imagine Mr Cook viewed his acts of sabotage as the right thing to do to raise awareness of not only his betrayal by Albion, but also his treachery towards Mr Mokano."

Cook suddenly began to sob.

"That was wrong," he cried. "So awfully wrong. Miss Althorpe convinced me it was not, saying I was being misused and I believed her. I thought, when I left the company, I was only taking my ideas. I had barely begun work on the Pearl Pink, it was just a notion I had one day when I was playing about with some colours. I didn't think it counted, but now I realise it did and that I should never have taken the idea away from Mr Mokano. I am so, so sorry and I would tell him so. I helped Albion steal the Pearl Pink from him."

"Shut up!" Mr Grundisburgh was almost hopping in anger. "All this nonsense, nothing was stolen, nothing! Mr Cook came to us of his own volition and his ideas were dreamt up in our own laboratories."

"You lured him away with deceit, Mr Grundisburgh," Clara said carefully. "You played on his emotions and used him wickedly. I have no doubt Mr Cook was an unwitting partner in the Pearl Pink affair, but you knew exactly what you were doing. You must have had a spy in their labs who spotted what Cook was about. You realised that if you let him do anymore work on the idea then Mr Mokano could make a case for it being created for his company. So you stole Cook away as quickly as you could."

"That sounds so underhand. It was nothing of the sort. I offered Mr Cook a job, he is a very clever researcher."

"Then why did you fire him so soon after the completion of the Pearl Pink project? It seems rather sinister, under the circumstances?"

"Mr Cook had warnings! He was dithering in his work, idling about! Wasting our time and money!"

"I can confirm that is what he is like," Mr Taversham huffed from the sidelines. "But I would also state that I never pegged Cook for a murderer."

Inspector Park-Coombs grumbled under his breath.

"So, you want me to believe that Cook would damage

property but not kill people because the latter was wrong? Where is the logic in that?"

"Mr Cook can explain," Clara said stoutly. "Mr Cook, how did you come to decide that sabotaging Albion's trade fair would not be wrong?"

Jeremiah Cook shuffled in the chair he had been sat in by the inspector when he was taken to the room. He thought for a moment, then looked up at Clara.

"I felt that Albion Industries had used me and made me betray Mr Mokano. I felt awful for that because Mr Mokano was always good to me and employed me straight out of university. I studied chemistry, you know, only I didn't get the best results because I tended to get distracted. That has always been my problem…"

"Stick to the point, Cook," Park-Coombs grumbled.

Cook sniffled through his tears.

"I knew no one was interested in what became of me, not even Miss Althorpe. I just wanted someone to know what had happened. I knew about the trade fair and I thought there would be no better place to get my message across. I told myself I would only use the Pearl Pinks in my acts of sabotage. That was my creation, and therefore my property, so to speak, and you can't vandalise your own property, can you? I made the banners and I used Pearl Pink to write on the floor. I thought people would listen, maybe someone would write about the sabotage in the paper, but nothing happened. So, I persuaded myself that as Albion was such a wicked company, hurting the rest of their products would not be wrong. I know that was stretching a point, but I was getting desperate. But I never touched products belonging to other companies, nor did I damage the Pavilion, or kill anyone!"

"Maybe you 'stretched the point' to persuade yourself murder was right too?" Inspector Park-Coombs suggested.

"No!" Cook cried out. "Why would I?"

"Let's start with Miss Althorpe, she betrayed you, perhaps it seemed appropriate to kill her? Or you just acted in the heat of the moment?"

"No!" Cook looked desperately to Clara. "I couldn't kill Esther, she was the love of my life. She broke my heart, but I never ever harmed her!"

"I believe Mr Cook," Clara announced, earning herself a scowl from the inspector. "It does not fit with his temperament to murder people. In any case, I think if he had it would have left him emotionally disordered. Mr Cook is not a person who can kill and live with the guilt. Besides, he had no motive for either Mr Forthclyde or Miss Owen."

"He needed the key off Miss Owen to get in here to cause havoc!" Mr Grundisburgh countered angrily. "You said yourself Clara that her key was missing and the person who murdered her probably took it."

"I didn't need a key to get in!" Cook said quickly. "I hid inside when the doors were locked. That is how I have always hidden in here. Mr Taversham will confirm it, because I was always the first man to be inside when work began."

Cook looked desperately to his employer. For a moment Taversham did not want to assist him, the fool had caused him a lot of trouble, but he could not quite abandon him. With a sigh, he said.

"That's true enough. I always thought it strange that I never saw Cook with the other men waiting outside, but he was always the first inside the Pavilion. It was about the only thing I saw in his favour, his punctuality."

"There has been someone else in this building," Clara persisted. "And I have proof."

She put the suitcase on the floor with a sharp thud. The inspector raised an eyebrow.

"I wondered why you were carrying that."

"Inside this luggage you will find the exact same cigars used to set the Pearl Pink stand alight, a crime I think not of Cook's doing."

"I never caused a fire," Cook agreed quickly. "It could have damaged the Pavilion!"

"Equally, Cook does not smoke, but someone was in the prince's bedroom smoking. While they were there they whittled a stave from a Cushing's Corset into a weapon. I can't tell you why they killed Forthclyde in the way they did, or what caused them to attack Miss Althorpe and Miss Owen, but I think this person is our killer."

"And who owns that suitcase?" Park-Coombs asked.

"Arthur Crudd," Clara declared, as she had expected everyone was surprised, especially Mr Taversham.

"The lad?" he said. "But why?"

"I don't know," Clara admitted. "Perhaps only Arthur Crudd can explain his motives. Unfortunately he has been missing since last night."

"Since the murder of Miss Owen," Park-Coombs sighed. "And I suppose Mr Cook you will state you were locked inside this building the entire time that crime was being committed."

"Yes," Cook said at once. "I only slipped out a little while after everyone had arrived. I was trying to avoid Mr Grundisburgh because I knew he would recognise me."

"Well, I am still arresting you, but in the meantime I'll have my constables start a search for Arthur Crudd. Perhaps the fellow has come to some misfortune and your suspicions are ill founded Clara."

Clara doubted that, but she allowed the inspector his moment. Time enough to prove him wrong once Crudd was found. Mr Grundisburgh was unimpressed.

"I know no one by the name of Crudd," he snarled. "Why would this person wish Albion any harm? I think you are being blinded by compassion Miss Fitzgerald!"

Clara had never been accused of being overly compassionate towards a murderer.

"I am not," she stated. "But until Arthur Crudd is in custody I can hardly prove it."

"Let's not start an argument," Park-Coombs grumbled. "I have this man to find you seem convinced is our real killer. For the time being, might I remind everyone to be careful?"

Clara thought that was a very sensible suggestion. Mr Grundisburgh merely grunted crossly.

Chapter Twenty-seven

The unfortunate Jeremiah Cook was discreetly led away by Inspector Park-Coombs. Clara could not help but feel sorry for him. He was a simple soul who had been easily misled and then used by Albion Industries. He had been blinded by love for Esther Althorpe, who had then broken his heart. In many ways it would seem natural for him to be extremely angry and set on revenge. If you took things at face value, it would seem perfectly logical that Cook was both saboteur and killer, but Clara never took things at face value. In her experience life was far too complex to do that.

Discreet as the inspector had been, the removal of Jeremiah Cook had not gone unnoticed, particularly by Mr Mokano who was keeping a very close watch on affairs at the trade fair. He was intrigued and wandered over to Clara.

"Why is Mr Cook being escorted away by that policeman?" he asked politely.

"It seems Mr Cook was behind the sabotage at the trade fair," Clara explained.

"Ah," Mr Mokano watched the departing figure of his former employee. "What of the murders?"

"He denies them, and I am prone to believing his

protests. Mr Mokano, Cook has been very ill-used by Albion Industries. They played on his feelings to convince him to betray you and then, as soon as they had the secret for Pearl Pink, they let him go. Cook feels very bad about what has occurred. I think, if you are looking for a star witness at your civil case against Albion, you will find Cook most willing."

Mr Mokano was amused.

"Fools come in many forms," he said. "Mr Cook, by most definitions, is extremely clever. He understands chemistry better than most of the men in my laboratories. But some fluke of his mind makes him utterly lacking in common sense. I should have perhaps been more careful of him. I should have guessed he would be easily deceived."

Mr Mokano gave Clara a polite nod then wandered back into the crowd. Clara glanced at her watch. The day was drifting away. Should she remain here or try to find more information on the mysterious Arthur Crudd? She had kept the secrets of his suitcase to himself for the time being. Supposing Arthur Crudd was simply inclined to be a female impersonator? Such men existed, and he would certainly be attracted to a large trade fair by the country's leading cosmetics manufacturer. Perhaps Arthur's appearance here was purely innocent? He might have come to look at the stands under the guise of being a workman, thus it would not appear odd for him to be wandering around. That did not explain his disappearance, however. Clara was beginning to think something had happened to him.

Clara decided to remain at the trade fair; she really had no idea where to begin looking for Arthur Crudd, so it seemed to make better sense to keep an eye on things here. There was still a killer on the loose. She was milling through the crowd when she spotted someone waving at her. Clara wandered in their direction and realised it was Gilbert McMillan. He was looking out of breath and had clearly been running.

"Miss Fitzgerald!" he declared. "I have news!"

Clara ushered him to a quiet corner, where they might not be overheard.

"Have you learned more about Mr Grundisburgh?" she whispered urgently.

"I have indeed!" Gilbert was almost falling over himself with excitement. "I contacted my colleagues in London, where Mr Grundisburgh lives. It seems his wife has gone missing!"

Clara was struck by this unexpected information.

"How long has she been gone?" she asked.

"She informed the neighbours that she was going to her sister's house the week before last. Her story was that her sister was unwell and needed to be nursed back to health. No one thought this odd and when Mrs Grundisburgh left with her suitcase, saying goodbye to her husband on the doorstep, it all seemed perfectly ordinary," Gilbert was in such haste to impart his information he was stumbling over his words. "Then Mr Grundisburgh was summoned here urgently. Not long after he had gone, his sister-in-law turned up on his doorstep for a surprise visit. She had come into London on a sudden whim to do a bit of shopping and decided to pay an unannounced call on her sister. Needless to say, she was surprised when the neighbours informed her that Mrs Grundisburgh was supposed to be tending her on her sickbed! The woman had never been ill and now everyone was wondering where Mrs Grundisburgh had really gone!"

Clara hefted the suitcase that she still clutched in her hand. A feminine suitcase. Expensive, well looked after. The sort of thing the wife of a professional might own, unlike Arthur Crudd who was supposed to be an impoverished orphan.

"Describe Mrs Grundisburgh to me?" Clara asked Gilbert.

"Short, not much more than four foot tall. Quite slender, with almost a boyish figure, according to my sources. She is younger than Mr Grundisburgh and takes very good care of herself. I hear tell she was a model for Albion Industries before she was married. She has dark hair and eyes, and she cuts her hair short in the latest fashion. You seem quite excited, Miss Fitzgerald?"

Clara was indeed excited, because it had dawned on her just where Mrs Grundisburgh might be and why no one had seen her lately.

"We must find Mr Grundisburgh quickly. I fear he is in danger," Clara glanced about the room she was stood in, but there was no sign of Mr Grundisburgh. "We must split up and look."

Clara started to move away, then paused and turned back.

"Is Mrs Grundisburgh a smoker?" she asked.

"Funny you should say that, she has quite a peculiar habit for a woman. She likes to smoke cigars. Apparently, it was a source of irritation to her husband and he insisted she always smoke them outdoors, which is why the neighbours knew about it," Gilbert answered. "She is a heavy smoker and the police have been visiting the local tobacconists to see if she has been in to buy her usual cigars. I should add that Mr Grundisburgh has yet to be informed of all this. No one was sure how to reach him."

Clara was certain Mr Grundisburgh would know very shortly that his wife was not visiting her sister. If her hunch was right, then Mrs Grundisburgh was very near at hand and, with Jeremiah Cook in custody, would be wanting to conclude her plans as soon as possible. Clara darted through the rooms casting her eyes around for Mr Grundisburgh, but he was nowhere to be seen. In one of the corner rooms she came upon Abigail.

"Where is Mr Grundisburgh?" she asked her.

"Oh Clara, it is good news!" Abigail smiled at her. "You know how you suggested I ask someone to fetch my copies of the sales figures from my home? Well I did. I contacted our family solicitor and he was very good and sent someone to my house with the police. They found the papers and they exonerate me completely! I just gave them to Mr Grundisburgh to compare to the forged ones Niamh had. He took them into the kitchen so he could look over them in peace."

"Thank you Abigail," Clara said to her, starting to dash off. "And that is superb news!"

She hurried down a corridor towards the kitchens. The Pavilion still retained the old facilities which had once been used to cook royal meals. Now they were only used when a function was happening at the venue. Since no food was being served at the trade fair they were empty of staff, though the Albion girls and stall holders were allowed to visit them and make themselves a cup of tea if they wished. As it was a busy part of the afternoon no one had the time to leave their stalls, so the old corridors were empty. Mr Grundisburgh had picked a good location for some privacy. It also happened to be an excellent place for a killer to find him alone.

Clara was coming down the corridor, glancing in side doors as she went in case Mr Grundisburgh had diverted into one of them, when she heard voices.

"What are you doing here?" Mr Grundisburgh's deep tones rang out clearly.

Clara increased her pace. Now a woman's voice answered Mr Grundisburgh.

"Did you think you would get away with it?"

"April, what is this all about?"

"I have had enough Albert! Enough of your lies and games! You won't make a fool of me anymore!"

There was the sound of a scuffle. A chair clattered onto the floor.

"Put the knife down April!" Mr Grundisburgh cried out.

Clara slammed through the kitchen door. Mr Grundisburgh had retreated across the kitchen and was trapped helplessly against a welsh dresser. His wife was poised over him with a long carving knife. She held it high over her head and was in the process of stabbing it down into her husband when Clara flew at her and knocked her from her feet.

The blade sliced through Mr Grundisburgh's sleeve and cut into his arm. He squealed in horror and stumbled sideways. Mrs Grundisburgh had fallen on her side as Clara toppled her, but she had not dropped the knife. Now she elbowed Clara in the stomach and twisted on the floor, bringing the knife up and around to stab down into her opponent. Clara was in time to see the knife dropping through the air and scrambled away, the blade striking harmlessly on the tiled floor instead.

"Mrs Grundisburgh, calm down!" Clara insisted, trying to grab the woman's arm before she could raise the knife again.

Mrs Grundisburgh, her face distorted with blind rage, lunged at Clara and the knife narrowly missed her as Clara dived to the side. It tore at the edge of her dress instead. Clara was tired of these games. She threw herself once more at Mrs Grundisburgh, trying to jolt the knife from the woman's hand, but April Grundisburgh would not give up her weapon so easily. She rolled her body and the knife came perilously close to striking down on Clara once again. This time Clara darted away and got back to her feet, moving a few feet from Mrs Grundisburgh and putting herself between murderous wife and injured husband.

Mr Grundisburgh was in a near faint behind her. He was collapsed against a cupboard, clutching his bleeding arm and looking deathly pale. He seemed too shocked to process what was occurring and was certainly in no position to help Clara. His wife, on the other hand, was alive with fury. Her eyes were wide and she had lost all hold of her senses. She was now wearing a dress and had discarded her ruse of being Arthur Crudd. She looked like some avenging wraith from a bad novel. She rose up from the floor like a demon and, knife raised over her head, ran at Clara.

Clara had mere moments to think what to do. When

she had raced into the kitchen she had dropped the suitcase she had been lugging about like a handbag since that morning by the door. It had skidded across the floor when she cast it aside, and now it sat tantalisingly close to her shoe. Clara had only a second or two to make a decision. Mrs Grundisburgh was running at her fast and if she ducked this time the odds were the blade would find its original target in Mr Grundisburgh who was collapsed just behind her. It seemed counterintuitive to bend down and pick up the suitcase, but in that instant it was the only chance Clara had.

As Mrs Grundisburgh thrust down her arm, intent on driving home the blade through Clara's heart, so Clara brought up the suitcase like a shield and the knife plunged harmlessly through its leather surface and wedged itself inside. Mrs Grundisburgh tried to drag out the knife, but the force of her deadly thrust had taken it right through the case and the blade was now entangled with the contents within and refused to be extracted. Clara released the case from her grip, letting the woman struggle while she went on the attack.

When Clara was younger she had played hockey. She knew how to take care of herself. As Mrs Grundisburgh wrestled with the suitcase, so Clara called her name. April Grundisburgh glanced up automatically, just in time to receive Clara's fist to her face. It was a blow fuelled by outrage and terror; Clara had come within inches of being fatally stabbed. She did not pull her punch and Mrs Grundisburgh rocketed back as she was struck. The knife was finally released as the woman flapped her arms, trying to save herself from a pitiful tumble backwards. It was to no available. She fell, clonking her head on the butler's sink as she went down. She was unconscious by the time she met the floor.

Clara shook out her hand, biting pain running through every finger and joint. She went to Mrs Grundisburgh and felt her pulse. Satisfied she was still alive she turned to Mr Grundisburgh. He had sunk to the floor, clutching at his wounded arm with a look of astonishment on his face.

"My wife…" he mumbled. "Tried to kill me…"

Clara looked at his arm and was relieved to see that though the cut was long, it was not deep. She took out her handkerchief and wrapped it around the wound, before returning to Mrs Grundisburgh. After a moment of consideration, Clara searched all the drawers in the kitchen and came upon some sturdy twine. This she used to tie up Mrs Grundisburgh's hands and feet tightly.

"I am going to fetch help," Clara told Mr Grundisburgh who was still sat on the floor in a daze. "I won't be long. Keep an eye on your wife."

"Tried to kill me…" Mr Grundisburgh mumbled, apparently unable to process what had just happened.

"Everything will be all right," Clara assured him. "I shall send someone to get help."

Clara departed the kitchen and ran as fast as she could back to the main hall. Spotting someone she could rely on to fetch help both swiftly and discreetly proved somewhat harder. It took her longer than she would have liked to find Abigail.

"Abigail," she quickly pulled her friend to one side. "You must fetch Inspector Park-Coombs and a doctor at once!"

Abigail stared at her in astonishment."

"Whatever for, Clara?"

"I can't explain just now, but you must hurry. When you find them, bring them to the kitchen."

Abigail was puzzled, but she didn't argue. She headed out to find help as she had been instructed. No sooner was she gone then Clara was running back to the kitchen. She had a killer to keep her eye on, and a man in deep shock. What a turn of events, she thought as she clutched her aching hand to her chest. She hoped she hadn't broken that too.

Chapter Twenty-eight

Mrs April Grundisburgh came around not long after Clara returned to the kitchen. She struggled with the twine about her wrists and then glowered at Clara who was sitting next to Mr Grundisburgh and keeping an eye on him. He had been close to a dead faint when Clara had returned, and his pulse had dropped alarmingly. Despite the wound being non-lethal, it looked ominously like Mr Grundisburgh might die of shock. Clara had roused him, made him get up and sit on a chair and had even found a stash of sugar cubes in one of the cupboards and was making him suck on one.

"Untie me!" Mrs Grundisburgh demanded.

"No," Clara replied. "You will remain like that until I hand you over to the police."

Mrs Grundisburgh gave a panged cry of anguish and wrestled with her bonds.

"Why April, why?" her husband asked with a look of abject misery on his face. "What made you want me dead?"

"You don't need me to spell it out!" April Grundisburgh yelled. "Oh, I know what you are like Albert! Every bit of skirt catches your eye!"

"April! What have I done?"

"I think it might be more prudent to ask your wife what she has done," Clara remarked. "Three murders, Mrs Grundisburgh? And an attempted fourth just now?"

"Who is this woman?" April Grundisburgh crowed. "Another of your fancy women Albert? She's not your usual standard. Bit on the plump side and isn't even trying with her hair!"

Clara was offended, but was not about to show it. She stepped away from Mr Grundisburgh and faced his wife, hands on hips, standing up straight.

"I, madam, am a member of the Brighton Pavilion Preservation Committee and your antics have placed this building, which I and my fellow committee members are responsible for, at risk of grave damage. It has therefore been in my great interest to track you down before any more harm could occur!"

"This stuffy old building deserves to be burned down!" Mrs Grundisburgh gabbled. "Pity Mr Mokano spotted the little fire I started. I could have taken out this whole place! At the least I could have made a mockery of the Pearl Pinks. Those damn lipsticks Albert, those are all you have drivelled on about for months!"

"I apologise for my wife Miss Fitzgerald," Albert Grundisburgh was regaining some of his colour, though he still looked fit to faint at the slightest provocation. "She is an emotional woman. She works herself up into such a passion over things."

"Don't speak as if I am not here!" April Grundisburgh screamed. "You always do that! Always!"

She started to wrestle with her bonds again. Clara had placed the knife in a safe place just in case the woman did escape. She still seemed intent on killing her husband.

"Esther Althorpe," Clara said the name sharply and Mrs Grundisburgh stopped wriggling. "Let's begin with her. You strangled her with one of the stockings she had made a bestseller. I don't think that was a chance thing. You knew of her, yes?"

"Little whore," April Grundisburgh puttered. "Always

her and Albert sneaking into a corner and talking in whispers. I saw them. I used to wait outside the head offices and watch for him. I needed to know what Albert was doing, he was always late coming home…"

"I was working April!" Mr Grundisburgh interrupted.

"Liar! I saw you take that harlot to a canteen after work and buy her a meal. I saw you!"

Mr Grundisburgh shook his head.

"We were working out a strategy to lure Jeremiah Cook to Albion. It was a secret plan and we talked about it in a place where no one would overhear us."

"Liar!" April Grundisburgh screamed. "You even invited her for Sunday dinner once! The nerve, the utter nerve of it all! Your mistress in my own house, eating off my best china! I don't know how I suffered it, but I did, because I was plotting my revenge."

"You killed Esther because you thought we were having an affair?" Mr Grundisburgh's face had fallen and he looked utterly broken by what he was hearing. "There was nothing between me and the girl. She did not deserve to die!"

April Grundisburgh preened at his outburst, instead of making her rethink her allegations, it seemed to satisfy her that she had been correct all along. She looked smug and it made Clara sick to see how wickedly she relished what she had done.

"What of Mr Forthclyde?" she asked to distract them all. "How had he offended you?"

"Cushing's Corsetry!" April Grundisburgh declared to Clara, as if the connection should be apparent. "I modelled for them for years! Before I married Albert I was close with Mr Forthclyde. Bertie. But he betrayed me too. I asked him to take me back once I realised Albert was a lying rogue, but he said he would not. He was too worried about his reputation!"

For the first time tears pricked April Grundisburgh's eyes.

"I thought we could be like before. It had been

glorious then. I never should have let him go for Albert, but I was foolish," the tears ran down April's face. "And all Bertie would say is that we were a thing of the past and he would not risk his career on a married woman! Still, he could not resist meeting me secretly in the dining room the night I killed him. He was surprised I was at the fair and wanted to know what I was doing. It was so simple to get him to agree to hang behind after the dinner. I hoped by writing the word betrayal I would deflect suspicion onto the saboteur. "

April Grundisburgh trembled with the emotion that was overtaking her. Her anger was faltering being replaced by self-pity. Clara moderated her tone too as she asked her next question.

"You began to plot revenge. The trade fair offered you an opportunity to take out those people who had hurt you without making you a suspect, but your husband was not going to be at the trade fair?"

"I knew…" April Grundisburgh choked on tears. "I knew that if some big calamity struck the trade fair my husband would be sent down to manage it. He is good at that sort of thing. All I had to do was stage the two murders and he was bound to be summoned. It was pure good fortune that it turned out someone else wished harm to the place and was prowling around at night sabotaging things."

"You told your neighbours you were going to your sister's to explain your absence from home," Clara continued.

"Yes. I told Albert that too."

"And you disguised yourself as Arthur Crudd to gain access unnoticed to the trade fair."

"That was easy," April smiled to herself, pleased with that part of her plan. "I have been disguising myself as a boy for many weeks now so I could spy on Albert. No one has taken any notice. Not that it was nice staying in that horrid lodging house with that ghastly woman, but I was prepared to endure it all."

"What about Niamh?" Mr Grundisburgh asked bleakly. "Miss Owen? What could you possibly have against her?"

"She was fluttering her eyes at you, Albert! From the very day you arrived here! Did you not see it? No, of course not, you were just too flattered by the attention!" April snorted, her anger returning. "That is how it always is with you! A wink and a smile and you are besotted! I saw you walk her home, arm-in-arm. My blood boiled! I had only just killed that other damn woman and you had found your next mistress! It was so callous, Albert. I actually felt bad for Esther. You didn't seem to care at all!"

"Neither Esther nor Niamh were ever my mistress," Albert had recovered enough to be cross and he spoke fiercely. "Listen here you stupid woman, those girls were employees and nothing more. I was sad when Esther died but I was not heartbroken because I never loved her, I was never having an affair with her! Niamh was feeling unwell the night I walked her home. You stupid, stupid fool! You killed three people out of misplaced jealousy, when the only person I ever cared about and loved was you! I worked hard for you! So you could have all the best things in life! And this is how you repay me?"

His outrage hit home. Suddenly the fight had gone from April Grundisburgh as realisation dawned on her.

"I thought…" she turned to Clara, perhaps hoping for sympathy. "I knocked on her door pretending I had a message for her. She was feeling bad and had to lie down on the bed. I… I put the pillow over her face."

"And you took her key to make it seem like she was killed for it?" Clara added.

"I don't know, maybe," April seemed to have shrunk in on herself. "She was holding it in her hand and it fell to the floor. So I picked it up…"

April Grundisburgh started to shake violently.

"Albert, I am so sorry," she looked to her husband. "I take it all back, every word I yelled at you!"

"Too late, my dear, too late," Albert Grundisburgh scowled at her.

"Albert?" April Grundisburgh's voice became wheedling. "Please Albert, I made a mistake. Don't be like that."

Her husband could not even meet her eye. Clara took hold of the conversation again.

"Where did you go last night, after you killed Niamh?" she demanded.

"I…" April turned her attention to Clara. Her eyes were big and damp and she seemed suddenly childlike. "After I killed the girl, Niamh, I felt strange. It was not satisfying like it had been to kill Esther and Bertie. I felt… sick. And… and I was dressed in my own clothes because I had been meaning to kill Albert. I thought I would catch him as the last person to leave the Pavilion, only he was with her, and I didn't get the chance. I had changed in the park, but when I went back the boy's clothes I had hidden under a bush were gone. I must have looked for them for over an hour, but they were gone. Someone stole them!"

This idea seemed to appal April more than the fact she had murdered three people.

"I could not go back to the lodging house dressed as a woman, so I stayed out all night. I thought I would have to abandon my suitcase," April's eyes suddenly darted across the floor to the badly damage leather suitcase. "That is my suitcase! You… you brought it here and ruined it!"

"I think you will find you ruined it," Clara said calmly. "But that is beside the point."

There were footsteps in the corridor and Inspector Park-Coombs arrived with two constables and Dr Deàth. He took one look at the scene, then glanced at Clara.

"Miss Sommers said you needed the police and a doctor? Dr Deàth happened to be in the station when she arrived so I brought him."

"Inspector, this is Mrs Grundisburgh, the woman

behind the three deaths here. And she came very close to killing her husband just now," Clara motioned to Mr Grundisburgh and his bloody arm. Dr Deàth moved forward to tend him.

"Mrs Grundisburgh, you best come down to the station with me and explain all this," Inspector Park-Coombs helped the trussed woman to her feet.

"Yes, inspector," April Grundisburgh stood meekly. "I have done some awful things. But I hope you will forgive me."

Inspector Park-Coombs glanced again at Clara, puzzled by Mrs Grundisburgh's demeanour. Clara merely shrugged. Murder, she had long ago concluded, was a form of madness and went hand-in-hand with other maladies of the mind.

The policemen departed and Clara was left with Mr Grundisburgh and Dr Deàth. The latter was humming as he bandaged Mr Grundisburgh's arm.

"Thank you, miss Fitzgerald," Grundisburgh turned to Clara. "The outcome is not what I would have wanted, but I am relieved you caught the killer. To think, it was my own April…"

"She had shown no signs before?" Clara asked.

Mr Grundisburgh merely shrugged.

"I was not looking for them. She was right about one thing, I was always working. April came second to my career," Albert Grundisburgh sighed. "We met five years ago. As she told you, she was a model for Cushing's Corsetry. I happened to be at one of their launch events for a new type of corset. April was modelling it. I took a shine to her."

Mr Grundisburgh winced as the bandage was drawn tight around his cut.

"I was never under any illusion April loved me, why should she? Look at me?" Mr Grundisburgh waved his good hand at his sizeable paunch. "But, I was content if she wanted me for my money, as long as I had her company I didn't mind."

"I think you were wrong, Mr Grundisburgh," Clara said softly. "April does love you. Jealousy is an emotion only stirred by strong passions. Had she only been interested in you for your money it would not have mattered to her you had mistresses. As long as she was your wife, that would have been enough."

Mr Grundisburgh smiled wistfully.

"It doesn't matter now. She has slain three people and tried to kill me. Whatever she once felt, whatever I once felt, it is all gone," he sighed. "I feel responsible. Especially for poor Niamh. April attacked her because she saw me offering her help home. I had only meant an act of kindness."

"You cannot blame yourself for that," Clara reassured him.

"I shall though," Mr Grundisburgh said mournfully. "Just as I shall feel guilt over Jeremiah Cook. This incident has made me realise how much our actions can affect others. It has made me rethink my position over Mr Cook's departure from Albion. I shall do all in my power to persuade head office to drop the charges of sabotage against him. If they do not choose to press them, then the police will not pursue it. I think that is the least I owe him."

Clara agreed. Albion Industries had treated Jeremiah Cook very badly and he did not deserve to suffer further.

"They will be busy enough dealing with the case Mr Mokano brings against them," Clara reminded him.

Mr Grundisburgh gave a hoarse laugh.

"We'll fight that one, don't worry!" then he became grim again. "Will my wife hang?"

"If they decide she was sane enough when committing the crimes, I suppose so, yes."

Mr Grundisburgh's face hardened.

"Good," he said. "Very good."

Chapter Twenty-nine

The trade fair was in its final hours. Soon the Pavilion would be restored to its usual self and the stalls and displays would be packed away. Clara did not think that could come too soon. But she was no longer at the Pavilion worrying about murderers and vandalism. That role had been deferred to Mrs Levington, for Clara had other matters to occupy her.

Owing to the steady determination of Dr Cutt, Captain O'Harris' discharge from the hospital had been obtained and he was now safely ensconced in Dr Cutt's spare bedroom. Dr Cutt had insisted on the arrangement, as it meant he could watch over the captain's recovery in a much pleasanter environment than the hospital. His housekeeper was equally delighted with the arrangement, having learned who Captain O'Harris was and being most eager to help a war hero. To assist them Dr Cutt had hired a nurse, a reliable soul he had known a number of years and who had specialised in psychiatric cases in the past. She would be on hand during the night should Captain O'Harris need help. Dr Cutt felt certain that between them they would have the captain back on his feet before Christmas.

Naturally Clara intended to keep her eye on them all.

"I shall visit every day," she informed O'Harris as they sat in his new accommodation. The bedroom was spacious and airy, with a comfy bed and a soft armchair. "You shall be sick of me and be glad never to see me again once you are well!"

O'Harris laughed. It was a good sound.

"I don't think I could get sick of you," he grinned.

"Many people do," Clara said with a raised eyebrow. "Mr Grundisburgh, despite my saving his life, quite never wants to see me again."

"Ah, well that might have more to do with his wife being discovered a murderer," O'Harris pointed out. He stretched out on the bed in the room and gave a peaceful sigh. "Did she confess to the police?"

"Yes. She was quite helpful to Inspector Park-Coombs. She explained how she had concocted this idea of murdering her husband while he was at the trade fair, so that she would not be deemed connected to the crime. She told everyone she was going to stay with her sister, but the sister spoiled that. Then she came to Brighton and started her plan by killing Esther Althorpe and Mr Forthclyde. They were really only the lure that would bring her husband down to the fair, but she had reason to want them dead too. She made the crimes seem connected to Albion by using beauty products in the crimes. But it was actually more personal than that. Esther had made her name via the promotion of a certain type of stocking, and that was how she came to Mr Grundisburgh's attention. Strangling her with the same type of stocking was something of a message. Similarly, killing Mr Forthclyde with a sharpened corset stave was because she had once been a model for Cushing's Corsetry," Clara paused. "When you think about it, Mrs Grundisburgh was actually leaving us messages all along. It was just we didn't know how to connect them."

"And Jeremiah Cook's presence was pure coincidence?" O'Harris asked.

"Just a lucky happenstance," Clara agreed. "After being

sacked from Albion Industries, Jeremiah felt a fool. He realised he had been used. He was jobless and the woman he had loved had abandoned him. I think any person in such a situation would contemplate revenge. But Jeremiah also felt guilty that he had betrayed Mr Mokano and he wanted the world to know what Albion had done. His message of betrayal had a double-meaning, firstly he had been betrayed, secondly he had committed betrayal.

"Jeremiah knew about the trade fair from his time at Albion and he concocted this idea. He would sabotage the displays at the fair and announce to the world what had occurred. He naturally targeted the Pearl Pinks. But the whole time he was masquerading as Ian Dunwright he had only the vaguest notion that someone else was in the Pavilion. As it happens, Mrs Grundisburgh kept her murders to the times when the Pavilion was open, while Jeremiah operated at night. He would deliberately let himself be locked in so he could get on with his sabotage.

"Mrs Grundisburgh, however, realised there was another person causing trouble and used it to her advantage. When she killed Mr Forthclyde she made sure he fell on the table where she had written the word betrayal. Her idea was to cast the blame for the murders onto the saboteur and it almost worked."

"And she framed Abigail Sommers?"

"She needed a scapegoat and Abigail was just too tempting. Abigail had perfectly ordinary reasons for often speaking with Mr Grundisburgh. She was the top sales representative in her region and she had been chosen to organise the trade fair. But, to a jealous wife, she looked to be another potential usurper. Abigail tells me that she asked for some of the samples to be brought to her hotel room, so she could go through them and check everything was there before the fair opened. The person given the task of carrying the boxes was Arthur Crudd. He, or rather she, was alone in the room for several minutes while Abigail ran down to fetch a message from the front desk. That was ample time to plant evidence."

"And killing Niamh Owen was a spur of the moment decision?" O'Harris asked, settling himself further on the bed.

"Yes, by that point I think everything had gone to Mrs Grundisburgh's head and she had lost all sense of reason. But the murder of Niamh was spontaneous and troubled her more. She had spent months convincing herself that it was right for Esther and Mr Forthclyde to die, but Niamh was a different matter. I think that murder brought Mrs Grundisburgh crashing back to reality," Clara thought for a moment. "I feel sad Niamh was killed, but I find it hard to feel the same sympathy for her that I do for Esther. Niamh had a nasty streak and she was intent on ruining her rival. She had a friend in the accounts department at Albion alter important documents and then send them to her. The forged documents made it look as though Abigail was cheating the company. Luckily Abigail kept her own copies."

"Sounds a dangerous business, being in cosmetics," O'Harris said thoughtfully. "I don't think it is a career I should choose. Still, it has certainly given the town something to talk about."

"To think Brighton was the place the Pearl Pink was launched, right before it became the item at the centre of a legal controversy," Clara smiled. "Well, that is none of my business. I caught a killer and that is that."

"Do you think Mr Taversham will ever recover from the fact he hired a woman disguised as a man?" O'Harris chuckled to himself. "I rather fancy it has hurt his pride that he couldn't tell the difference."

"Nor could anyone else, to be fair," Clara laughed with him. "Mrs Grundisburgh does not have a feminine figure and years of heavy cigar smoking have deepened her voice. She might have tried to insult me by calling me plump, but I personally feel I have a far more natural and favourable appearance than she."

Captain O'Harris gave her a wink.

"I like my ladies with curves."

"Jolly good," Clara said with mock sternness. "Because you are stuck with me. Now, I am going to head off to see poor Mr Taversham and hopefully console him in his misery by offering him the task of getting your house liveable again. If you are all right with that?"

"Perfectly," O'Harris said. "Tell him to strip the place and redecorate it! I want the old memories all gone. I need a fresh start."

"It shall be done," Clara promised.

"Though…" O'Harris hesitated. "I think the cars could stay?"

Clara rolled her eyes.

"Naturally!"

She started to move away, to head out of the room and get on with making arrangements. O'Harris called her back and she stood by the side of the bed. He took her hand.

"Just needed to check you weren't an hallucination," he said, a frown creeping onto his forehead. "Sometimes, I am not so sure."

"My dear Captain," Clara said drily, "do you really imagine your mind could concoct anybody so complex and irritating as me?"

"Well, perhaps not, but to be sure…" Captain O'Harris pulled her down towards him and kissed her on the lips.

Clara blushed. She stood up quite flustered. O'Harris was laughing to himself again.

"You ought to know by now I am impulsive," he reminded her.

"Just as long as you are feeling better," Clara flapped. "Now, I really must…"

Captain O'Harris' good-natured laugh followed her from the room. Clara reached the head of the stairs and had walked two steps down before she allowed herself a smile. A warm buzz of excitement and happiness raced through her. Clara knew a new adventure was beginning for her, and this one did not involve any sort of crime. Now that was very satisfying.